W9-BPS-750

FATAL SECRETS

0-812-53451-4-00499-5

9 780812 534511

50499

THE TEMPO IN THE BLACK LAMP CLUB QUICKENED.

The wild beat and exploding lights made it seem that the guests were inside a giant fireworks display.

The sexual tableau in each cage overhead seemed to become more graphic, more authentic with the passage of time. Lovers in dimly lit corners began to sink to the plush carpets and soft leather couches—mimicking the antics performed in the four giant cages.

Tor books by Ralph Arnote

Fallen Idols
Fatal Secrets

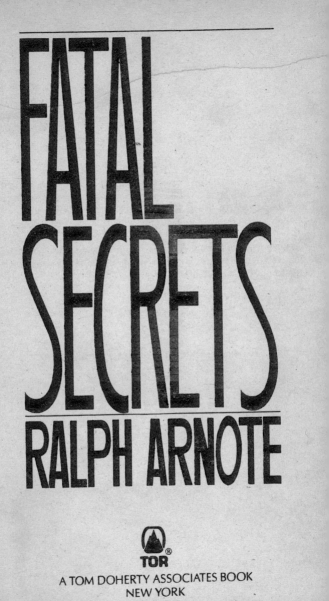

FATAL SECRETS

RALPH ARNOTE

TOR

A TOM DOHERTY ASSOCIATES BOOK
NEW YORK

FATAL SECRETS

Cover art by Joe DeVito

A Tor Book
Published by Tom Doherty Associates, Inc.
175 Fifth Avenue
New York, N.Y. 10010

Tor® is a registered trademark of Tom Doherty Associates, Inc.

ISBN: 0-812-53451-4

First edition: January 1994

Printed in the United States of America

0 9 8 7 6 5 4 3 2 1

To my sons, Glenn and Joe

All these people have shared their wisdom and given me boundless support. Without their confidence, Willy Hanson would still be working nine to five in Manhattan.

Nancy Murphy, Bob Gleason, Ed Gabrielli, Richard Wheeler, Glory Roseman, Patricia Arnote, Maria E. Melilli, Angelique Dubois, Bob Lofgren, Jennifer Royce and Lynn Sutherland.

"Three may keep a secret, if two of them are dead."

—BENJAMIN FRANKLIN

Prologue

Sawyer Lyman didn't want to be a juror. When the notice had arrived a couple of months ago, Emmy had assured him that he needn't worry about actually serving because he was too stupid. The only reason he'd not thrown the summons in the trash was to prove Emmy wrong.

The days dragged on, and Lyman often had a hard time staying awake. The lawyers seemed to go on endlessly. Occasionally the attorney for the defense would crack a joke and everyone would laugh. Lyman would wake up then.

Every night Emmy asked him about the day's court proceedings and every night he told her it was none of her business. In fact, the judge had clearly instructed the jury not to discuss the case with anyone, even family members. Emmy, of course, claimed to be more than just a family member. She was his wife. And then she would call him stupid again.

Lyman didn't hesitate to remind Emmy that he had been promoted to expediter down at the packing house. Of course, he would never tell Emmy that he was still ignored by his bosses as completely as ever. He told her instead that since the promotion he was always called Mr. Lyman. Mr. Sawyer Lyman. Nobody called him Old Sawface anymore.

No sooner had all the jurors been seated this morning than Miss Onyx Lu was brought back into the courtroom. Lyman's position in the jury box gave him by far the best look at the defendant. He was appreciative of his good luck every time she crossed her legs, which seemed to happen an awful lot. He could have sworn that she smiled at him once right after flashing him an especially provocative view of that tiny patch of pink. He could feel the surge of blood through his groin, and he crossed his own legs to relieve the mounting pressure. He stared at the defendant and imagined what they would do if he could get her alone in the attic. That Onyx Lu did have a nice leg.

His reverie was jolted when the judge slammed the gavel down to quiet the courtroom.

Onyx did have a nice pair of legs. But there

was something helpless and almost juvenile in her overall appearance today. The faded print dress that hung loosely over her five-foot frame made her look like a pathetic waif, caught unexpectedly in a storm.

Onyx had been found beaten, bound and gagged in her own sailboat, a luxury ketch named the *Windsheer*, near Jack London Square in Oakland. In the hold of the boat the Coast Guard had found enough cocaine to supply all of San Francisco for months. The evidence against Onyx seemed to be damning. But the prosecution had yet been unable in the eyes of the press to disprove her contention that she had been set up. Witnesses of any sort had been almost impossible to find. In fact, as the trial progressed, it was learned that several of the witnesses had recently died, apparent victims of a raging war between drug barons.

Onyx Lu came off as a poor little ship of a woman who could only poorly express herself in broken English. The defense contended that she was a Hong Kong citizen whose boat had been commandeered by drug smugglers. She told the court how she had chartered her boat, inherited from her father, to a group of young students celebrating their graduation with a Pacific crossing. She testified that the students had abandoned the trip during a stop in Hawaii. Within hours after that, she claimed, the *Windsheer* had been hijacked by a group of men involved in cocaine trading. Her complicity in their operation had not been proved to the press covering the trial,

3

the only adverse witness being one Miss Jade Baker, a real amazon, herself a drug user with a history of numerous arrests for drug abuse and prostitution. Miss Jade, in fact, had been a witness for the defendant, who botched her testimony to such a degree that she had become the hope of the prosecution.

The courtroom hushed at the bang of the judge's gavel. Onyx Lu stiffened in her chair, and for an instant she looked like an angry woman instead of an innocent. Sawyer Lyman noticed, and knew in his heart that she was a vile, wicked bitch who needed the attention of his swelling manhood.

"Has the jury reached a verdict?" The judge's voice was low, but audible in the silence of the courtroom.

"Yes, we have, Your Honor." The jury foreman was a well-dressed black man.

"Will you please tell the court your decision?"

"Your Honor, we find the defendant . . . not guilty!"

For a moment, the courtroom continued to hold its breath. Then the spell was broken. The defendant stood to be embraced by her attorney, and the noise of conversation and controversy resumed.

Onyx Lu was alone except for the statuesque Jade and a slightly built Oriental man who remained at a distance from her. She walked over to the jury box to shake hands with the members of the jury, the last being Sawyer Lyman.

She grasped his hand firmly, then brushed his

fingertips with a soft kiss. Then for an instant their eyes locked. He would swear later that she flicked the tip of her tongue provocatively across her lips.

She's a real hot bitch, thought Lyman. And she's guilty as sin!

1

Logan Phipps swirled Glenlivet in his glass at the Admirals' Club in San Francisco International Airport. It had been only an hour and a half since Carlos had called with the good news from the courthouse. Phipps smiled with satisfaction. He had been especially impressed with the paucity of living witnesses for the prosecution. Onyx certainly had a way of taking care of business.

Phipps moved his tall frame from the plush lounge chair and strode over to the receptionist. Though it was late in the day, the expensive dark silk suit held its shape as if it had just come from the presser. Phipps was tall and thin, over six feet, with a combination of Caucasian and Oriental features that blended to create a very distinguished appearance. He spoke English with a trace of British accent from his years in the Crown Colony of Hong Kong.

"Excuse me, please, do you expect my Los Angeles flight to leave on time?"

"I'm showing six-oh-five, sir, about forty minutes. You were waiting for a companion, weren't you?"

"Yes, and I will not leave without her. Just in case she is not here in time, will you check the availability of the next flights?"

No sooner had the receptionist turned her head toward the computer than Onyx Lu appeared in the lounge.

"Logan! It's been so long." There was a warm handshake that lingered just a bit. "I must look a mess. I had no time after the verdict to prepare for the trip. Carlos brought me directly from the courthouse."

"The verdict came so quickly, Onyx." Phipps handled her strictly as he would any other business associate. But in truth, he needed her badly. Her sources and connections were totally reliable. "Only two hours!"

Onyx drew close to him and whispered, "They were so stupid, Logan. They had even *me* believing I was not guilty!" She chuckled at her little joke.

Phipps remained stonefaced, thinking that the

best thing they could do was to get aboard the plane, where they could talk more privately.

They took their seats in the last row of the first-class cabin. Phipps had chosen those seats with security in mind.

"Oh, Logan! I never doubted the outcome of the trial for a second. The lawyers were superb. I know that was no accident." Onyx clasped his hand tightly.

Phipps responded by staring at her fixedly and touching his forefinger to his lips. "We have much to talk about before we land. However, we must talk very quietly, even here."

"Forgive me, Logan, I will be so very careful. It is just that even I get excited. It has been so long since I have seen anyone who really cares. I have been out in the cold for a very long time."

"That is over now. You will take our new operations base in Palos Verdes. It is close to everything, extremely comfortable and secluded. Just the place for our rare sweet bird to rekindle her fighting entrepreneurial spirit."

"I too have an agenda." Onyx grinned provocatively. "The Americans would call it 'an ax to grind.'" It was good to have a confidant at her side. It had been many years since she had actually seen her Hong Kong connection.

"That's fascinating, Onyx, and I will look forward to hearing about that later. Right now, however, it is imperative that I bring you up to date concerning what is happening in Los Angeles. We have a chance to recover a very large inventory of product, perhaps more than fifty kilos. It is rightfully ours, but a few roughnecks have taken the position that it is not. Onyx, you don't know how much you have been missed. There was never a defection in the ranks when you were running things."

"Tell me about it, Lo. I want to get back to it. I do have some of my staff left over from the old days. When they hear Onyx is back, they will seek me out."

Logan Phipps again put his forefinger to his lips and squeezed Onyx's wrist firmly. "I don't know how much you have heard about the news in Los Angeles. But there are some events that are working in our favor. Have you heard about the black fellow who was beaten up by the local police on the freeway? The entire incident was filmed by a private individual using a home video camera. The chap who took the beating was only speeding, but the police got carried away and made a living martyr out of him."

Onyx listened intently.

"The black community is up in arms, demanding that all the police officers involved be suspended or fired. If the officers are exonerated, we have information from the streets that all hell will break loose. And therein, my dear, lies our golden opportunity."

Onyx let her mind race ahead. "Don't tell me. I can see your plan. We can fan the fires of a riot and do a little looting of our own."

"You haven't lost your spirit. The jury's decision is due within a matter of hours. Even if it happens while we are in the air, Carlos will have all our street people on the move. Authorities will have no chance of keeping control over central Los Angeles. Our forces, on the other hand, will have total control over the small strip mall where our goods are held. Jade has already been flown south to handle a critical assignment." He paused. "By the way, she is expendable, is she not?"

"Oh, yes," said Onyx without a flicker of emotion.

The two of them sat quietly for the next several minutes. Hand in hand, they made a striking couple. They might have been newlyweds or lovers.

The flight attendant brought Phipps another scotch. He released Onyx's hand to swirl the swizzle stick in his glass, thoughtfully contemplating the violence ahead.

"Now, my dear, you spoke about having an agenda of your own. I hope it doesn't interfere with our plans, which, of course, must move forward swiftly. Why don't you tell me about it?"

She looked at him earnestly. "There are two people out there who could have caused me a lot of trouble if they had surfaced for my trial. They are the people responsible for my capture. They are still alive and will be very unhappy with the outcome of today's trial. For some reason I don't understand, they are fugitives."

"You mean Willy Hanson?"

"Yes. And his girlfriend. They came very close to destroying my organization. There is plenty of time, of course. It will be a little game to take my mind off business once in a while."

Phipps grinned. It was the first time Onyx had seen him smile since they had met in the Admirals' Club.

"Really!" he said. "I thought Wong was your little game."

Onyx was shocked to realize that news of her virile and perverted gofer had evidently traveled all the way back to Hong Kong. She grinned back like a child caught in the cookie jar.

"As I described," Onyx said, returning to her inscrutable, serious demeanor, "I can be patient. But when opportunity comes, be it a day or year from now, I will kill the girl first, just to cause him grief. And then I will kill him."

"He is a rank amateur," Phipps assured her. "Someday he will present himself as a target, and you will take care of business."

The Fasten Seat Belts sign came on as their plane prepared for landing at LAX. Further details of their plans would have to come later.

Logan Phipps and Onyx strode rapidly through the arrival lounge, down the long concourse and outdoors to the arrival level. There was a repetitious flickering of lights from a long black limousine that moved curbside. The dark glass made the interior impossible to see. Onyx and Phipps entered the rear door. She was flabbergasted to see that her old friend, the stoic Wong, was their chauffeur.

Phipps observed them both with another satisfied grin. "All the comforts of home, my dear Onyx. It is important to have someone around whom you can totally trust." He leaned forward to address Wong.

"Take us directly to Palos Verdes. I want you to make Onyx comfortable. You are to stay close to her unless she otherwise instructs you."

The balance of the trip to the Palos Verdes estate was made in silence.

2

The sudden wind gusted strongly through the marina and rattled a hundred halyards that weren't tied down. The result was a din that wiped out the sound of the radio from the cabin below. Willy scrambled below deck with catlike agility to listen to the startling broadcast.

Willy stood over six feet, broad-shouldered and muscular; his appearance belied his rapidly approaching fiftieth birthday.

He had heard it right. Onyx Lu, infamous international drug dealer, had been freed by a jury in San Francisco. During her long trial, she had gained the sympathy of the press, the public and ultimately the jury.

This was the worst sort of news. Willy Hanson had been hiding out for almost six months aboard the *Tashtego*, sailing up and down the coast while working furiously on the book he had promised his publisher. The book would detail all the events leading to the capture of Onyx by the coast guard in Oakland aboard the yacht *Windsheer*. Now the credibility of the whole book could be questioned. And worse, it would have no ending. His vile leading character had been vindicated by a jury of her peers, and Willy was apparently doomed to remain a man on the run.

"Willy, how can we let it be destroyed?" He turned as Ginny lowered herself through a hatch into the main cabin. He followed her descent inch by inch; her lithe body never ceased to please him. Finally he was looking squarely into her warm brown eyes.

As Ginny spoke, the news returned to the bigger story of riots in Los Angeles. There was a rumble in the distance and a plume of black smoke boiled into the sky from far inland. From his distant vantage point in the small marina near Long Beach he estimated the smoke to be rising well north of Los Angeles airport. The radio reported that the rioting was out of control and getting worse.

All at once Willy's personal problems seemed dwarfed by the events before them. One fire was raging now well south of the airport. The wave of anarchy was certainly not limited to South-Central L.A., as the earlier report had described.

"Ginny, we're looking at something horrible," Willy said quietly. "The National Guard should have been here hours ago."

Even the massive problem in Los Angeles, however, couldn't push the news from San Francisco out of Willy's mind. His name had come up at the trial. Just as Ginny had warned him, the defense had made hay of the fact that a witness was avoiding subpoena who could shed significant light on the case.

By not answering the subpoena Willy had definitely strengthened Onyx's case. Without him, there was no one to rebut her testimony that she knew nothing of the drug-laden hold of the *Windsheer* and that she herself had been a prisoner aboard the ship. After all, Willy had left her bound and gagged in the aft cabin.

But to testify at the trial would have delayed his commitment to Reinard Gossman and exposed Ginny and his daughter to painful interrogation. And, of course, Willy had killed a man.

Ginny poured a brandy for both of them and then grasped Willy's hand. "I guess we've made a mess of things, and I suppose I've contributed greatly to that. Right now it looks like we're doomed to spend the rest of our lives on this boat. As much as I love her I have no desire to live aboard her permanently. Willy, the *Tashtego* has become a prison. Onyx is free and we are unable to rejoin the human race."

Willy became strangely relaxed and sent a big

grin Ginny's way. He quickly realized that she needed much more than flippant humor to reassure her right now.

"Ginny, baby, I've thought a lot lately about making a clean breast of everything. We could tell the authorities all we know. 'Idealistic publishing exec blows cover off the rich and famous and traps drug queen in the process.' We could fill in all the gaps of the trial. A sharp prosecutor could probably get a new trial, and maybe we could still see Onyx Lu sent to prison."

Willy paused before he continued. They had both been over this ground many times before.

"But we just can't do it. The fact of the matter is that I made a couple of mistakes. Real bad mistakes. I killed that scoundrel Forbes in the airport parking lot. As much as it was a him-or-me situation, it was hardly legal. Also my old friend Leslie got herself fed to the sharks because of the chain of events I created." He shook his head. "The best thing that came out of it all is that I met you that day. An innocent just standing by the ocean, probably wishing to avoid a guy who would bring you as much trouble as I have."

"I'm not so innocent," Ginny said. "And I'm not terrifically attracted to martyrdom either. We just can't surface and face the music. Why should a jury believe us? I thought the state still had a strong case without us, but they blew it.

"So what do we do?" She rose to tie down a slapping halyward. "Willy, the *Tashtego* has always been a second home to me, and I love your company! But it's all so temporary. What if one of us needed medical attention? Or the coast guard might pull up alongside for a routine inspection. Any one of a dozen things could happen, and I really doubt you would have a chance of defending yourself if you were caught on the run."

"And what if I turned myself in?"

"Oh, Willy, I'd probably lose you either way!" Ginny tried to force one of her big toothpaste-ad smiles but it just wouldn't come.

Willy wrapped his arms around her as they stood in the cabin of the *Tashtego*. He wanted to measure his words well. Ginny deserved to know exactly what he was thinking. As nebulous as his plans were, she deserved to know them.

"Our biggest problem at the moment is that I am Willy Hanson. I need to be able to move about freely if I'm to get us out of this mess. I might even need a false passport. My own won't do me much good with a murder warrant out on me." The memory rushed back through his mind. That bastard Forbes clinging to the door handle of the van back at LAX, smashing the window with his pistol. Willy could still hear the deafening roar of his own revolver in the van as he sent a bullet into Forbes's chest. Self-defense would be tough to prove now.

"Ginny, an old acquaintance of mine in San Pedro can turn Willy Hanson into someone else. He worked for the Immigration Service and was a cop for years, but he sort of dropped off the edge of respectability. Now giving people new identities is his business. He works on both sides of the law. He owes me a big favor, and there will never be a better time to collect."

"I suppose we should sail to San Pedro in the morning," she said matter-of-factly.

"Want to duck out on our whole deal, gorgeous?" He marveled at her ability to adapt to all this.

"Not in a million years. I don't know what lies ahead, but it can't be more dangerous than what we've already been through."

Willy hated to tell her otherwise. "I seriously doubt that you're right about that."

They didn't sleep much that night. Their preoccupation with each other knew no limits. The orange orb of the sun rose over a burning Los Angeles as they awoke, united against the world.

3

"**I** saw him." The muscular Oriental spoke with a tone of authority. There was no questioning what he said. "He lives on a boat in the marina at Seal Beach. A big ketch named the *Tashtego*. I saw him leave the boat for a few minutes to pick up supplies at the ship's store in Seaport Village."

Onyx, waist-deep in the blue waters of a swimming pool, watched Wong carefully. She had been prepared to spend many months searching for Willy Hanson. For Wong to have had such immediate success was totally unexpected.

"How, Wong? How did you find him so quickly, and are you sure it is him?" With a nimble flip that gave testimony to her remarkable fitness, she vaulted her nude form up out of the pool.

Wong stared at her exquisite female perfection. Then he hastily scrambled to the other side of the pool to fetch a large towel.

"Please sit down, Wong, and tell me all about it."

Wong pressed the towel into Onyx's outstretched hand, then sat down as she stood squarely in front of him, skin glistening wet. He watched as she maneuvered her body, drying carefully but never allowing the towel to cover the tiny triangle that held Wong's gaping attention.

"Wong, didn't I ask you a question? If you can be distracted by such a tiny morsel, how can I trust you at all? Maybe you didn't really see Willy Hanson. Maybe you imagined it while ogling some sexy woman on the beach."

Onyx moved ever closer until the object of his attention was only inches away. She handed him the towel. "Here, Wong, finish drying me off."

Before his trembling hand could reach its mark, Onyx released a karate chop that dropped him to his knees. She abruptly wrapped herself in the heavy towel and strode to the other end of the pool. She turned toward him with fiery eyes and an accusing finger.

"You miserable horny pig! You haven't got the strength to deny yourself something you've had a half dozen times since yesterday. I ask you one more time. How did you find Willy Hanson?"

Wong, holding his hand to his cut upper lip, was trying to stem the copious flow of blood provoked by Onyx's vicious chop.

"I remember a long time ago. I remember when there was a shooting at Long Beach Marina. We thought Willy Hanson shot dead. But our people miss him."

Onyx fixed an icy stare on the kneeling Wong. Wong had never been known for his cogitative powers. His reasoning was accurate, however. Someone had assisted Willy in his survival that night. Maybe he had a friend in the marina. Maybe that was the mysterious woman who had been talked about at the trial. Onyx smiled. Wong had succeeded at something beyond the slavish perverted attention he loved to lavish on her. It couldn't be all luck. The police, the courts, the FBI and God knows how many private investigators had tried to find Willy Hanson. Only Wong had succeeded. She crooked her finger toward the still cowering Wong.

"Come here, dear Wong."

Wong quickly sprang to her side and she pulled him close to the heavy bath towel that separated them.

"I want you to go back to the marina. Pretend you are a gardener, a fisherman, a handyman for hire. Whatever you choose to be, I leave that to you. Without hair and a mustache, you appear much different than you did two years ago. But watch the *Tashtego*. Find out if Willy Hanson is alone on the boat. If he has a companion, I suspect it will be a woman. Get her description."

Wong struggled for words, trying to find his dignity. His lip still dripped blood from Onyx's chop.

Onyx kissed him full on the wound she had inflicted.

"My dear, sweet Wong. What would I do without my wise soldier?" As she spoke, she licked the blood from his lips and smeared it across both their faces.

Wong could only muster an idiot grin in response. Onyx had forgiven him, and that was all that was really important. He would get his reward much later and many times. He could tell by the gleam in Onyx's eye and the soft stroke of her caresses on his cheek and neck.

"Wong, while you are keeping track of our Mr. Hanson and reporting back to me, I will be setting up our new operation. I will find you and let you know when I need you. Now go!"

Onyx turned to survey the sumptuous estate her Hong Kong friends had arranged for her to occupy and enjoy while she set up the new sales operation. She had toyed with the idea of making this Palos Verdes mansion a headquarters for the scheme she had worked out with her Colombian friends. But that would have to wait. Locating Willy Hanson had put those plans on the back burner for now. All her connections had advised her to wait a while anyway. Her celebrity status had to cool down.

Revenge was going to be so sweet. She would

plot a real masterpiece. The world just wasn't big enough for Onyx Lu and Willy Hanson.

Her thoughts returned to Wong as she plunged back into the pool. She wished she could call him back and set him to work at his specialty. Vengeance could certainly have waited a few more hours.

4

The *Tashtego* had fairly soared in the fresh breeze off an ideal beam reach, and the trip north to San Pedro had taken only a couple of hours. They were much closer now to the disaster festering in Los Angeles. The black pall from the burning buildings hung with an acrid stench in the morning air.

His contact met him in a small hotel coffee shop in the Port of Call shopping complex.

There was certainly an economy of conversation as Willy handed over his old passport. No questions were asked about why he wanted the new identity. The man obviously knew his business and wanted to get it over with.

The man grimaced. "Same place, same time tomorrow morning and you'll be a new man." Sirens wailed in the distance as the man rose to leave. "Just one thing, pal. I never knew you before and I don't know you now."

Willy nodded his understanding and departed, not relishing the overnight stay in the marina so close to the trouble just north of San Pedro.

The guy was right on time the next morning. He walked over to where Willy was having coffee and without a hello or a see-ya-later dropped an envelope in front of Willy and left immediately.

The photograph on the passport was his own, but the name William Conrad Hanson had been replaced by Caleb Jones. It would take a little time to get used to the sound of it. Along with the passport was a Social Security card and a San Francisco voter registration card, each bearing the name Caleb Jones.

Later, aboard the *Tashtego*, Ginny was not at all pleased. "Caleb is much too biblical for a guy like Willy Hanson. It makes you sound like a Puritan from Cotton Mather's time." She was sprawled out on the cabin bunk with her hands clasped behind her head. "Couldn't you choose your own name? I just can't imagine Caleb being a very sexy guy."

Obviously, Ginny found the whole thing amusing.

"Lover, you are going to discover that Caleb is

just about the sexiest guy to come along since Cotton Mather was a kid."

She closed her eyes as if to help power her imagination. "Maybe I could call you Cal."

"You can call me Willy when we're at sea. When we're on land, feel free to call me Cal if you like."

"That takes care of the land and the sea. What do I call you on airplanes?" She was enjoying this.

"For me to finish this manuscript, to write the last chapter, we are going to have to find Onyx. That may well take us to South America or to Hong Kong, given her profession."

Ginny rolled onto her side in the narrow bunk. "You know, Reinard is one hell of a friend to agent a book for you after what you put him through. You disappeared once and had the whole world believing you were dead. Now you're going for an encore."

"I'm not so bad," Willy said. "Where in all the world could you ever hope to find another guy who offers such high adventure, world travel, sparkling days on the high seas, and incredibly hot nights in the sack?"

"I know I could never find another guy like that who was named Caleb," Ginny replied.

5

Within the publishing community in New York City, the West Coast trial and acquittal of Onyx Lu had created a frenzy of interest. The alleged marketing tactics of ConCom Publishers, involving orgiastic parties staged by sexy Onyx Lu, had kindled the fires of every tabloid. Therefore, when super-agent Reinard Gossman was able to offer an explosive insider book concerning the case, every publisher in town was interested. His not-so-gentle hints that the book was being written by missing publishing executive Willy Hanson allowed him to sell the book, as yet uncompleted, for a six-figure advance.

Communication between the agent and his author had to this point been scant indeed. About once a month Reinard would receive a phone call from somewhere up or down the West Coast. Willy was low on funds and Reinard had expected him to call immediately after the book deal was publicized in the papers. It was a full two weeks later, though, before he received a call from a phone booth in San Pedro, California. Reinard had recorded the brief telephone call, which he listened to one more time now before erasing the tape. He wanted to make dead certain he had committed it to memory.

"Hi, old pal!"

"I've missed you. Everything okay out there?"

"The city's burning, but you probably know more about that than I do. Ain't got much time for television. I hear I'm rich."

"That's right, you are. It's two hundred thousand dollars." Reinard heard a long, low whistle.

"I want you to write down this bank account number." With that, Willy read off a series of digits, which Reinard then read back to him.

"Send twenty-five thousand to Mr. Caleb Jones at that account number. I need a new pair of shoes, among other things."

"Have you gone insane?"

"Put fifty thousand in an account for my daughter. Take your cut, of course, and sock the rest away for a rainy day. If you learn that I got laid out on a slab someplace, take it and throw a big wingding."

"Be careful. No book is worth that." Reinard

was surprised to hear a catch in his own voice. "When do I get some pages?"

"Look, old buddy. There ain't nobody getting nothing until the last chapter is done."

"Same old Willy! Listen, the city misses its big-time editors when they suddenly up and disappear. Any desire yet to return to the wonderful world of publishing?"

"Not really, considering it would likely involve a detour through Leavenworth."

Reinard laughed. "You be careful out there. If you want a good professional private investigator to work with you, give a yell."

"Remember, Reinard, happiness back there in the big brick-yard is having a lot of money in the bank. If I buy the ranch, you got it all. Get real, Reinard! We are both going to be famous and rich whether we want to or not."

Reinard rewound the tape. Rich and famous indeed. Reinard was already so rich he couldn't spend it all in his lifetime if he tried.

6

Wong rubbed his eyes in disbelief. No sooner had he slammed the door on the old Cadillac and taken two steps toward the marina than he caught sight of the big ketch *Tashtego* abandoning her slip. A deeply tanned woman stood at the helm. Long, dark hair trailed in a ponytail from under a Dodgers baseball cap.

He observed the progress of the ketch as it worked its way through the labyrinth of slips into the main channel. The *Tashtego* showed no sail, content to proceed under power along the jetty toward the open sea.

Finally, the barely visible ketch sprouted a

mainsail. For a few moments, Wong could make out a second figure scrambling to winch in a billowing jib. Then the big ketch leaned into the Catalina Channel and moved north toward Los Angeles.

It was a clear day, and Wong was able to see the ketch until it faded to a speck. It seemed to follow a line that would not clear the Palos Verdes Peninsula, perhaps taking a course to San Pedro.

Wong decided to inspect the slip vacated by the *Tashtego*. His experienced eye told him the *Tashtego* would return. There were some lines and some gear stacked on the finger that probably would have been stowed aboard if the ketch were to be out for any length of time.

He hated to talk to Onyx about this, but of course he would have to. And as he thought about it more, his confidence increased. Onyx should be pleased. There was nothing he could do about the *Tashtego's* leaving its slip. He had followed it with his eye and could guess that it was probably pointed toward San Pedro. And if it was San Pedro, he could in all probability find it somewhere along the channel.

The phone call to Onyx was brief. She listened without comment as he told his story, then instructed him to maintain his surveillance of the *Tashtego's* slip in Long Beach. She told him she would have the harbor at San Pedro checked out by someone else or would perhaps do it herself. Disappointed, Wong hung up the phone. He didn't really want to know about the existence of "someone else," and a surge of jealousy hit him. He would have preferred to pinpoint the *Tashtego* in San Pedro himself. Besides, San Pedro was just a stone's throw from Palos Verdes, where he could amuse Onyx with some new little tricks that had been racing through his mind.

Wong was struck in the face by a fresh onshore wind when he returned to the marina in Long Beach. The slip was still empty. However, he broke into a broad grin at the sound of banging halyards all over the marina. All the pennants that were flying were flapping stiffly toward land. That made it even clearer to him that the *Tashtego* would have tacked well within his sight had the ketch intended to maneuver past the Palos Verdes Peninsula. He felt good about his assessment. So good, in fact, that he decided to call Onyx again to give her further assurances.

The phone rang endlessly. Damn her, he thought, she had decided to go down to San Pedro herself! Someday he would have to teach her a lesson. After all he, Wong, was a man and she was merely a woman.

Reluctantly he returned to the Long Beach marina to maintain his vigil.

Meanwhile, back in San Pedro a small Oriental woman in a floppy-brimmed straw hat stood on a boat, scarcely fifty yards from the ketch *Tashtego*. The ketch had tied up at an itinerant dock alongside the Ports of Call shopping complex. The man and the woman crewing it were casting off lines. Soon the *Tashtego* was motoring westward in the heavily trafficked channel to the main Port of Los Angeles.

Onyx motored to a high point near Fort Mac-Arthur overlooking the whole harbor basin. She trained her powerful glasses on the *Tashtego* as it came about to move south along the coast. It was the unmistakable figure of Willy Hanson at the helm, feet wide apart. She would know him anywhere.

A broad smile broke across her face. Onyx watched the *Tashtego* until it was a speck. It would soon be coming into the view of Wong, standing vigil at the slip in Long Beach.

Onyx told herself she was about to have her day. The game of cat and mouse had begun, and Willy was about to become a diabolically tortured mouse. And what of that handsome woman, thought Onyx. "She will be a bonus!" Onyx said out loud as she watched the *Tashtego* fade into the coastline to the south. She couldn't remember having this much fun since Willy had beaten her half to death more than a year ago that afternoon in Oakland.

7

Aboard the *Tashtego*, the view of the smoldering Los Angeles basin was truly startling. Willy turned over the helm to Ginny once they had pointed the *Tashtego* toward Long Beach. In the distance, columns of smoke still marred the sky.

"You know, Ginny, this is really no place to be. I must have six weeks of work to do on the manuscript before I can think about anything else. Let's do a run up the coast and enjoy the fine weather while I work. If we are going to take this baby across the Pacific, I could stand a little practice."

"What's in the back of your mind, Willy? We

don't have to sail the whole West Coast to practice a little navigation."

"No, but I just can't sit here and watch Los Angeles burn. I've got work to do and don't want the distraction. I suppose I have a guilty conscience. I owe Reinard a manuscript and he deserves to get some of it while all the facts are straight in my mind. We could go on up the coast, maybe all the way to Vancouver, and by then get some stuff off to Reinard. We could do it just in time to sail to Hawaii for the change of seasons."

Ginny tried to understand what was really in Willy's head. Not that she didn't want to make the sail north. It was just too idyllic for the dynamic Willy she loved. Willy had something on his mind and wasn't quite ready to talk about it yet.

"It couldn't be that you have in mind a little stop in San Francisco? Maybe we could find Onyx and you could beat a confession out of her? We could tie her up below deck and you could pummel her until you had every bit of information you wanted. Then you could toss her overboard and write the last chapter."

Willy listened. As idiotic as it all sounded, it was not far off the mark.

"Ginny, someday soon, I hope we can confront that bitch and nail her to a life sentence for murdering that girl. This time we have to do it right."

It was dusk in the marina when the *Tashtego* returned. Ginny expertly inched the big ketch through the maze of docks while Willy readied the lines. As he stepped onto the dock, he noticed a large china dinner plate that had been left on the dock and shattered by something. It was lying face down, broken into a dozen pieces. Nothing else on the dock seemed to have been disturbed.

Ginny stared at the plate and spoke first. "I guess we've had a visit from those kids from the next gangway." With that, they dismissed the incident.

Willy decided to relax in the cockpit after Ginny offered to prepare the evening meal. Trolling in the channel coming down from San Pedro, he had been lucky enough to catch a small yellowtail. They would be able to savor a couple of beautiful fillets, given Ginny's expertise in the galley.

The marina was dead calm. Willy's eyes followed a single stocky fellow making his way down the floating dock by the shoreline. He was carrying what appeared to be some lacquer cans and a small tool kit. Vaguely Willy recalled seeing this fellow before during the past several hours. Willy thought he saw the man glance over at the *Tashtego* for an instant. But the man continued to shuffle ahead until he disappeared in the parking lot.

8

About a dozen miles away from where Willy sat aboard the *Tashtego*, a fire raged in a strip mall on South Crenshaw. The blocklong facility contained a dozen stores, and all of them, with the exception of a small hardware store, burned fiercely. Black smoke mushroomed skyward as a panel truck backed up to the rear entrance of the store.

The door opened, and several men moved in and out carrying what appeared to be small nail kegs. When about a dozen such kegs had been loaded into the panel truck, two of the men climbed into the back. Another man slammed the rear door. A tall black woman, statuesque in tight black jeans, climbed behind the wheel.

The panel truck roared up the alley behind the strip mall, narrowly missing a crowd of looters and spectators. The woman drove with furious abandon, expecting the crowd to either get out of the way or get killed.

The two burly occupants in the rear sat on kegs behind the driver, automatic weapons held across their chests at a ready position. Behind them came the thump and deafening roar of dynamite as the hardware store exploded.

The van sped south on Vermont, ignoring all the traffic lights, narrowly missing the panicked rioters in the streets. The burning and confusion ended as they got farther south. When the entrance to the San Diego Freeway appeared a few blocks ahead, the black woman suddenly felt the sharp prod of the automatic in her shoulder.

"Pull over and get out!" One of the men slapped the woman's head with his weapon.

"Why are you doing this? Onyx will not like it if you leave me here. What are you doing with the stuff?"

As the panel truck pulled to a stop, the woman was thrown to the street. A hail of bullets from the machine pistol cut across her abdomen, and her screaming stopped as her body slumped in a heap near the curb. A squeal of rubber against pavement filled the night air as the van roared ahead to enter the San Diego Freeway going north.

Forty minutes later the van eased quietly into

a parking area behind a magnificent ranch house in Palos Verdes. The twelve kegs were quickly transferred to a space under a tarp in a small greenhouse. The two men from the van were laughing jovially as they strode up the driveway to the showy hillside mansion. Onyx Lu met them at the door and led them to a small patio just off the foyer.

"One-hundred-thirty-one kilos."

"And Jade?"

"She has joined the African ancestors."

A tear welled in the corner of Onyx's eye as she dismissed the two couriers and told them to wait in the van. She returned to the study of the sprawling Palos Verdes villa, where a tall, swarthy man in a silk business suit paced impatiently.

"Carlos, the mission was a success. I don't know what you have planned for our friends waiting in the van, but they are now in your capable hands." Onyx stood across the room from the man she addressed, obviously not wanting any further conversation.

"I will take them back up to the riot area and kill them there, right in the van. Another couple of bodies in all that mess will not arouse any suspicion at all." Carlos waited for her approval.

"Just make sure I've seen them for the last time. I really do not care to know all the sordid details. Go now and get it over with."

With that the man called Carlos went out the door.

Onyx picked up the telephone on the ornate

desk in the lavishly decorated study. She dialed the pay phone in the Long Beach Marina. It rang a dozen times before Wong picked up the receiver.

"Wong, is that you?"

"Yes. Wong here. The *Tashtego* back in slip. Willy and young lady are aboard."

"Wong. I want you to come to Palos Verdes right now and tell me about it."

"I will be there in half hour."

"I want you here in twenty minutes. Understood?"

"Yes, yes! Twenty minutes."

"That's better. And Wong, dear. We have something to celebrate. When you get here I want a very special fucking. I want you to think about how you are going to please me. Remember, Wong, I want this to be very special."

Onyx hung up the receiver before Wong could finish his stammering reply.

9

It was the next day about noon. Willy was working on notes for his book, and Ginny had brought a sheaf of navigational charts topside to plan the first leg of their sail north to Santa Barbara. It was a windless day, perfect for plotting a course while soaking up a little sun. The marina was quiet, as it usually was on a weekday.

Then she saw him again. The same workman, a stocky Oriental man in spanking-clean overalls. He had two cans of lacquer in one hand and a small open tool kit in the other.

"Willy, come topside for a minute."

"Just give me a few moments."

"I mean right now, Willy."

Willy bounded topside, approached her from the rear, encircled her in his arms and buried a kiss in the hollow of her neck.

"Mmmm! Just keep doing that and without looking directly, check out the stocky workman in overalls over beyond the next gangway."

"Okay, I see him. Now what?"

"What is he doing?"

"He's sitting under a palm tree on the fence by the parking lot."

"Willy, that's brilliant. But what is he doing?"

"Nothing. He's doing nothing but sitting on the fence by the palm tree."

"That's the point. This morning he was sitting way over there on that fence under that palm tree. Once in a while he gets up and walks and sits on the steps by the rest room near the parking lot. He just kind of hangs around like he's waiting for someone who never shows up."

Willy stiffened. He continued to hug Ginny while scrutinizing the figure in the distance. A chill caused the hair to rise on his neck. He realized it was the same person he had noticed at least twice before.

"Honey, I think we're being watched. You stay right here. I'll saunter down below and put the binoculars on him through a porthole. I think he has a face I want to memorize."

"Who could he be?"

"I don't know, but he can't be good news. Unless he just likes to gawk at tall brunettes in bikinis."

Willie went below and drew the binoculars from the portside keep.

Adjusting to the slight movement of the boat, he fixed the lenses on the figure now standing near the marina bathhouse.

"Goddamn it!" Willie tossed the field glasses onto a bunk. "Ginny! Come down here."

Ginny dropped into the main cabin to find him pacing nervously, stopping frequently to peer through the porthole at the man who sat a hundred yards away.

"I know him. I know the son of a bitch." Willy was actually breaking into a sweat.

"Who is he? Why are you so upset?"

"His name is Wong. He works for Onyx Lu. He has been her lackey and her lover for years."

Ginny stared at the man, who had now made himself comfortable on the steps. The positive identification by Willy set their minds racing along the same lines. If it was Wong, Onyx had sought them out and found them. There was only one reason why she would do that: to dispose of the only people alive who might bring her to a retrial.

"I can't believe our good luck," Willy said.

"Our good luck? Willy, there is only one reason she'd want to find us and that would be to kill us."

"You're forgetting one thing. That guy, Wong, can lead us straight to Onyx. He doesn't know we've discovered him. You might say that he's working for us now, though he doesn't know it. We'll just watch him and let him lead us to

Onyx. He must have a car in the parking lot. We'll watch him until he climbs into his wheels, then we'll follow him."

"What if he comes right down here and climbs aboard, takes out a big gun and blows our brains out? My God, Willy, that would be a hell of a last chapter to your book."

"Not a chance. Wong is strictly a pussycat she uses for all the nitpicking chores. He is a big-time gofer. When she wants to get rid of us, she'll send a pro." Willy realized that what he was saying would not put Ginny at ease.

"Or maybe she'll just blow up the boat sometime when we're asleep," Ginny said.

It was now approaching dusk. They had both seen Wong make several phone calls from the pay phone near the bathhouse. Now he strolled around the marina, pausing occasionally to study the boats, some of which were marked For Sale. Suddenly he broke into a sprint and ran back to the telephone, which must have started ringing.

Wong's conversation lasted only a few seconds. He then strode swiftly back to the bathhouse to pick up his paint cans and the tool kit before heading toward the parking lot.

"Ginny, get your car keys. Fast! We've got to see where he goes."

Ginny's Porsche was parked near the *Tashtego* in the general direction in which Wong was headed. When they reached the parking lot, they saw Wong climbing into a vintage white Cadillac. He would have to pass right by the Porsche to exit the lot.

Ginny and Willy huddled low in the Porsche, hoping they wouldn't be seen. The Cadillac roared by them, Wong evidently preoccupied with getting someplace in a hell of a hurry. Ginny revved up the Porsche and drove out, getting them about a hundred yards behind the speeding Caddy.

Wong turned north on Pacific Coast Highway, driving like a madman. The reckless speed began to make Willy visibly nervous. The Caddy was going well over seventy.

"The idiot must think he's on the freeway. He's going to draw cops for sure if he doesn't slow down."

Ginny was trying to keep Wong in sight and make the traffic lights work for her as they sped up the highway.

"At least with everything going on north of here, I doubt the police will be around to care about a couple of speeders," Willy offered.

The Caddy suddenly swerved sharply to enter the Harbor Freeway going south toward San Pedro. They both breathed a sigh of relief. Ginny was easily able to keep the big car in sight now. But soon the freeway ended, and Wong began to make his way down the Palos Verdes Peninsula using a network of local streets that were totally unfamiliar to both Willy and Ginny. The streets were narrow and winding, so the Caddy was forced to slow some.

Ginny tried to keep her distance as dusk turned to darkness, fearful that Wong would spot her lights in his rearview mirror. There was no other traffic now as they climbed higher and higher up the winding roads of a residential area. The dazzling lights of the coastal communities to the south sparkled in the night air.

Ahead of them Wong hesitated at every intersection, and Willy wondered if he had become suspicious. Finally he made a right turn that took him higher up the mountainous road. Rambling, opulent ranch houses with magnificent landscaping bordered the winding road. Privacy fences of redwood, vined and ornate, hid most of the homes, but here and there it was possible to peek in at a lanterned garden or a pool area.

Without warning the Cadillac stopped. A solid redwood gate flush to a narrow sidewalk opened silently, and the Cadillac and Wong disappeared.

Willy committed to memory the gold numbers on the garage door: 12755. The street sign at the crest of the hill read "Ventana Drive."

By comparison, the drive back to the marina was relaxing.

"Hey, gorgeous, that was some pretty fancy driving. I think you're a natural-born private eye."

"So what's my reward?" Ginny lingered when a red traffic light turned green, there being absolutely no one behind them. She leaned across the console to let Willy bury his tongue between her parted lips.

"What do you think your reward should be?"

"Caleb, I think fancy driving like that should be rewarded with fancy screwing."

"They don't make these Porsches big enough

for what I have in mind. Let's get this crate back to the marina."

"Caleb, I don't think I'll be able to relax in the marina. I think I'd rather go back in the daylight."

"Okay, pull up ahead and we'll give Mr. Hilton a break. Nobody will look for us there."

"Oh boy. We'll register under your assumed name."

Willy grinned.

The night spent at the Hilton was not one they would soon forget. Ginny and Willy were hopelessly restless. There was no way of telling how long they had been observed by Wong, though neither could remember seeing him for more than two days. They wondered about the mansion in Palos Verdes. Could Onyx be living in those palatial digs so soon after her acquittal?

"We have to abandon the marina, Caleb. We can leave by land or sea, but we absolutely must go."

Their lovemaking was furious, each of them trying to get lost in the other, trying to erase everything from their minds except the sheer pleasure they were feeling. But it didn't work. Even postorgasmic exhaustion left them wide awake. A short respite and then one or the other would begin burrowing around under the covers. It was the only escape possible, however temporary, from the specter of Wong.

They awoke in the morning, unrested, in a bed that was a mess.

"You know, Willy, you are a steamy, horny bastard. How many women did it take to make you like you are?"

Ginny had walked over to the draped window to inspect the Porsche parked a few feet away. Women all seemed to have one thing in common, Willy thought; they all wanted to know sooner or later how many others there had been, as if you kept a file somewhere and updated it routinely.

"There are one hundred and twenty-nine. You are very much like number eighty-one, except that she never once jumped out of bed to stare out the window."

The flying telephone directory hit him right in the gut.

"Hey, watch it! You know I could ask the same question."

"But you know better, don't you?" Ginny returned to the bed and fell into his arms. He seemed always to let her win the arguments eventually.

They left the Hilton shortly after 9 A.M. to drive back to Palos Verdes. They located the Municipal Office Building, where they inquired who the tenant at 12755 Ventana Drive was. The clerk was initially tight-lipped about the exclusive community, until Ginny took charge with her big smile.

"We've driven all the way up here from La Jolla to look at a piece of property at 12755 Ventana Drive. A Mr. Clarence O'Grady was to meet us there but he never appeared. Could you please tell us who the owner of record is so we can contact him by mail before driving all the way back up here?"

The clerk leafed through a file, took out a sheaf of papers and spent an unusually long time studying one document carefully.

"There is no one named O'Grady listed for 12755 Ventana Drive."

"Oh, there wouldn't be. He's a real estate broker from La Jolla, a friend of the owner, I believe. It's possible that we had a miscommunication about our meeting time."

"Well, that's too bad, but I doubt if you'd have any more luck discussing the property with the owner. The owner of record is Mr. Logan Phipps of Hong Kong."

Ginny's heart pounded as she concentrated on maintaining her composure.

The young clerk spun the file around for them to read:

Mr. Logan Phipps
711372 Nathan Road
Kowloon, Hong Kong

Ginny made a careful note of the address.

"I think we'll be driving back to La Jolla today. We will be corresponding with Mr. Phipps, and we thank you for your help."

"Very, very exclusive property. One of the nicest properties in Palos Verdes. Mr. Phipps takes very good care of it," offered the clerk.

He returned the file to its drawer, then promptly sat down at his desk. They exited the office and returned to the Porsche.

"Logan Phipps, Hong Kong. It all ties in, Ginny. That place has to be worth millions. Phipps must be Onyx's Hong Kong connection."

"And they know where we are."

"But they don't realize we know about them."

Willy looked out across the channel toward Catalina. They were still driving high up on the Palos Verdes Peninsula. The sky was black beyond Catalina. About half of the island was obscured by a storm moving north.

"Darling, I guess we'd better get back to the marina and batten down the hatches."

Ginny looked unenthusiastic.

"We'll make a couple of stops on the way. I want to pick up some ammo for the thirty-thirty and for the revolver. When the wind starts blowing, we'll get going."

"What about Wong?" Ginny knew what he was thinking.

"Two things about Wong. He probably knows that people don't go out sailing in storms. He probably also has sense enough to come in out of the rain."

Willy flipped on the car radio to get a weather report. As far as he could tell, it was just an ordinary rainstorm moving north. Winds would be tolerable and visibility would be nil. Just what they would need. Secretly, he relished the idea of taking the *Tashtego* out in some real weather. After all, most of their sailing was pretty ordinary stuff.

The *Tashtego* was already pretty well loaded with provisions. They stopped at a sporting goods store to pick up some ammo and then at a supermarket to pick up a few nonperishable staples. Their decision had energized them both. They dropped the Porsche off at a long-term storage facility near Long Beach Airport and took a cab from the airport back to the *Tashtego*.

Entering the marina parking lot, they spotted Wong's old white Cadillac parked near the cluster of shops that made up Seaport Village. It had started to drizzle, making the gangway slippery underfoot. They carried their provisions below, stowed them and then doused the cabin lights. From topside, the white Cadillac was barely visible in the hazy drizzle. It was doubtful that Wong could pick out much detail aboard the *Tashtego*.

Willy put on dark foul-weather gear and sat low in the cockpit of the ketch peering under the low brim of his hat toward the Cadillac. Suddenly Wong was near the public phone.

Willy adjusted the small roof-prism field glasses under the brim of his hat, focusing them on Wong, who still carried the paint cans and the tool kit.

Ginny stood in the darkened hatchway and observed what she could.

"You know, Willy, the guy is pretty stupid. I wonder how many other people in the marina are beginning to wonder who he is."

"I don't know, but he's staring right at this boat. Douse the cabin lights up forward and see if we can convince him that we're sacked in for the night."

The wind began to kick up and halyards began to slap all around the marina. It was no longer a drizzle, but a steady rain. Yet for a half hour longer, Wong kept his vigil. Then he took the few steps to the public telephone. His conversation was brief. After hanging up, he paused for perhaps a full minute to stare at the *Tashtego*. Then he pivoted on his heels and paced rapidly toward the old Cadillac.

"Halleluia!" exclaimed Willy. "I betcha he's going back to Palos Verdes to catch some shuteye."

Willy kept the roof-prisms focused on the car for as long as he could. He watched the Cadillac pause for the light, turn left on Pacific Coast Highway and then accelerate north. He could hear the blowers hum to life as Ginny flipped the switch to clear out the fumes from below deck. The rain began to pepper down faster and the rigging began to sing.

The big ketch stirred in the slip as the diesel rumbled to life. Willy flipped himself over the rail to clear the dock finger of all the things they would need. He could feel the excitement in his chest as he thought of the adventure ahead. The ketch nudged the dock as he began to clear all lines.

As he vaulted back aboard, Ginny, now in foul-weather gear too, stood at the helm. Gently the big craft lumbered in reverse toward the next dock. Ginny was a master at maneuvering the ketch in tight quarters despite wind. Willy locked his arm around the mizzen, continuing to scan the parking lot until it was out of sight.

The diesel rumbled louder as the *Tashtego* left the maze of docks and entered the channel. In less than five minutes they were in the open sea, headed west by northwest. Soon the weather closed in around them, and the *Tashtego*, sealed away from the world, plowed ahead through the heavy chop.

In all the time since they had left the slip they had not spoken. Willy went forward to set up a reef in the main. It was obvious that a full sail was not called for in the weather ahead. The reef secured along the boom, Willy gave Ginny a thumbs-up and she broke into a smile of assent. God! They sailed well together, he thought. She was a better sailor then he, but she had turned him into a good skipper.

Of course, he thought, they did everything well together. Willy marveled at the perfection with which their feelings seemed steadily to evolve. The only thing he felt sure of now was that he wanted this to last forever.

10

Carlos Lopez liked the way Onyx worked. She just didn't believe in "leaving footprints," as she called it. She had told him that as her chief of security, he must above all things run a clean store. She had told him that even he would not know everything. As she had explained it, sometimes in order to motivate people you have to give them a certain piece of knowledge. When they have completed their task, it must be determined whether or not they know too much about the company. If the decision is made that they know too much, then they must be unceremoniously terminated.

"And who makes the decision that one knows too much?" he had naively asked.

"I do, Carlos. You should never forget that." Then she had quickly added, "I have my own judge and supervisor also."

"Do you have a girlfriend, Carlos?" she had asked. He had lied, not wanting to tell her about Luisa Maria back in Ensenada.

"No one special," he said.

"That is bad, but it is also good. Perhaps you would like to get it on with me." She had leaned forward aggressively to fondle his trousers and had smiled unblinkingly when he immediately stiffened. "Someday when I say so."

Carlos thought about her management style as he sat in the back of the van. The two men who knew too much were up front, weapons at the ready as they approached the riot-ridden streets ahead.

"Stop right here," he demanded. He had already selected a Molotov cocktail from the dozen or so that lay in the crate next to him.

The van slowed down and stopped. Several buildings were burning in the next block of South Vermont.

"Gentlemen, you will wait for me right here. I have an errand which will take me only a minute or two."

With that he exited the rear door of the van. With his back toward his comrades in the front seats, he paused to light the crude rag wick of the Molotov cocktail. He took a couple of long strides and heaved the makeshift firebomb back into the van, then scrambled to put as much distance between himself and the truck as possible before the explosion and billowing fire made an inferno of the van and its occupants.

The havoc of the surrounding riots let the execution go virtually unnoticed.

Onyx would be so proud, he thought, so proud!

11

It was dark by the time Wong got back to Ventana Drive. He was soaked to the skin from his vigil at the marina. The storm had gathered strength, and the latest forecast was for dismal weather for the next two days. On the drive back from the marina Wong had reasoned that perhaps Onyx would permit him to stay in Palos Verdes for the next day or so and had fantasized some especially lascivious games to occupy the rainy days.

That illusion was soon shattered. "Look at it this way, Wong. With the storm at sea, we have them trapped right there in a little hole in the water. We have two days to decide how to capture the woman. That is what I want to do, Wong. I want the woman. She can fill in all the blanks as to what Willy is doing. She is also insurance against him doing it, whatever it is."

Wong listened to her remarks without comment or motion. Isolating the woman would not be difficult, he thought. She frequently left the *Tashtego* alone, though she hadn't for the past couple of days.

"What is her name?"

He shrugged. That was not part of his assignment. He thought to himself that it was awfully unfair of Onyx to demand information that he had not been required to collect.

"I do not know her name. I no get close enough to find out. Willy would know me if I get too close."

"Her name is Ginny Du Bois."

"How you know that?" Wong looked like a child who had been slapped.

"Oh, for God's sake, Wong. You yourself gave me the coast guard numbers of the *Tashtego*. We ran a check on the ownership."

"Oh, yes! That very smart."

"Is she pretty, Wong?"

"Oh, yes! She beautiful. She tall and sexy." Wong gave Onyx his idiot grin as he contemplated the memory of the bikini-clad Ginny.

"So your job of spying on the *Tashtego* has not been without its satisfaction, has it, Wong?"

"She not as pretty as Onyx."

"Really!"

"Oh, that for sure. I only know that in the morning she exercises on deck with bathing suit on. So I notice she is pretty. That is all."

"Tell me, Wong, do you sit in that stinking old Cadillac of yours and masturbate while you watch her?"

Wong's grin turned to a frown. "No. Of course not." Onyx was playing games with him, but he did not like it. "I only do that when I think of you." Wong blurted it out almost proudly. A flicker of a smile crossed Onyx's face and Wong's grin returned.

"Wong, were they aboard the *Tashtego* when you left the marina?"

"Yes, they were preparing for the night. All lights were out aboard the boat when I talked to you on the phone."

"Are they together most of the time?"

"Most of time. Sometime she go away but never for long. He hardly ever leave boat. Today they both go away and come back by cab." All of a sudden Wong realized that he had not actually seen them as they had left or returned. But Onyx need not know that, he thought.

"Wong, come here, please." Onyx rose from the sofa on which she had been sitting. "Get down on your knees, Wong. You are so much taller than I that you terrify me when we stand together."

"Onyx, I understand." It was always the same feeling for Wong. Desire for Onyx wiped everything else from his mind. She began to remove her few pieces of flimsy clothing just inches before his eyes.

"Was it storming when you left the marina? Do you think our friends would go sailing tonight?"

"No, only a fool would go sailing on a night like this." Wong, entranced by the teasing Onyx, eagerly awaited the end of her questioning.

"Wong, we have only a few hours. No matter how hard it storms, I want you back watching the *Tashtego* before daybreak." With that, the last piece of her clothing slipped to the floor at Wong's knees.

"Tomorrow I want you to keep a written record. Write down the times either or both of them leave the boat. Try to figure out when we would most likely find Ginny Du Bois alone. Do you understand what I am asking of you, stupid Wong?"

"I am not stupid."

"Then what are you doing there on your knees?"

"I am crazy for you, Onyx."

"If you understand that you must leave before daybreak, you may begin to amuse me now. Start taking care of our business, Wong. We have only a few brief hours."

12

Come morning, the *Tashtego* was seaward off the Channel Islands off Santa Barbara. By the miracles of radar and compass, the night's sailing had been accomplished with visibility of, at best, only a couple of hundred yards.

"We've done it, Caleb. The worst is behind us, and I speak particularly of those murderous friends of yours. I wonder if Wong returned to the marina." They were both feeling the effects of a night without sleep, but at least they had put a hundred miles between them and the Long Beach Marina. Even despite the foul weather, they felt safe, sealed away from the rest of the world.

The storm was moving inland, and after they turned the great bend northward along the California coast the weather began to brighten up considerably. They agreed to take turns running three-hour stints at the helm and catching up on their sleep. San Francisco was still three hundred miles away, and that meant thirty to forty hours of sailing if the current winds prevailed.

By early evening, they were forty miles offshore, shrouded by a coastal fog bank. A moonless night brought millions of stars out to light their way.

"I think we should put in at Monterey and take on some diesel." It was Ginny who spoke after studying the charts spread out below. They had used more fuel than expected, keeping themselves on a course that would put distance between the *Tashtego* and Long Beach as quickly as possible.

"Aye-aye, Skipper. I'm all for it. Actually I want to call Reinard anyway. When I talked to him last he said to give a yell if we needed a private investigator."

"You're right. We need one. But only if we can get someone we totally trust."

"Don't worry, we'll get the best. We're going to need some eyes and ears ashore. We've got to keep an eye on Onyx and try to nail her before she gets the whole L.A. basin addicted to crack."

"Caleb, I think our eyes and ears ashore should be a lawyer as well as an investigator. We're in a hell of a mess, and you can't surface unless you answer a bunch of subpoenas that would wipe out your credibility."

"Aye-aye, Captain. Monterey it is."

Ginny nodded.

"I'll try not to get us both killed," Willy offered. "If we can build a case that is airtight against Onyx and turn it over to professionals, we will. At least I'll be able to finish Reinard's book in jail."

During the morning they had kept the radio tuned to a commercial all-news station in Los Angeles. The rioting seemed to be under control now, and unrelated stories were again back in the news. It was midmorning when a news summary included a bit that drew Willy out of his bunk.

"Jade Baker, star witness in the recent Onyx Lu narcotics trial in San Francisco, was found dead of multiple gunshot wounds today in Los Angeles. The body of the controversial witness was found at the off ramp of the Harbor Freeway where it joins the San Diego Freeway. Baker's death brings the fatality total to over fifty since the rioting began two days ago in South Los Angeles." The short bulletin ended and the announcer went on to other items.

Willy bounded topside, where Ginny was tending the helm.

"It was an execution, Ginny," he said after filling her in. "There was no rioting near there. Onyx was probably counting on them writing this off as a riot casualty. She's wiping out anyone who could possibly have anything on her."

Ginny shook her head. "Isn't there anyone else from the old days who knows enough about Onyx to put her behind bars?"

"Just you and me, sweetheart, as far as I know."

"Willy, maybe we should do a ninety-degree change of course and point toward Pago Pago or Tahiti. Under the circumstances maybe we should choose a life in paradise."

"No matter where we went or how far, she would find us. Her connections are worldwide. Sooner or later we'd turn around and she'd be there."

"Maybe she'll meet a quick unnatural death. She travels in the fast lane all the time, after all."

"I wouldn't bank on it. I'm only sorry that you're implicated."

"Onyx doesn't know me at all."

"Sorry, sweetheart, but your anonymity ended when Wong found us at the marina. The numbers off the *Tashtego*. Bingo! They check the registration, and then they check other things. And they just keep on checking. Onyx Lu knows just about everything about you by now."

Ginny rose to put her arm around Willy. "Let's get that investigator onshore. We need another pair of shoulders, Caleb."

Willy nodded his agreement. It was Ginny's turn at the helm. He sat down next to where she was standing in the cockpit, close enough to touch her now and then.

"Ever been to Monterey?" he asked.

"A number of times. It's a great little place to stop over. I took a glance at the charts and nothing has changed. It will be a piece of cake for us getting in and out. Willy," she said suddenly, "maybe I'm paranoid, but I just thought of something. I did a stupid thing."

"You mean when you hooked up with me?"

"No, Willy. This is terrible. The charts down below are all new. I bought them for the trip."

Willy drew in a long breath. "Actually, Ginny, the odds against them checking on something like that are prodigious. They've got to have their hands full of other problems right now. I would guess that Wong will get bloody hell for letting us slip away. Onyx will throw a temper tantrum and that will be that."

"I hope so, Willy." Try as she would, Ginny just could not feel comfortable about her purchase.

"Ginny, it's pointless to dwell on it. There is absolutely nothing we can do about it. Even if someone goes into the Olde Charte Shoppe to check, chances are the clerk wouldn't remember the details. Besides, you bought charts for the entire West Coast! It's not like you've pinpointed our destination for them."

"I guess I'm being paranoid, but I can't get it off my mind."

"Well, I can get it off your mind for you. When we hole up in Monterey, I will give you old Caleb's special mind-clearing, mind-blowing remedy."

Ginny smiled just a little as Willy rubbed her thigh.

13

Wong was exhausted. He had run off the shoulder of Pacific Coast Highway twice, once narrowly missing a mailbox. Onyx had drained him of every drop of energy. The smell of Onyx was all over him and permeated the interior of the old Cadillac. It was 5 A.M. and drizzling rain. Hardly any traffic traveled Pacific Coast Highway at this hour, yet the trip back to Long Beach Marina seemed to take forever. At last he arrived, in a downpour.

Wong pulled up close to the public rest rooms and bathhouse and turned the engine off. The rain was sheeting down so hard he couldn't really see anything beyond the docks at the close edge of the marina. He rolled himself over into the backseat and collapsed into a deep sleep. He dreamed that Onyx was naked beneath him and that he was crushing her into submission.

It was midmorning before he was awakened by the blazing sun burning into his eyes. The taste and smell of Onyx still overwhelmed his senses. He opened the door and got out to stretch in the almost empty parking lot. Raising his arms, he looked out across the marina.

A shock of fear jolted him awake. A hundred yards away, the *Tashtego* was not in its slip. He walked swiftly toward the marina, rubbing his eyes in disbelief. He walked quickly down the gangway and out on the dock finger where the *Tashtego* had been tied up. All lines had been cleared from the dock except for one small coil.

Wong's heart started to pound and he broke into a sweat. His first instinct was to run toward the public phone and call Onyx. But as he neared the phone fear gripped him again. Of course she would expect him to tell her when the boat had left. There had been at least five hours of daylight, and he reasoned that the *Tashtego* surely must have set out during that time. They certainly would not have left earlier, during the storm. He tried desperately to remember whether he had actually seen the *Tashtego* when he arrived in the rain. Once again the smell of Onyx engulfed him and he cursed aloud.

"Dumb stupid bitch. She make me lose the *Tashtego!*" His mind became clearer with each minute. The *Tashtego* could be fourteen hours at sea. That was the last time he had seen the ketch.

His mind raced through all the possibilities as he dialed the number of the Palos Verdes ranch.

"Hello, that you, Onyx?"

"Yes, you fool, who else would it be? Wong, I hope this call is very important. You woke me up. All those stupid perverted games you play wear me out. I think you better think up some new ones, Wong."

"I will do that, Onyx. I will do that for you." As he spoke he could feel his manhood stir, and he wished he were back in Palos Verdes now.

"There is something I must tell you. The *Tashtego* is gone ... I mean, *Tashtego* leaving right now." It was the first time he had ever lied to Onyx. There was a long pause at the other end of the phone.

"Wong, where is the *Tashtego* right this second?"

"It in channel between breakwaters, motoring."

"Does she fly any sail?"

Wong hesitated, glancing up at the flags and streamers around the marina, trying to get a sense of the wind. "She raising main right now."

"Right now! They raising main in the breakwater channel?"

Wong realized he should probably not have said this. It was done occasionally, but there was no real advantage to raising the mainsail in the channel. Onyx would know this.

"Wong, go out to the beginning of the jetty. Take your glasses and keep the *Tashtego* in view for as long as you can. When you are absolutely certain that they have changed course to go either north or south along the coast, call me immediately. Then keep them in sight for as long as you can. Do you understand, Wong?"

"Oh, yes. I go to jetty right now."

"And Wong, when the *Tashtego* finally disappears from sight, you will come back to me here in Palos Verdes. We will talk. I will have some special instructions for you."

"Yes, I be right there, as soon as *Tashtego* is out of sight."

"Wong, you must call me just as you leave, the minute that you cannot any longer see the *Tashtego*."

"Oh, yes, I understand."

"And Wong, when you get here you and I will have time for a nice swim in pool. Of course you will have to return to the marina soon to let us know when the *Tashtego* returns."

With those last words, Onyx hung up. Wong went back to his old Cadillac. There would be no use going out to the jetty. The *Tashtego* was long gone and there was no way of telling in what direction.

He would have to hang around the marina for an hour or so before calling back. Actually he welcomed this time to decide whether he should tell Onyx north or south. But this dilemma was soon squeezed out of his mind with the vision of

Onyx swimming nude as she always did in the pool in Palos Verdes.

He looked at his watch impatiently. In a little over thirty minutes he called Onyx again.

"The *Tashtego* go straight out. She no go either north or south as far as I can see. She sail straight toward Avalon. I think they make overnight in Catalina before coming back." As he spoke, he realized that he had now told Onyx at least three lies. I shouldn't worry about that, he told himself. I am a man and that dumb bitch is a woman.

"Wong, I hope you are correct. They will be easy to find in Avalon. We have someone over there who will look for them."

Wong felt his stomach churn. Oh well, it would be easy to explain. He could say that they had gone north or south from Catalina. Or maybe he would be lucky and they would actually be found in Avalon.

"Wong, I feel very warm. I am slipping out of my clothes now and going out to the pool."

The phone clicked as Onyx hung up the receiver. Wong took a long last look at the marina, his eyes coming to rest on the empty slip. He thought of Onyx waiting in the pool.

The vintage Cadillac roared out of the parking lot, leaving a wake of blue smoke as it sped north on Pacific Coast Highway.

14

Office complexes in Irvine, near Newport Beach, were springing up fast between the freeways, creating new skylines seemingly every few months. Upscale engineering firms, property management companies, international traders, and particularly big banks were all eager to locate their headquarters there. Already settled in was the Sino-Americo Trading Company.

Carlos Lopez parked his nondescript car next to a meticulously polished black Jaguar in the sprawling lot adjacent to the Sino-Americo Bank Building. The building featured well groomed gardens of bonsai trees, waterfalls and stone walkways.

In the well-lit marble lobby stood a security desk with two uniformed, armed attendants. Carlos, as he had been instructed, handed one of the men a card that identified him as an international representative of the Cheung Chau Trading Company. He was immediately directed to the fifteenth floor.

The elevator opened up to a slick marble floor. Several steps led down to a sunken foyer highlighted by a large oval reception desk and several glass cases holding priceless treasures of the Orient. Carlos was particularly drawn to a carved jade Buddha almost ten inches high.

The receptionist was a young, svelte Chinese woman clad in a severe pinstripe suit. The severity of her suit, however, was undercut when she stood to greet Carlos. The tight pinstripe skirt was short enough to reveal almost the full measure of her thigh.

Ah, thought Carlos. Even his Luisa Maria did not have legs like those.

"Mr. Lopez, you are right on time. That is very good." She gave the hint of a smile.

The large carved rosewood door behind the receptionist suddenly opened.

"Señor Carlos Lopez, you honor our house." The deep, rich voice carried a strange mixture of British and Chinese accent. "I am Logan Phipps," the man announced, and then circled the desk to extend his hand toward Carlos.

Carlos grasped the extended hand firmly, then

stepped back. He had never seen this man before, though he had heard stories for years.

"Carlos, we haven't much time. Beryl, please join us in my office. Carlos, Beryl is to be your contact here. It is my wish that she know everything about our work together. You can be assured of her reliability, and your own security. Now let's get started."

Carlos Lopez and Beryl sat across from each other in plush leather chairs. A large Oriental rug covering the floor between them extended flush to the front of a massive carved rosewood desk. Logan Phipps didn't sit at his desk; instead he began pacing around the room as he talked.

"Carlos, Onyx Lu wisely selected you as her security chief for the new West Coast marketing operation. In this capacity you will be under the absolute supervision of Miss Lu." As Phipps talked, Beryl's dark eyes never left Carlos. The magnificent legs were on maximum display. She held a small clipboard and pad, but never used them. He realized suddenly that she was very nearly a young clone of Onyx.

"That is not to change," said Phipps, emphasizing the word "change." "However, we are here to discuss an additional facet of your employment. You will keep four other people under your surveillance and report on any activity that you think negatively affects the development of the company. Since Onyx is one of those people, it is absolutely forbidden for her to know of this added responsibility. Is that clear?"

"So far it is," replied Carlos. "But Onyx is a

very shrewd person. It will not be easy to delude her."

"I am sure, Carlos, that you have the ability to do that. You must be very careful, however." Phipps hesitated for a moment and then went on. "She can be very persuasive. I suppose the word I really mean to use is 'seductive.' In this case we must be careful that business does not become twisted up with pleasure."

He hesitated once again, then leaned forward with his two hands spread on his desk. "Besides, you have your Luisa Maria."

Carlos tried not to show his anger. He wondered how in the hell Phipps knew about Luisa Maria.

"Of course. This is a business matter." Carlos wondered what Phipps would say if he knew that Onyx had already contacted him to make clear her intentions.

Carlos turned from Phipps to face Beryl for a second. Her eyes were still riveted on him, but now she wore an open smile. She still did not speak. His gaze traveled down to her legs again and then he looked away. God! he thought. She certainly is as close to an Onyx look-alike as anyone could be. If anything, she's younger and more exotic.

He could feel Phipps studying him closely and turned his attention away from Beryl.

Phipps cleared his throat and spoke again. "As I said before, there will be four people under your scrutiny. Onyx and Wong you have met. The other two are Willy Hanson and Ginny Du Bois. Do you know of them?"

"No, not at all."

"Beryl will bring you up to date. Onyx will be able to fill in the details, especially about Mr. William Hanson. Encourage her to talk about him when she mentions his name. She holds a vendetta against him that could be a great distraction from business."

Phipps walked over to the window, which overlooked elegant Newport Beach, with a splendid view of the Pacific Ocean in the distance. "Hanson and Du Bois are of no immediate concern. They are presently at sea on a small sailing yacht, several days out of San Francisco. As I said, Beryl will bring you up to date."

15

It was a sparkling day along the Monterey Peninsula when the scenic coastline came into view from the *Tashtego*. An onshore breeze of about twelve knots rammed the big ketch forward. She passed Lovers Point and then made a perfect tack to sail directly into the mouth of the romantic old California port. Both Ginny and Willy had gotten some rest over the past couple of days, but they still looked forward to stretching their legs.

It was decided that Ginny would oversee the fueling of the *Tashtego* and then pick up a few groceries. Willy climbed onto the transient dock and headed for the first public telephone he could find that offered some degree of privacy. Luckily he caught Reinard at home back in New York.

"Hey, Willy, it's about time! I'll bet you've called to tell me you have a manuscript ready."

"Not a chance, pal. We've got big problems. Ever since Onyx was freed by the jury in San Francisco, she's been looking for us. We've given her the slip for at least a while." Reinard was the only person, other than Ginny, Willy felt he could trust. "I need some eyes and ears back in Los Angeles. I need a private eye with real talent. It'll cost some bucks but at least maybe you'll have a living author rather than a dead one."

"Willy, I may have just the guy. He did some work out there for a friend of mine who ran into trouble with a major mob character."

"You mean I'm not the only friend you've had on a hit list?"

"His name is Coley Doctor. He's a tough guy, but he can do a lot of low-key stuff without getting in trouble."

"Hey, I'll take your word for it. Tell him to meet me in San Francisco at Alioto's down on the wharf. We'll have dinner there Tuesday at seven, and mingle with the tourists."

"Wait a minute. I'll have to talk to him first."

"Look, tell him this is the opportunity of a lifetime. If that doesn't work, tell him you'll pay him double. If he's good, I want him. Ginny and I will be at Alioto's Tuesday night. That gives you three days. If you draw a blank, leave word for Caleb Jones with the bartender."

"I would bet he'll be there. He needs the money. I'll have to pay him well. He has three ex-wives to support. Where the hell are you now?"

"We're in Monterey, aboard the *Tashtego*. Of course, no one knows that, even you."

"Are they really trying to kill you?"

"Of course. They already got Jade, you know."

"Yes, I caught the piece in the press. Sounded like she was caught in the riots."

"Riots, my ass. She was dumped nowhere near the riots."

"Maybe the police should handle this, Willy."

"Look, old boy. We tried due process of law and they dumped Onyx right back on the system. This sweet innocent bitch is already set up in a mansion in Palos Verdes. When I finish with her this time, it will really be over."

"For a man who has a contract out on him, you sure have a lot of confidence."

"My confidence is only as good as your man Coley Doctor is. He'd better relish excitement. By the way," lied Willy, "your book is coming along great. I'll have a big chunk for you before we reach Seattle."

"Sure, Willy. Just like California is all fast horses, pretty women and butter-pecan ice cream."

"Reinard, you've got your priorities mixed up, as usual. See you soon, pal."

When Willy got back to the *Tashtego*, Ginny was still shopping. He did not relish her being out of sight. Even here he found himself scrutinizing everyone. He was jumpy, edgy, just plain paranoid.

A check of the gauge revealed that the diesel tank had been topped. He sat in the cockpit reading a copy of the *Examiner* he had picked up in town. After he'd scanned the entire paper, anxiety hit him hard again. Where the hell was she?

Then, far down the dock, he saw her coming, toting a large shopping bag. His sigh of relief was audible, and he didn't take his eyes off his striking companion until she had once again boarded the *Tashtego*.

"I thought you went for groceries, not a vacation. I don't like us being apart. After this we do everything together. Okay?"

"Hey, wait a minute! I didn't know we started serious conversations without a kiss."

Willy kissed her lightly on the cheek as she handed over the shopping bag. "I'm sorry, but I'm nervous as hell."

"Caleb, did you make your phone call to Reinard?" Ginny was beginning to like Willy's having two names. Caleb served very well when he got a little grumpy.

"As a matter of fact, I did. We're seeing our new contact on Tuesday night on Fisherman's Wharf. He's helped Reinard out before. Supposed to be a top-notch undercover guy."

"Are you going to tell him everything?"

"Just about. We've got to trust somebody. We've got to keep an eye on Palos Verdes while we are out here on the *Tashtego*."

"I'm with you, baby. Let's sail up to San Francisco Sunday afternoon. I know a couple of people in the marina. I'll call ahead and get a slip assignment."

"Let's not call ahead, Ginny. I'd rather put as little on record as possible. There will be a lot of boats out on cruise, and overnight slips should be easy enough to get. I don't think we ought to put our name on a reservation list. In fact, maybe we ought to rechristen the *Tashtego*."

"Willy, the *Tashtego* is a one-of-a-kind ketch. We can't hide her behind another name. We've put a lot of distance between here and Long Beach. At this point I think we're kind of like a needle in a haystack, the haystack being the Pacific Ocean."

Willy merely nodded, not wishing to press the matter further. After all, the odds were against their being discovered in the vast reaches of the Bay Area waterfront. But his mind drifted to other concerns. One was Ginny's visit to the Olde Chart Shoppe in Long Beach, where she had purchased the charts for their trip. The other was the Golden Gate itself. The Golden Gate was a narrow strait, a bottleneck. Every single vessel that passed in or out of San Francisco had to go through it. A land-sea stakeout of the Golden Gate could easily record a list of all boats that sailed that way during the course of a day.

"Ginny, I'd like to amend our itinerary just a bit. I think we should pass through the Golden Gate as inconspicuously as possible. If we time our passage with a friendly fog bank, that's all the better."

"You're right, Willy. We should hang around a few miles out and wait for the morning fog. Then we'll go in by radar. It's duck soup, Willy. If anyone were looking, it would take a miracle to spot us."

16

The message light was blinking on Onyx Lu's telephone in Palos Verdes. To her immense surprise, it was a message from Logan Phipps. He wanted her to join him for dinner in his cliff house at Dana Point. He had never done that before. In the past, it had been only business meetings in business places.

After slipping into her thin, cream-colored silk sheath, Onyx stood spread-eagled before the large mirror with a bright light burning behind her. She wore nothing at all under the dress, and every detail of her female perfection showed clearly in the mirror. It was almost as good as being naked.

She drove herself to the house on Green Lantern Street. A sleek young woman who could have been her younger sister answered the door.

"Ah yes." The young woman bowed. "Mr. Phipps is expecting you."

Logan Phipps was dressed casually, in contrast to his usual business attire. There was a table for two set on a deck overlooking the Pacific. The shore below them was a sheer three-hundred-foot drop.

"Onyx, thank you so much for coming. I think it is past time for you and me to celebrate."

"For what, Lo?" Onyx had once been introduced to him by his mainland name, Lo Fong. It gave her a feeling of power to call him by his real name, a name few others knew.

"There are actually two reasons for celebrating. The first is by far the most important." Phipps paused for emphasis and then continued.

"We are opening a new cabaret and restaurant in Redondo Beach. We will call it the Black Lamp. Onyx Lu will have complete control over the officially listed proprietor. Onyx, it is very chic and upscale. We will see to it that you have your mecca for all those friends in Southern California who, shall we say, just want to have."

Phipps hesitated, giving his rare broad grin. "The crack market is expanding. The Black Lamp will enable us to capitalize on the rapidly increasing public demand."

"Lo, I don't know what to say. It will be exciting to get back into business again. How soon do we open the Black Lamp?"

"At the latest, it will be three weeks."

"That's wonderful! It gives me time to plan an opening that will be, as they say, a bombshell!"

"I thought you would be happy. Now I would like to talk about the second reason for our little meeting." Phipps hesitated, choosing his words carefully. "How many people in addition to you and me know the whereabouts of the *Tashtego?*"

"None. Absolutely no one. When Wong told me about the *Tashtego* sailing, I handled the investigation myself." Onyx rose from her chair and walked casually around the small terrace, cocktail in hand. Finally she positioned herself directly between Phipps and the rapidly setting sun. Her silhouette through the flimsy sheath was revealed totally, even to the darkly etched tuft of pubic hair.

"So tell me about it, Onyx." If Phipps was ruffled by the erotic display, he gave no indication of it, keeping his eyes fixed on her face.

"I sent Wong away on other business and went to the marina as a stupid tourist. I pretended to look for the *Tashtego* as a friend of Ginny Du Bois. No one on their dock could remember seeing the *Tashtego* leave and expressed surprise that they would have left during the storm."

Onyx turned her back for a moment and stretched before the setting sun. She pivoted quickly and was delighted to catch Phipps appraising her. She stood perfectly still for several seconds until he lifted his eyes again to lock his gaze with hers. Onyx paced quickly to the other side of the terrace.

"So tell me, Onyx, how did you get the information that the *Tashtego* was headed north?"

"Among other shops, I went to the Olde Chart Shoppe near the marina. It was much easier than I expected. There was an old fool behind the counter."

"And did you charm him by standing in front of his doorway in that same dress?"

Onyx flashed a radiant smile at Phipps's acknowledgment of her charm. "He too was puzzled that the *Tashtego* would leave in a storm. He knew Ginny Du Bois well. She was a regular customer. He offered to go through recent cash receipts and let me make a list of all her purchases."

"And just why would he offer to do that?"

"Because he let me get behind counter and he stood behind me while I copy. I think I could have written a novel as long as I stand there. He was dumb bastard. He said he would lock front door and let me blow him."

"Onyx, spare me the details."

"Imagine that dumb bastard. In a day and age like this he would take a chance like that. But just then I find information I was looking for. Ginny Du Bois had bought navigational charts from Santa Barbara all the way to Puget Sound. She told the old fool that they were leaving on a cruise when the weather broke."

"How did you come to the conclusion that they went north?"

"Wong said he saw *Tashtego* leave slip. He say she headed straight for Avalon as far as he could follow her. My contact in Catalina never see *Tashtego*. I believe they went north because they buy northern charts."

"I think you are right, but we'll know soon. I have a land-sea stakeout on Golden Gate Channel. However, I think you should consider whether or not Wong was telling the truth. If they were headed north they would have pointed well within his vision. Wong is a sailor. He lied about the Avalon bearing. I doubt that he ever saw the *Tashtego*."

Onyx flushed with anger. The same thought had crossed her mind, but she hadn't put it together the way Phipps had. Of course, Wong might have mistaken another far-off boat for the *Tashtego*. But then, as Phipps said, Wong was a sailor. Onyx turned from Phipps to look out the window over the sprawling marina below.

To her surprise, Phipps closed his arms around her from behind. One hand dropped firmly against the tantalizing tuft that had been so clearly silhouetted by the setting sun.

Onyx arched her back against him. "Oh, yes! Lo!"

Rudely, Phipps spun her around and held her at a distance by her shoulders.

"Onyx! Shame on you. In this day and age you would let me do a thing like that? Beryl! Show Miss Lu to the door, will you, please?"

Onyx shook with anger and humiliation at

Phipps's rejection, obviously witnessed by the girl.

Beryl smiled and shrugged in half hearted sympathy. Phipps had left the room. It was time to go home, home to Wong in Palos Verdes. Oh, there would be hell for him to pay tonight. He had lied to her, and she had let him get away with it. As she climbed into the sleek Jaguar, she thought that rejection by Logan Phipps was really to be expected. Someday she would find the key to that man, though she cared little about going to bed with him. But Beryl! Ah, she would be more like it!

But tonight Onyx would have to occupy herself with Wong. First he would have to be disciplined for telling lies. She would push him to the brink, maybe even over the edge. She thought of the derringer hidden in her headboard, thought of Wong humiliated and crazed. One day he would eat the bullet right out of that derringer.

17

At the northern end of the Golden Gate Bridge, on Highway 101, on the way to Sausalito, there is a scenic overlook. Countless thousands of tourists take photographs from that spot every year. On a clear day, San Francisco stands out like a jewel. But the shifting fog banks and winds can create an entirely different view. On many mornings the giant piers holding the bridge thrust up through the fog, seemingly suspended in air. That is the way it was on this day.

At the corner of the scenic overlook nearest the bridge stood Casey Larkin. Larkin tried to focus his powerful field glasses on the waters below the bridge, but except for an area close to the shore, the main channel was closed to his vision.

Larkin was a diesel mechanic. He freelanced work from the various marinas around Sausalito, but his current assignment was certainly different from anything he had ever done before. Captain Alexandros, aboard the trawler *New Territories*, had described the *Tashtego* to him in vivid detail: a forty-six-foot ketch with fancy deck hardware and a rigging that stretched higher than most of its kind. Alexandros even furnished a Polaroid. Larkin's job was to scrutinize the channel that entire day and try to identify the boat, though the job would be almost impossible until the fog had lifted.

Out in the channel under the main span, traffic was minimal. There were hardly any pleasure craft sailing in the crisp air. Now and then a big tanker or giant container ship would move slowly through the Golden Gate. The *New Territories* rumbled back and forth across the channel, crossing aft of the giant ships to make certain the *Tashtego* didn't use them to run interference. It was a difficult job, but not impossible, unless the fog thickened. Alexandros could see that the lookout on the cliff above Sausalito would be useless until the fog lifted at about noon. The next two days were supposed to be sharp and clear, so the captain figured the *Tashtego* would try to slip through today. But supposedly those on the vessel had no inkling they were being sought. If this was really the case, they might wait for tomorrow's fair weather.

18

The water was mirror-flat. The big container ship stretched a thousand feet ahead of the *Tashtego*, now tucked alongside the port beam of the massive vessel. The bow disappeared into the fog as it inched ahead under the main span of the Golden Gate Bridge. The *Tashtego* would be invisible to anyone unless he was in the main channel and perhaps less than a hundred yards from the container ship.

The giant vessel, *Nagasaki Maru*, was heavily laden with container boxes piled four deep fore and aft. The *Tashtego* positioned itself about a hundred yards abeam of the pilothouse of the

Nagasaki Maru and motored alongside at four or five knots, letting the sophisticated radar of the big container ship knife the way through the fog.

All at once, high above both vessels loomed the main span of the Golden Gate Bridge. Within another couple of minutes they were surrounded by the waters of San Francisco Bay and the bridge was lost behind them in the fog.

Less than a mile away, the trawler *New Territories* crossed ahead of the *Nagasaki Maru*.

Captain Alexandros swiftly scanned the sides of the big ship, whose stern disappeared into the fog, and then proceeded to another point, where his radar indicated a second large vessel making the Golden Gate passage.

Directly astern of the *Nagasaki Maru* the diesel engine of the *Tashtego* rumbled to life as the ketch angled off the stern of the huge ship and pointed toward the waters off Fort Baker lookout toward Sausalito. Within minutes the *Tashtego* was alone in the foggy waters and the *Nagasaki Maru* vanished astern in the dense fog. Other than the container ship, neither Ginny nor Willy had spotted a single vessel in the morning fog.

Running along shore with Sausalito dimly visible off the port beam, the *Tashtego* proceeded for several miles to a small marina near Marin City. Ginny expertly pulled alongside a fueling dock and Willy vaulted over the handrail to secure lines.

"We've done it, sweetheart! We're inside the

bay and I'll bet nobody knows it." Willy was elated.

Ginny was eyeing the small marina carefully. "Let's pick up a mooring offshore. That way we won't be accessible to any landlubbers."

Willy wondered about the wisdom of an off-shore mooring openly visible to passersby on the shore road. But they were well above the busy harbor at Sausalito, so maybe Ginny was right. They would only be there for a day or two. The bay was well sheltered and it would be great for catching up on some much-needed rest.

Ginny talked to a dock attendant, who pointed out a mooring at the far northern tip of the small harbor. A harbor launch was available, so getting ashore and ultimately across the bridge to Fisherman's Wharf by taxi or rental car was no big problem. Both agreed that this was a more obscure place to stay than any of the busy marinas close to the Wharf, where they were to meet Coley Doctor the next day. If they happened to be blessed with another morning fog the next day, they could sail the *Tashtego* across the bay to the downtown area, tie up at any one of a thousand docks, rent a car and have the run of the city.

Meanwhile, high on the ridge overlooking Marin City, Casey Larkin couldn't believe his good fortune. He trained his powerful binoculars on the handsome ketch, moored now at the northern tip of the marina below. It had come through the fog and passed by his vantage point unnoticed. The *New Territories* had also missed the fancy ketch. But now, easy, it was right in his front yard.

Larkin walked over to the telephone and dialed Captain Alexandros's number. He left a message on the answering machine, saying that if the *Tashtego* left its mooring, he would follow her in his runabout and check in later. They had the *Tashtego* caught in San Francisco Bay just like a model ship inside a wine bottle.

For his good work, Alexandros would no doubt favor him with a handsome reward.

19

Willy and Ginny arrived at Alioto's early so that they could sit at a table near the bar. Outside, the sea lions did their best to entertain the patrons, cavorting on the dock and doing flips into the water.

At the stroke of noon a tall black man emerged from the stairwell and strode toward the bar. He was lean and fit, fully six feet six and neatly dressed in casual sports clothes. The bartender poured a shot of Chivas Regal neat as the man turned to scan the restaurant. His eyes came to rest knowingly on Willy and Ginny. He tossed several bills on the bar, walked directly to their table and sat down without saying a word.

He watched the sea lions for a while, then finally said, "They're fun to watch, but they stink." The man extended his hand toward Willy. "Reinard Gossman sent me. I'm Coley Doctor."

Willy extended his hand and saw it disappear into the massive grip of Coley Doctor. "What else did Reinard tell you besides what we looked like?"

The man studied Willy carefully. "He told me you single-handedly smashed a major drug ring and sent the major conspirator off to trial. But the trial fizzled because the bodies of all the key witnesses were way too cold." The man paused. "He told me I would get two hundred bucks a day until you've seen enough of Coley Doctor. That would for tracking down people and evidence. I'd submit bills for extra expenses. What I will not do is get shot on your behalf. If that kind of heat comes down on me, Coley Doctor will no longer recognize your faces. I am a technician, not a hero."

Willy smiled at the man's appraisal of his job. He had the gut feeling that Coley Doctor would not be so quick to run and hide if there actually was trouble.

"That's all fair enough. Reinard is a man with exceptional judgment. If you're okay with him, you're okay with me. I must warn you that we're playing with people devoid of ethical fiber. You need to recognize this as you proceed with your investigation. No one is asking you to be a hero, but the job carries a lot of dangerous baggage. If they ever figure out who you are and what you're up to, you're dead."

The man's expression did not change. "I can always up my fee."

"Tell me about yourself. Fill me in just a little."

"Born in Watts, 1960. Basketball, Syracuse. Passed the bar exam, 1983. Convicted on a drug rap, Florida, 1985. Disbarred, Florida, 1985. They didn't waste any time. Conviction reversed, 1987. Justice was done, but my name scares the wits out of respectable law partners. Private eye since 1987, mostly in and around L.A. I like it. I make a lot of money."

Willy liked his candor. He looked too good to be true. "Let's have lunch. Ginny and I will bring you up to date on everything that has happened since we last saw Onyx Lu."

Coley Doctor smiled. "I'd like to hear your whole story. I think I might be able to update you on a few things already. I was in Watts during last week's riots. There were some strange goings-on that had nothing to do with the cops beating up that guy. But you tell me your story and I'll tell you mine."

Willy liked Coley Doctor better all the time.

Their entrees came: two plates of fresh salmon and Dungeness crab. Willy started his story at the point over a year ago when he had left Onyx Lu bound and gagged in her own boat, waiting for the coast guard to arrive. Coley Doctor nodded his acknowledgment of Willy's audacity. He scribbled occasionally in a small leather note-book.

By the end of the meal, Coley had been brought fully up to date. Willy described Wong's spying on them and how they had followed him to Palos Verdes.

Suddenly, Coley spoke. "Pal, you're living on borrowed time. What if Wong had discovered you? You would have been dead in five minutes. You just can't take chances like that. From now on, leave the detailed investigations to me. There are ways of getting information without putting your life on the line. If you keep wandering out solo, you'll get us all iced. Trust old Coley and we'll slam-dunk all these bastards."

"Where's the *Tashtego*?" Coley had been scanning the distant boat slips, thinking they might have sailed right into Fisherman's Wharf.

"We rode sidesaddle to a container ship through the Golden Gate. The fog was thick and we think we got through unnoticed. Once inside the bay, we veered north and tied up in a small marina near Marin City." The more Willy talked, the more he realized he had done the wrong thing. He had put the flashy *Tashtego* in a spot where it would stand out instead of tying up with a thousand other vessels at some monster of a marina within the bay.

Coley, who had listened carefully all this time, now seemed genuinely perplexed. "Why did you think you had to sneak into the bay?"

Ginny felt her nerves tighten. She decided to

make Coley Doctor aware of her visit to the chart store.

"You see, Coley, I bought these charts, navigational charts for the whole Pacific Coast. I picked them up right there in a chandlery near the marina where Wong found us. I realize now that it was a stupid thing to do."

Coley Doctor stared at her before speaking. "Yes, it was. How many people in the marina knew you were leaving?"

"We made a decision to leave so quickly that we didn't have time to discuss our plans with anyone."

"Nevertheless, you did talk to the clerk in the chart store and bought charts from L.A. to Seattle." Coley looked glum and a little disappointed. "You ain't going to like what I'm going to say. But I'm going to say it anyway. We can assume that they inquired around and that they did visit the chart shop. From that point forward we should assume that they know exactly where you are. Hell, they might be right here in this restaurant!"

Willy's eyes quickly swept the room.

"The people you are involved with have endless resources," Coley said. "They have learned to be very thorough. It is inconceivable to me that they would not have checked the marina thoroughly."

"Okay, let's say you're right. Let's say they're right on our asses. What do you recommend we do now?"

"Hey, friend. I supply information, not advice.

As soon as I get back to L.A., I'll check out the marina and visit the chart shop."

"Willy, I'm so sorry!" Ginny's comment went unanswered.

Coley spoke again. "Incidentally, I know about Logan Phipps. His real name is Lo Fong, and he is as slick as a greased weasel. The Feds have known for a long time that he oversees a massive narcotic ring, but so far they have not been able to nail him."

Coley paused for a few seconds. "By the way, how did you get from the *Tashtego* to Alioto's?"

"We hired a cab for the day. I struck up a deal with a taxi driver who brought someone to the marina. He's parked down the block. We gave him a couple of hours. He's probably having lunch right now." Willy recalled hailing the taxi as it was pulling out of the marina. The driver had taken the fifty bucks eagerly, with the promise of another fifty when they got back to the *Tashtego* at the end of the day.

"Good. You did good." Coley Doctor nodded. "You could have done something stupid, like renting a car, or just sailing right out front and tying up. You'll have to start thinking cautiously all the time."

Coley glanced around the room as if to demonstrate his point.

"Why don't you put the *Tashtego* back out under the Golden Gate in the next morning fog? I think you guys are a menace on land."

Coley broke into a sudden big smile. "Logan Phipps!" He shook his head slowly. "Man oh man! We've got a chance to catch the biggest and the baddest red-handed. If he is openly messing around with someone like Onyx Lu, we just might be able to nail him." Then, sobering quickly, he added, "Let's just not get overanxious. Okay?"

"Are you armed?" Coley asked, unbuttoning his loose-fitting sports jacket to reveal a Glock nine-millimeter snugly holstered under his massive arm.

"I have a thirty-eight police special and we have an old thirty-thirty Marlin aboard the *Tashtego*." Willy realized how pitifully weak his arsenal was as he spoke.

"Man, those are toys!" Coley said. "Of course, the guys you're up against are no doubt set up with automatic weapons, grenades and God knows what. So it really doesn't matter. Do you want to be buried with family?" He was only half joking.

"Okay, okay!" Willy responded, irritated now. "Obviously we have to win this battle with our wits. Your job is to supply information. We'll do the rest."

"Hey, look, we've talked some and I've learned a little. But there has to be a lot I missed. I'm going back to L.A. as soon as I leave you guys." Coley was rapidly flipping through several pages of notes. "I want you to check in with me every third day when you're sailing and every day when you're holed up someplace."

"Look, Coley," Willy said, uncomfortable with the way things were going, "I want to get this thing over with. I want to nail Onyx in such a way that a jury of idiots will send her up for life. From you, I want to know when she's vulnerable. That's all. You can leave all the dirty work to me." Willy made a motion toward the waiter. "Of course, Reinard can act as an intermediary if necessary."

Coley fixed a hard gaze on Willy. "You don't know what you're getting into. You care about her?" Coley glanced at Ginny. Willy said nothing. "If you want to keep her alive, you'd better get her to a fast jet and hide her away until this is over. I don't think you're aware of who you are dealing with in Mr. Logan Phipps. I have friends down in Watts who tell me he was the major activist in the L.A. riots. He aided and abetted the whole thing as a smokescreen for a major drug deal. He saw an opportunity and he took it. Having the blood of fifty or sixty people on his hands meant nothing to him."

"Street talk," Willy said dismissively.

Coley's massive hand firmly grasped Willy's shoulder. "Believe me, and we got a chance of pulling this thing off. Doubt me, and you stand a good chance of being a dead man."

With that, Coley Doctor rose from the table, touched his forehead lightly in farewell and strode toward the stairs leading down to the street. The man exuded confidence, and Willy had to hope he actually knew what he was talking about. He and Ginny seemed to have no choice but to put their trust in Coley Doctor.

Ginny interrupted Willy's thoughts. "I think he's a pompous ass."

"Maybe you're right, but he does come highly recommended. We should start for the taxi," he said, then added, "He evidently knows the turf around L.A. pretty well. The fact that he knows of Logan Phipps is obviously a plus."

They were about a half block from where their taxi was parked when they noticed a small group of people clustered around the cab. The driver himself was squatting on the curb.

As they approached, Willy could see a deep scratch in the yellow paint running from the rear of the vehicle to the rim of the headlight on the front fender. When they reached the driver, he was inspecting a shattered headlight.

The driver pointed wildly to the long scratch in the yellow paint. "Look what some dumb jerk has done to my new cab." He pointed to the headlight. "If I find the punk who did this, I'll rip his goddamn liver out!"

"Where were you when it happened?" Willy asked.

"Hell, I went across the street to get a bite to eat. When I got back, I found this! This city is getting as bad as New York. I left New York because of bullshit like this!"

Willy looked more closely at the damaged headlight. It had been hit dead center with a sharp object. Jagged lines radiated from the center to the rim, dividing it into wedges. For an instant his mind flicked back to the broken dinner plate he had found on the dock at Long Beach Marina.

Ginny looked at the broken headlight. "I'll pay for the repair," she offered.

The driver shook his head. "Why should you?" The man smacked his fist firmly into his hand. "It just pisses me off that some young punk has got nothing better to do. Nowadays I guess this is just a cost of doing business."

Ginny and Willy climbed into the back of the cab for the trip back to the *Tashtego*. Both were quiet until they drove across the Golden Gate Bridge.

"Willy, do you remember that broken dinner plate we found on the dock back in Long Beach?"

Willy nodded. "I thought of that too. Great minds think alike. But I'd have to say there could be no connection. It's called paranoia. I don't think either of us will relax until we get the *Tashtego* back out on the other side of the Golden Gate."

Ginny agreed, then put her head on Willy's shoulder. The thought of putting out to sea in the morning was comforting to both of them.

20

Casey Larkin didn't reach Captain Alexandros aboard the *New Territories* until the morning after the *Tashtego* tied up in the Marin City Marina. He had positioned himself at a fisherman's coffee shack near the north end.

"They're removing sail covers and show every indication of leaving the marina. Captain, there's hardly any visibility down here. I can't believe they're going to put out in this soup."

"Of course they are. They're going to sneak out just as they got in. Follow them as far as you can from the shore. Take up your post at Fort Baker and try to spot them going under the span. I'll position the *New Territories* at halfway under the span. If they're leaving the bay, they ought to be under the bridge in less than half an hour."

At Fort Baker, the soup was thick but visibility was still close to five hundred yards. An empty tanker riding high in the water was barely visible out under the span of the Golden Gate. On the starboard side of the tanker just below the wheelhouse the tall mainmast of the *Tashtego* was clearly discernible, moving seaward. Larkin watched until both vessels had passed under the giant span and then picked up his cellular phone and dialed the number of the *New Territories*.

"Captain, she's all yours. She's pointed north tucked in alongside that big tanker on the starboard side. If you need me again, you know where to find me."

In the quiet morning air, Larkin could hear the rumbling of the revved-up diesels of the *New Territories* bearing up on the stern of the tanker.

"Good job, Larkin. Stand by at home for further instructions." Alexandros revved up until the *Tashtego* came barely into view. He then fixed his radar on the big ketch and dropped his speed enough so that he was well out of sight in the morning fog. About five knots farther at sea, the *Tashtego* split sharply away from the tanker and pointed due north along the coastline toward Point Reyes.

The morning sun dazzled and sparkled a million beads of light on the water as the *Tashtego* burst free of the fog bank. A fresh morning breeze filled the full jib and main. Ginny cut the diesel kicker and let the big sails of the showy ketch push them forward swiftly and silently.

The magnificent morning revived Ginny's and Willy's sagging spirits. They were alone on the ocean except for a tiny speck, apparently a trawler, several miles to their port stern.

"Where we bound for, Captain?" Willy's face broke into a broad grin. The bright sun and the spirit of adventure had replaced the dour thoughts of the previous evening.

Ginny flashed the bright smile that had attracted Willy from the beginning

"I think we'll trade watches until we get to Humboldt Bay near Eureka. Can you stand two or three days of this?"

Ginny flashed the bright smile that had attracted Willy from the beginning.

"You betcha, kid. I could stand this forever. I've been thinking, maybe you could rig up the autotiller for a while so we could catch up on some friendly homework."

Ginny responded by unsnapping her halter and flipping it into the cockpit below the wheel. Her shorts quickly joined the halter and she stood like a bronzed goddess at the helm of the *Tashtego*.

Willy knelt between her and the wheel to lavish kisses on toes and ankles. Slowly he worked his way up the sleek legs, ankles spread apart for balance against the stiff breeze.

"Willy! You damn fool!"

Ginny gave the big wheel a spin. The ketch, pilotless, pointed into the wind, the big sails flapping uselessly with no hands on the tiller. Their two bodies went down and meshed with the gently pulsing motion of the cockpit, out of view of the entire world save for a circling gull seemingly curious about the peculiar ritual taking place below.

21

Onyx and Carlos had just finished their inspection of the Black Lamp. The new, upscale restaurant was dimly lit, the walls and tables of black and gold reflected hypnotically in mirrors that magnified the place's elegance. Looking out over the ever-fascinating activity of the Redondo Beach waterfront, it was the perfect location for the wealthy customers Onyx planned to cater to.

Onyx and Carlos stepped into the small elevator at the rear and took it to the third floor above the restaurant. They stepped out into a small foyer decorated sparingly with a few pieces of red and black lacquered furniture. A large black Oriental lamp hung from a gold chain in the corner of the foyer, its small, flickering bulb providing the room's only light.

Onyx pressed a small remote-control button she carried in her purse. Before them, a sliding teak panel opened onto an immense room that took up the entire third floor. This was the cabaret room, where the most special guests of the Black Lamp would be entertained. Here Onyx would use her special talents to tease the appetites of California's most decadent and affluent citizens.

She looked at the dazzling room and imagined it filled with bejeweled guests plunging into the depths of hedonism. A long bar was elevated several steps above the rest of the room. A stage for performers started behind the bar and wrapped around the corner of the room, spreading into a small circle in the middle of the area where the cabaret patrons would sit.

Electricians were still at work installing special track lighting that would focus on groupings of plush furniture. The room would comfortably accommodate more than a hundred people.

"A hundred dollars per person for a hundred people is ten thousand dollars a day, Carlos. A hundred days, a million dollars. What do you think?"

Carlos nodded without speaking. Secretly, he wondered how much of the million would trickle down to him. Probably not much, he reasoned. His duties were clearly defined. His retainer was handsome but contained no escalator clauses.

"And that is just the beginning," Onyx went on. "When the really big spenders come to Onyx's playpen, the figure will double."

The two of them wandered into the women's rest room. The handsomely lacquered door, not yet hung, was propped inside against the wall next to a long leather sofa. A row of dressing tables lined another wall, each table with a large well-lit mirror above it.

"These are for our stars, the ladies who bring the men who spend all the money." Onyx sat on one of the leather stools with her back to the mirror.

"Carlos, come here. Stand before me and look at the mirror behind me. Closer, Carlos." Onyx moved her hands along Carlos's hips.

"What are you thinking about, Carlos?"

"I am thinking that you will make a lot of money here at the Black Lamp. I remember a similar place I saw once in Macau."

"Is that all you think of? Just money?" Onyx's hands moved to the zipper in front of her. "Do you think of nothing else, Carlos?"

"I am trying very hard at this moment to think of nothing else. But it is very difficult, Onyx." The zipper moved down quickly at Onyx's gentle tug.

"You know, Carlos, I don't believe you. And I can see now that you do not believe yourself. Let me take a good look at this and see what it is that you are so selfishly saving for your Luisa Maria."

Carlos grasped both Onyx's wrists and jerked her to her feet.

"Luisa Maria! Who! Who told you about Luisa Maria?"

Onyx stared down at his open zipper, refusing to meet his angry eyes. "Everyone knows about your precious Luisa Maria. We even know where she is."

"She is no part of this life. She is none of your business. She is not part of my agreement with you." Carlos released Onyx and backed away quickly, zipping himself up. To his surprise, she did not look angry. In fact, a hint of a smile played at the corners of her mouth.

"You are a big damn fool, Carlos. I was going to give you special treat. You could be special friend. Business and pleasure would work together very well in our case. All you would have to do is stand there and let Onyx make you feel like king. You are a bad boy, Carlos."

Carlos backed farther away, tantalized by her proposition, but much too furious to succumb. Logan Phipps had also been aware of Luisa Maria. Their knowledge was a threat to Luisa Maria's life, and could be held over him like a dagger to his throat.

"Onyx, the electricians are still working out there. They could walk in." Carlos was immediately sorry he had spoken. What he had said only made him look weak, as if he were postponing her invitation, instead of refusing it.

This time a broad smile crossed Onyx's face.

"It is wonderful that you are so rational and

sensible, Carlos. The wisdom of most men is overwhelmed by that thing they carry around in their pants. You are so wise, Carlos."

He could see that she was taunting him, enjoying the job of destroying his Latin machismo.

Onyx walked over to where he now stood in the doorway. The electricians worked industriously at their task, paying no attention to the two visitors. She reached up to put her hands on Carlos's broad shoulders and spoke softly into his face.

"Carlos, you are so naive. Someday we will have each other and you will think back and realize how silly it was to back away today. It really isn't very manly, dear Carlos."

He grabbed her arms firmly and took them from his shoulders.

"We will have each other, Carlos," she repeated. "Many times. Most of the time it will be when I say so, at my command. But the first time we do have each other, I promise you that you will have to beg. You will have to get on your knees and beg and beg and beg!"

With that said, Onyx strode forward, brushing against him as she made her way to the elevator in the foyer. For just a moment he was sorry he had not let her have her way. It would have meant nothing, and avoided trouble. Then he remembered again Logan Phipps's warning.

During the rest of the afternoon Onyx acted as if nothing had happened. When Carlos dropped her off in Palos Verdes, she turned to him with a full smile and spoke. "Oh, Carlos, I am so happy.

We open the Black Lamp in only a week. You should see my guest list. Right from the beginning, it will be the 'in' place to go in all of California. Of course you will not be there. You will have to tend to the security room, watching the television monitors. Logan and I will depend on you to do that well, Carlos."

She departed without saying good-bye. She was all business.

22

Lolly Penrose eyed the envelopes on the small oval desk in front of her. They were all unopened. Her thoughts rambled back to a few years ago, to the glory days when her fan mail had been delivered to her opened and banded together. It had filled large baskets then. Though most of the letters had been glowingly similar, there had always been a few that were downright nasty or even pornographic. She had always particularly enjoyed reading the most unflattering and suggestive ones. They were rarely repetitious or boring. On the contrary, they were sometimes extremely imaginative and outrageously decadent. Their authors would never know how close they came to hitting the real personality of Lolly Penrose right on the head.

Lolly studied the small mirror over the small desk. The tiny lines and puffiness remained constantly visible to her, though she was always complimented for her youthful beauty.

She counted the envelopes. There were nine. There were always fewer than ten these days, and some days there were none. One of the envelopes was black, small, and addressed in white script. Because it was different, she opened it first.

It turned out to be an invitation to the grand opening of a new restaurant and cabaret. The Black Lamp. She had almost flipped it into a wastebasket before she noticed a handwritten note appended to the invitation.

"Penny Rose, long time no see you. Hope you come to Black Lamp and party-party with Onyx. It be kinda like old times. You will love Black Lamp. As always, your most wild wish is your command to me. I love all of you!" The note was signed "Onyx."

Lolly pushed the other unopened letters into the waste-basket, then tucked the invitation to the Black Lamp into the top dresser drawer. She flushed warm as memories of past parties with Onyx and her friends flooded through her mind. She thought of the times when she and Willy Hanson would plunge into days of revelry together along the Orange County coast. Onyx had always been there with fancy booze and cocaine.

She walked over to the liquor cabinet and poured three fingers of scotch neat. It was eleven in the morning. Time for a drink. Lolly tucked her legs beneath her on the sofa, unable to get Willy off her mind now. He would really raise hell with her about drinking in the A.M. She could almost hear his voice from years back, warning, "Try a little screwing instead. Drinking in the morning will take you right out of the big game."

Lolly smiled and downed the scotch in one gulp. By God, she thought to herself. I need a little party. Black Lamp, here I come. She returned to the desk to memorize the date of the opening, then strode back to the liquor cabinet. She poured another three fingers and made a pact with herself to sip this one. She would nurse it along until it was time for breakfast. Lolly Penrose had made more than fifty pictures during a career which had made her a household name to America's cinema fans. Lily Hinkle's gossip column had recently made much of her turning forty-seven years of age, harping on "how lovely she looked." Lolly turned again to the mirror. Of course, she was really fifty-one. And there hadn't been a role in the past three years except that disaster of a horror movie.

Leaning over the desk, she removed the mirror from the wall and stooped to slide it under the sofa. The light was just not right for a mirror there, she told herself.

The flood of memories continued. It wasn't long ago when she had escaped her industrialist husband's indifference by trysting with Willy Hanson. Willy had filled her life with excitement and nourished her insatiable appetite for sex and cocaine. It had always irritated her that Willy had done nothing to throttle her need for cocaine. He had never used it himself, though his mania for good scotch had been a fine companion for her addiction.

When Willy had vanished from the face of the earth well over a year ago, she had managed to clean up her act a bit.

Her mind raced over the brief, torrid affair she'd had then with Reinard Gossman, Willy's friend. Her shrink had suggested that the affair was just a way of getting back at Willy for dumping her. She didn't think that was really true, but it had given her a magnificent excuse to dump Reinard and retreat into her daily bottle of scotch.

She walked out onto the balcony of her condo. She gazed over the Los Angeles Basin toward Redondo Beach and the Palos Verdes Peninsula. She tossed the three fingers of scotch down in one swallow and then spoke aloud. "By God, I will go to the Black Lamp. Maybe that bastard Willy Hanson will be there."

The scotch too was bringing back memories. That was another piece of wisdom from Willy. He always called scotch a thinking man's drink. It forced you to think about things that were better left buried. Lolly's face flushed again when her mind raced back to the time she had caught Willy and Onyx naked and drunk, grotesquely interlocked in a cabana near her pool.

Lolly Penrose walked back to the bar and poured another three fingers. It would help her sleep, she reasoned. It would soon be time for a little nap.

23

Coley Doctor watched the kids going one-on-one in the park on Crenshaw. Of the half dozen shooting buckets, one kid stood out from all the rest. He was six ten, gangly, with hands that had no trouble at all palming a basketball the way most people would hold a softball. Again and again he would snake skyward, sidestepping his coverage, and deftly guide the ball through the rusty netless hoop.

"Hey, Stringbean!" Coley yelled and motioned for the kid to pass the ball to him.

It came like a shot. Coley caught the pass and drove in toward the basket, spun around and launched himself skyward, only to find the big gangly kid right in his face to bat the ball half the length of the court.

"Not bad, kid. You can't do that again."

The big kid frowned and whipped the recovered ball again to Coley, who drove hard at the basket only to have the young giant thwart his shot again.

"Where do you go to school, kid?"

"What's it to ya? Who the fuck you think you are to start askin' questions?"

"If I could defense like that, I'd be in the NBA."

"That's a lot of shit, man. You had your chance and you blew it with those crackheads in Miami. You're Coley Doctor. We ain't stupid. We all know you."

With that, the tall kid rifled the ball short-range at Coley, who miraculously hung onto the hard shot as it thumped against his chest.

"Hey, punk, don't believe everything you hear." Coley slammed the ball hard into the nineteen-year-old's chest. "Let's talk."

"Hell, man, why should we talk? You leave the neighborhood, go to Syracuse, average twenty-two points, get the MVP and the next time I hear, you get busted in Miami. Now you're back trying to slam-dunk with the rest of us losers. Fuck you! I don't have nuthin' to say."

"I don't suppose it would do any good to tell you that my bust was turned around and I was reinstated to the bar?"

Stringbean sat on a bench that served as a

baseball dugout in the small park. "Why would you want to be a lawyer when you could have been NBA?"

"Look, you just beat me twice in a row. How do I make the NBA?"

Stringbean grinned at Coley Doctor. "Yeah, man. I'm pretty good, but I ain't no Jabbar. Still, if I got the breaks you did, I'd be NBA some way. What the hell you want with me anyway?"

"You used to work in the hardware store up the street in that burned-out strip mall."

Stringbean's eyes got big and he became very sober. He reached for a sweatshirt and quickly pulled it over his head.

"So, what's it to ya?"

Coley flipped out a badge just long enough for Stringbean to catch a glimpse of it.

"Why did you punks burn down the mall?"

"You're real crazy, man. Nobody around here burn down nothin'. Nobody liked what happened up in Simi Valley with those cops getting off scot-free. But we didn't burn down no mall."

"Were you working in the hardware store that night?"

"You're damn right. I just checked in a shipment of twenty kegs of nails when all these guys with nine-millimeters popped up all over the place. They was nobody I had ever seen before."

"So what did you do?"

"Man, I lit out! They was throwin' Molotovs all around and shooting off their guns in the air. Sometimes not in the air. I actually saw one guy drop. Hell, man. I was lucky to get away."

122

"Would you be able to identify any of these guys?"

Stringbean looked at Coley, his eyes widening with fear. "You gotta be crazy! Next week I start junior college. I'm gonna play basketball. I'm going to the NBA. If you keep asking questions like that around here, you're gonna be dead! Goodbye forever, Coley Doctor."

With that final remark, Stringbean started jogging rapidly out of the park and down Crenshaw. Coley sat on the old wooden bench and watched the kid until he was out of sight.

24

Logan Phipps paced the antique carpet in front of his teak desk. The man he was addressing was slumped comfortably in the large leather club chair.

"Your job will be to track someone. They must not suspect that you are doing so. If they do, I will be forced to discontinue your retainer and drop your services immediately. Your fee will be a thousand dollars a day. For this kind of money, our interests do not tolerate failure."

Phipps paused and studied the face of the man who had come so highly recommended.

"I understand that you were a lawyer once.

This background should assist you in covering your own tracks. I do not want any paper trail to your activity. Periodically you will furnish us with worthless objects of art. You will receive payment for them through the Sino-Americo Trading Company."

The prospective private investigator stirred nervously in his chair. It was a peculiar agreement, but the money was incredibly good for what would be an especially simple task.

"Somewhere between San Francisco and Seattle there is an ornate little sailboat named the *Tashtego*."

"*Tashtego*. That's a peachy name for a sailboat. Tashtego was one of Ahab's harpooners, I believe." The tall black private detective was sorry he had spoken. He had obviously interrupted Phipps's train of thought, and Phipps looked annoyed.

"The *Tashtego* is a forty-eight-foot ketch owned and skippered by a Miss Ginny Du Bois. She has one passenger aboard, a Mr. Willy Hanson, who is wanted by the law for all sorts of things. It is important that the authorities do not find him and that I deal with him first. You will have the use of a small plane currently on a landing strip near Humboldt Bay in Northern California, should you need it. The woman purchased detailed charts to Puget Sound. That appears to be their destination."

Phipps stared at the man. There was something strange about him. His eyes were fixed on the endless legs of Beryl, Phipps's assistant, who was taking notes. Oh well, Phipps thought. He appreciates women. That is something useful to know about a man.

"Beryl will take you into her private office and show you the file we have on Willy Hanson and his lady friend. She will be your contact when you can't reach me."

Coley Doctor unfolded his lanky frame from the plush leather chair. He was trying very hard to suppress a big grin. A thousand bucks a day sure beat the hell out of Willy's retainer. He wasn't sure right then that he wanted ever to take up law again. He forced himself to move his eyes away from the exotic Beryl. Phipps obviously wanted to say something else.

"By the way, Mr. Doctor, how did you manage to get reinstated to the bar so quickly?"

The question caught Coley Doctor by surprise. Phipps had obviously done his homework.

"Let's just say that it would have been very embarrassing to a lot of politicians if they hadn't acted fast. When people start shoving stuff up their noses, it finally gets to their brains. There ain't no goin' back for some of them, Mr. Phipps."

"I think you and I will work together very well, Mr. Doctor." Phipps paused, then spoke again. "I am going to tell Onyx Lu at the Black Lamp in Redondo Beach to be expecting you. I want her to bring you fully up to date on what she knows of Willy Hanson. Do you know anything about Onyx, Mr. Doctor?"

"Nothing except what I've read in the papers."

"Well, you can't believe any of that. She was totally exonerated, you know."

Phipps let Coley exit his office and then called Beryl back in for a few words. "Get in touch with Carlos and tell him it will not be necessary for him to pursue surveillance of Willy Hanson and Ginny Du Bois any longer. Onyx has him much too wrapped up at the Black Lamp, anyway. Tell him to stand by on this assignment. When it comes time for the hit, we may use him. I'm sure that is not Mr. Doctor's forte."

Beryl emerged from Phipps's office and led Coley Doctor into her own. The elaborate rosewood desk was a close match to the one in Phipps's office, but there the similarity ended. Behind her desk was an elaborate computer setup. She gave it some instructions, and shortly a printer began spewing out page after page of what turned out to be Willy Hanson's file.

After a brief inspection, she put the whole thing in a large envelope. She then rose from her desk and walked over to where Coley had seated himself on a large red leather sofa that extended the length of one wall. To his surprise, she sat down next to him.

She handed him the envelope.

"This file is for your eyes only. Be careful with it. Perhaps after you have read it several times you should codify a few notes for yourself and destroy it."

Coley took the file, very much preoccupied with the heavy jasmine scent that followed her wherever she went. He couldn't keep himself from rudely staring at her incredibly long legs, which extended from under a tight micro-mini skirt.

"You were a great basketball player, I hear, Mr. Doctor."

"Please call me Coley." He had the urge to just grab her and squeeze her. He had done stupider things with women, with less provocation. "I was pretty good in college. I don't know about 'great.' If I thought I would be good enough, I guess I would have tried the NBA. Something inside me told me to be a lawyer." He resumed looking at her legs and inhaling the jasmine.

"You have strange voices inside you, Coley. I bet you are still plenty good. It would be good fun shooting some baskets with you sometime. It's good exercise. I try to keep in shape."

"And you succeed. Now don't tell me you are a basketball player."

"I played on a team in Taiwan once."

"You got a date, kid. Would it be against the rules for you and me to work out together?"

"Not at all. Keeping fit is part of both our jobs. Perhaps we can exchange a few pointers."

Having said that, Beryl rose from the couch and walked back behind the rosewood desk. The ball-bearing hip action was spectacular.

"We'll get together as soon as I've finished my homework." He fingered the thick file in his hand and wondered if it would reveal anything about Willy Hanson he didn't already know.

"Don't be too long arranging it. We are all

busy, but I can always free myself up for a workout."

With that, Coley Doctor arose from the sofa and walked over to let himself out into the foyer. Beryl did not move, but he was certain she was watching his every step.

The drive back to Redondo Beach took almost an hour. It seemed to Coley there was never a good time to be on the freeways.

His thoughts returned to the question that had been bothering him for several days: Who could have recommended him to Phipps? It had to be someone in East L.A. A number of people had followed his career there, no doubt. And the press had covered the story when he had opened his private investigation company.

He laughed at his situation: Each of his clients had hired him to tail the other. So where would he place his loyalty? A thousand dollars a day against two hundred was no contest.

Only a real fool wouldn't go for the bucks, especially with the sleek Beryl for a bonus.

25

The second day out of San Francisco the winds ceased to favor the *Tashtego*. What little wind there was came from offshore, making swift passage to Humboldt Bay and Eureka impossible. Ginny and Willy began to feel safe in their isolation from the world. Once in a while a passing freighter or cruise ship would appear in the distance. Every now and then a small trawler that seemed to be working the waters south of the *Tashtego* would appear on the horizon and then fade again below the curve of the earth.

The relative calm was welcome. Willy and Ginny shared a love for the sea that matched their affection for each other. Hours were spent in silence, broken only by the occasional identification of some new landmark on the distant California coast.

Willy began to flesh out an outline for the last portion of the book he had promised Reinard. The book had been brutally frank up to now; so frank that he had concealed parts of it from Ginny. Of course, the book did not have an ending yet. A long prison sentence for Onyx would have been the perfect conclusion, but the justice system just hadn't worked.

His thoughts went back to the day when he had beaten Onyx and then bound her to the stanchion in the cabin of her own boat. His temper had got the best of him and he had wrongly played judge and jury, enacting in the process a scene which created a long litany of defenses for Onyx. The prosecution's case had raised a tide of reasonable doubt among the jurors.

"I've known Onyx for too long, Ginny," he had blurted out one afternoon. "She only knows how to do one thing well. She is an extraordinary marketer. She has a knack for identifying customers and then selling them all the coke they can possibly stuff into their noses or their veins. She doesn't fool around with street users. She concentrates on the bored and spoiled offspring of the affluent, and breeds chaos among some of the most influential people in society. She's like a powerful virus eating away at the strength of our nation."

"Willy, maybe everything has happened for the

better after all. If the jury hadn't set her free, she wouldn't have had a chance to lead us to Logan Phipps. Phipps must have lots of marketing people like Onyx. Getting Onyx would be satisfying but very objectively, nailing a big fish like Logan Phipps might mean a lot more."

"A lot more to who?"

"To the Feds, Willy, to the Feds. Maybe you could go to them with everything you know and make a deal with them. They might let you cop a plea if they could nail one of the major drug pipelines."

"You still have more faith than I do in the system, Ginny. We handed them Onyx on a silver platter and they let her go free. The system is so liberal that even a smoking gun doesn't help a prosecutor most of the time. Ginny, it is you and me and Coley against the world. Onyx comes first. Onyx comes first because I think it is possible to do that. I know her methods of operation. I know her weaknesses, right down to the last perversion. Logan Phipps is a name I never heard before until we saw it on that property tax record in Palos Verdes."

"Coley knew of him," persisted Ginny. "Willy, have you ever considered that the prosecution of Onyx might have been weak on purpose? Maybe the Feds didn't want her locked up. Maybe they were letting her run free so that she would eventually lead them to Phipps and others."

Willy was suddenly paying closer attention to what Ginny was saying. "It seems preposterous but possible. If you're right, we have a bear by the tail, or more correctly a dragon. It's one thing to nail a local drug pusher and another to take on an international cartel that could swat us down like a pesky fly. We'll have to bounce that one off of Coley when we get to Eureka."

Willy stood up and walked aft until he could stand behind Ginny at the wheel. He put his arms around her and clasped his hands over hers, just holding them gently as she moved the wheel. The wind was now very light and it took a deft touch to keep the big sails fully inflated. Her skill was magnificent.

"You are pretty good, you know."

Ginny beamed her big smile and squinted toward the horizon. "In the sack, you mean?"

"I mean at finding the wind when there isn't any. That's a much more important talent."

"You won't say that when we get to Eureka and we can stop alternating watches."

Ginny took his hands and placed them under hers on the wheel. She let her hands ride lightly on his as he tried to keep the sails full.

"You're pretty good too." But a big flap of a jib falling limp gave the lie to her praise.

"Caleb, have you noticed that trawler working the horizon back of us? He's been there all day, working back and forth. What kind of fish run in these waters this time of year?"

"Damned if I know." They both looked aft to observe the trawler, which was just a speck on the horizon. Now it seemed to be working a pattern that would take it farther out to sea.

Willy felt a gnawing twinge of concern in the pit of his stomach.

"I think we should forget about the trawler. If he were up to no good, he could have caught us by now and eliminated all his problems. The water has been warm this year. He's probably chasing yellowtail."

With that, Willy went below. He unstrapped the .30-.30 from the bulkhead, snapped a clip of shells into it and gently placed it in the portside keep. He realized the weapon would be of little use if the big trawler meant business.

26

From all outward appearances the *New Territories* was a state-of-the-art trawler designed to go anywhere in the world to chase albacore in season. It was a huge vessel by fishing trawler standards. Close inspection would reveal that it was fully equipped with nets, davits and fish lockers. An abundance of electronic gear could identify the location and movement of the vast swarms of ocean denizens below the steel hull. Besides the sophisticated fish finders, an inspection of the trawler's topside would reveal the latest in radar equipment for scanning the surface of the sea. Captain Alexandros was easily able to fix on the movements of the *Tashtego* without ever coming within identification range.

The double-decked captain's quarters were just a bit longer and wider than usual for such vessels, and the superstructure hid a dozen separate cabins fitted out with a luxury that probably would never be found in similar trawlers. Far aft on the second deck was an even more ornately furnished duplicate of the captain's digs. The opulent decor featured art and treasures of the Far East. Specifically, the suite featured the valued artifacts of the Crown Colony's most northern province, the New Territories, the childhood home of Logan Phipps.

The elegant aft cabin was locked most of the time except for the rare instances when Logan Phipps would use it as a hideaway for a tryst with the exotic Beryl. Their visits to the *New Territories* usually lasted two or three days.

Alexandros really didn't appreciate having a woman on the trawler, though when Beryl did come aboard she would disappear into the cabin with Phipps and not be seen again until just before she went ashore.

Alexandros gazed now at the *Tashtego*. The ketch was lumbering along at three or four knots, seemingly unconcerned about time. Alexandros was annoyed at the slack wind, bored by endlessly crisscrossing the waters all around the *Tashtego,* staying just out of sight.

After a full three days he concluded that the *Tashtego* was apparently headed toward Eureka and decided to bring Logan Phipps up to date via radiophone.

Phipps's voice came through loud and clear in Mandarin Chinese.

"I am transporting a new member of our surveillance team to Eureka. Proceed ahead of the *Tashtego* and meet him ashore at Harry's Landing on Friday morning. His name is Coley Doctor. He is a tall black man, a private investigator. He is not to come aboard the *New Territories*. Mr. Doctor will keep track of our friends when the *Tashtego* is not at sea. At some point when they are obviously holed up for a while, we will send a party ashore and take the woman. Once we have accomplished this you will be hearing directly from me."

Alexandros broke into a sweat under his parka. Bringing in drug shipments was one thing. Kidnapping was quite another.

"And how do you propose to do that?"

"We'll let Coley Doctor and Beryl work all that out. Captain, you are just an innkeeper, a host in this operation. A rich lady is paying her way aboard for a little coastal cruise."

"Aye-aye. I just don't want to attract attention."

"Captain, maybe you should take a few albacore, just in case. You really should look like a working trawler."

"No problem there. How soon do we take the woman aboard?"

"Could be two days. Could be two weeks. We must wait until they put in for a few days. What is your concern, Captain? All you really have to do is skipper your boat and catch some fish."

"Aye. I will be ready for the lady."

That said, Phipps broke off communications. Alexandros stood motionless, pondering the exchange. Personally he thought a better course of action would be just to ram the *Tashtego* with all hands aboard and forever put an end to the problem. The whole thing would be a cinch. In the thick soup of a morning fog, a spindly ketch would be no match for the *New Territories*.

27

The empty bottle of scotch was terrifying. Lolly tried desperately to recall the events of the night before. She had been alone. Looking around the room and then out on the deck of her condo, she could find no evidence that she had had any company. Her eyes fell to the invitation from Onyx. She vaguely remembered it and her desire to go. She would have to arrange an escort. Lolly Penrose just couldn't do it alone. Not the great Lolly Penrose.

The headache began to build. She ran to the bathroom, tripped and fell heavily to the floor. Momentarily dazed, she pulled herself together and crawled to the stool, her insides heaving. Dizziness overcame her efforts to crawl back up to the edge of the stool, and her head cracked against the porcelain. Lolly Penrose passed out.

She had evidently lain on the bathroom floor for many hours. When she woke, the throbbing headache and nausea returned. The noonday sun was pouring through the open drapes in front of the deck. Suddenly, she felt that if she could just get to the sliding door, open it and go outside, the fresh air and warm sun would cleanse her body of the torture she had perpetrated on it.

She started across the living room on her hands and knees. Her robe kept catching under her knees and impeding her progress, so she paused to let it slip off. About halfway to the sliding doors she caught a glimpse of herself in the floor-to-ceiling mirror across the room. There was the great Lolly Penrose, moving like a big dog across her own living room floor because she was too hung over to stand up.

"Hey, baby, you've still got quite a body there." Lolly spoke aloud to herself in the mirror. Then she squinted, scrutinizing her face. She touched a huge red mark on the side of her forehead and remembered. "I see the great Lolly Penrose has smacked herself in the head with her own toilet bowl. You dumb bitch!" She resumed her doglike walk to the doors, watching herself in the big mirror as she did.

All at once she focused on her famous derrière and began pumping in a fornicating motion. She grinned at the image and began an exaggerated circular grinding.

"Oh Jesus! Willy Hanson, where are you now that I need you, you horny bastard!" She closed her eyes and tried to imagine that Willy was mounting her and pinning her to the carpet. Then her mind went back to a night at one of Onyx's parties in San Clemente when she had found herself in the same position and turned to find that it wasn't Willy pinning her down but some monstrous stud of an Oriental.

"Damn you, Willy!"

Once again she slumped to the carpet and passed out. When she woke up again, the big orange sun was setting. She had lost the entire day to the now empty bottle of scotch.

She dialed a weather number and was informed that it was 7:10 P.M. on Wednesday and seventy-nine degrees outside. She breathed a heavy sigh of relief. She had all day tomorrow and the next day to work on her face before seeing the old crowd at the Black Lamp. If Willy Hanson wasn't there, there would at least be others whom she hadn't seen in months.

28

It was a full moon, and you could almost see forever. "Air-line pilots call a night like this 'severe clear,'" Willy remarked to Ginny as they raced along the Northern California coast at almost ten knots on a fresh wind just slightly off the port beam. Eureka was out there somewhere and they were getting close.

Instead of hanging around until morning, Ginny had made the decision to complete the run to Eureka that evening. It had been several days since they'd talked to Coley Doctor, and Willy was anxious to make telephone contact. While

Willy stood at the helm, Ginny went below to study the charts. This was a port she had never made, and though the weather was offering no problems, she wanted to make certain that the tie-up for at least one night would be uneventful.

Back at the helm, Willy saw the lights of Eureka appearing in the distance. It seemed as if getting into the harbor would be a piece of cake unless Ginny had discovered something to the contrary on the charts.

Willy could hear the far-off rumble of a powerful diesel engine astern of the *Tashtego*. Well in the distance he could see the running lights of a small freighter pursuing a coastal route beyond Eureka. The still bright western sky yielded a faint, now familiar silhouette of what appeared to be a fishing trawler.

A faint uneasiness gave birth to a tightness in his chest, which vanished quickly enough when the trawler plowed past the harbor and proceeded north beyond Eureka. These were, after all, prime fishing waters, and hundreds or perhaps thousands of fishing vessels dotted the eastern Pacific north of San Francisco all the way to the Aleutians.

Ginny came topside and smiled at Willy when she saw the harbor lights ahead strung out like a diamond necklace.

"Let's drop the jib and we'll coast on in. When we get within the jetty, I'll start the kicker and you can secure the main." With that she flipped on the blowers, and they both sat quietly watching the coast before them. One by one they began to pick up the harbor buoys. The diesel rumbled to life and Willy went forward to prepare lines for a tie-up at the long transient dock which already loomed.

There was no activity in the small harbor. Willy stepped onto the dock, secured lines fore and aft and walked down the long float toward what appeared to be a dockmaster's office about a hundred yards away. The feel of solid footing was welcome. To him, the first few minutes ashore after a long sail were always exhilarating. The small office was locked, but he found several public phones lined up alongside the facility. He quickly dialed the voice mailbox of Coley Doctor in Los Angeles and instructed Coley to call him as quickly as possible. He said he would stay within earshot of the public phone until morning.

Willy was about to return to the *Tashtego* when he saw Ginny walking toward him. The smile on her face made it obvious that she was also glad to be ashore.

"Sleepy place," she said. "Looks like we have no company at all."

"I'm glad of it. It's good to know we're alone and there's nobody around who gives a damn about us. I called Coley's voice mail. If you hear the phone ring it will probably be for us. If we don't connect, we'll go on into town in the morning."

"Hey," Ginny said, "we've got company."

A tall man on a small bicycle was pedaling along the shore road in the distance. He had on a baseball cap and seemed to be very much a stranger to the bicycle he was riding. He was pedaling slowly and moving in a choppy zigzag. It seemed he had to maneuver the handlebars to avoid hitting his knees.

Neither Ginny or Willy could take their eyes off the man, who was still almost a quarter mile away. It was as if he were a cartoon, but a very serious cartoon. Closer and closer he came, with both Willy's and Ginny's eyes riveted on him.

"My God!"

"It can't be."

Willy looked directly at the man on the bike until he pedaled right up to where they sat.

"But it is."

Coley Doctor dismounted from the clumsy little bike and stood before them wearing an ear-to-ear grin.

"Howdy, folks. Fancy meeting you here. I got your message off the voice mail and decided I'd better hurry."

Willy sat quietly, preferring not to speak until Coley had explained how he could be standing right before their eyes, five hundred miles from where they had seen him last.

Ginny just stared at Coley. Since that day at Alioto's in San Francisco, she had had reservations about Coley. Logically there would seem to be no way for Coley Doctor to know where they were.

"Okay, Coley, quit playing games. How did you find us? This better be very good."

"Good! Man, it's wonderful. Now, I warn you, you ain't going to believe it, but it's true. But you will believe it all in good time, just because Coley Doctor said so."

Neither Ginny nor Willy said a word.

"Of course, the *Tashtego* helps. I've been watching you through the glasses all day long as you passed the cliffs south of here. The wide spreaders, the thick mast and the long mizzen boom make it a cinch to pick out in a crowd, which there wasn't."

Coley paused and removed a small tin of miniature cigars from his jacket pocket. He selected a cigar, unwrapped it and lit up. He took a deep drag of the acrid smoke.

"No wonder you didn't make the NBA, smoking those stinking bastards." Willy couldn't resist taking the jab at him. "Coley, am I supposed to believe that you have been driving the California coast for six days watching us from Highway One? Bullshit!"

"Okay. Okay! Just give me time, man, I'm trying to figure out where to start. There's a lot happening."

Coley took another long drag. Ginny stood to move upwind from him, never once taking her eyes off the giant investigator.

"Sorry, Miss Du Bois, sorry." Coley looked genuinely apologetic and flipped the offensive cigar into the sea, where it died with a brief sizzle.

"First of all I guess I had better explain that I have got a brand-new job. It pays a thousand dollars a day, which makes your two hundred a day look like little tiny Spanish peanuts."

"And you drove all the way up here from San

Francisco to tell us that?" Willy was beginning to get hot under the collar, furious with himself for his poor judgment of Coley, and pissed off at Reinard for recommending him.

"Of course not. If you just relax a little, I think you may like what I've got to say." Coley pulled another tiny cigar from the tin, moved downwind from both Ginny and Willy and lit up again.

"First of all, I didn't drive up here from San Francisco. Actually I flew up here in the company jet." Coley paused.

He would have made a great actor, Willy thought.

"Coley, I am happy for your good fortune. I am also sorry we ever met."

"Hey, wait one minute, man! You haven't asked me who owns the company jet. I think you'd like to know. I would if I were in your shoes."

Ginny's curiosity surfaced first. "Okay, Coley. Who owns your company's fucking jet?"

"My, my, the lady does get salty. Now listen up. My new employer's jet is owned by the Sino-Americo Trading Company of Newport Beach."

Dead silence greeted his pronouncement.

"And my friends, the Sino-Americo Trading Company is wholly owned by Mr. Logan Phipps of Hong Kong."

Willy swallowed the news. Coley couldn't be joking, he decided. It was too bizarre not to be true.

"And what is the nature of your assignment with Logan Phipps?"

"Now this you are not going to like. But I do hope you can see the possibilities in what I have to say. My assignment is to find the *Tashtego*, keep my eye on it, and report to Phipps daily about your whereabouts. I am to report your activities whenever you venture off the *Tashtego*."

"How did you find us here? Eureka is hardly a significant port of call."

"The operative words in my assignment are 'on land.' Somebody else is responsible for keeping track of you on sea."

"The trawler!" interjected Ginny.

"Let me make one thing clear," said Coley. "They must have some way of keeping track of you at sea, but they did not tell me about any vessel. I did notice one this morning, though. When I was observing you from the cliffs south of here, there was a large trawler in the distance working the waters south of you. It disappeared for a while and later showed up going full speed to the north of us."

"We are being kept track of by land, sea and air," Ginny said. "Mr. Phipps is going to a lot of trouble and expense."

"By the way, Coley," Willy said, "you haven't told us how you managed to find us yet."

"My daily phone call, remember? Yesterday morning I got a phone call from Miss Beryl. Oh, you don't know her. She works directly for Phipps. I get the distinct feeling that she is Phipps's right arm. Quite a dish. We are going to shoot some buckets together. Miss Beryl is my control."

"I bet she is, Coley."

"You interrupted. Miss Beryl passed me information that the *Tashtego* was fifty miles south of Eureka and would probably put in there. I have no idea how she figured that, but she was obviously right."

"And?"

"I was told that the corporate jet was waiting for me at Van Nuys airport for a flight to Eureka. I flew to Eureka, rented this sporty little bicycle, and here I am."

"And?"

"And what?"

"Why don't they just kill us and get it over with?"

"Remember back at Alioto's? I told you it wasn't my job to think, only to furnish information. Well, there is one more piece of information I haven't told you about yet."

Coley took a long drag on the stinking cigar.

"I'm pretty sure that someone else is following you besides me and the trawler."

"Why would you think that?"

"Early this morning when I was down on the coast south of here with my bicycle, I saw an old Chevy Malibu. Some guy in a business suit kept getting out of it and looking out to sea with binoculars. But this ain't the time of year for whale watching. As far as I could tell he might have been keeping his eye on the *Tashtego*. Once he sat down on a big rock and kept you in focus for a half hour."

"What do you think?"

"I told you that I am not getting paid to think. But if I did think, I would be pretty sure that this guy was fuzz."

Willy's mind was racing. All those days he and Ginny had felt so alone and so secure. Now it seemed that scenic Highway 1 had been like an endless bleacher seat for the *Tashtego* watchers.

Coley's last bit of news worried him the most. The warrant out on Willy for obstructing justice at the trial in San Francisco was serious business. If the FBI really wanted to bring him in, they could do so anytime. So why didn't they?

"So Coley, what's your next move?"

"I'm going to keep my eyes on you folks for a day or so. Then I'm going to take the corporate jet back to L.A. and see if I can dig up some information. I'd like to give you your two hundred bucks a day's worth."

"How are you going to do that?"

"The first thing I'm going to do is shoot buckets with Miss Beryl."

There was something about the whole thing that just didn't make sense to Willy. Coley was either brilliant or he was the luckiest man alive.

"Coley, how did Logan Phipps come to pick you for his private investigator out of all the hundreds that must be in the L.A. phone book?"

"I've thought about that, and believe it or not it all seems logical to me. First of all, where have his contacts been lately? He has been active in moving a big drug shipment through Watts.

Watts is my home turf. Now, how many private investigators with a law degree do you think come from Watts? Me! So our Mr. Phipps asks a few questions, finds out about my bust in Miami and says to himself that here is a guy who must be pissed off at the system. Here is a guy who would probably sell his soul for a thousand dollars a day. I can tell you I had never seen him until he called me and asked me to come to Newport Beach for an interview."

"So how do I know you're working for me and not him?"

"I'm working for both of you. I'll hang in there with Sino-Americo until the heat gets unbearable. With my inside help we might nail Onyx and Phipps both."

"You're crazy, Coley. Phipps would stuff a hand grenade up your ass the minute he had the slightest suspicion about you."

"I've thought about all that. But do you really want to know what the kicker is here?"

"I haven't the slightest idea, Coley. What is it?"

"It's Miss Beryl."

"What about her?"

"Man, I ain't seen a pair of legs on a babe like that since Melissa Montez back in ninth grade. And you know what?"

"What?"

"She wants to shoot buckets with me every day in the gym. She's crazy about basketball."

"And you're crazy about dying if you think you

can pull the wool over the eyes of Mr. Logan Phipps. From what you've said, he must regard her as private stock."

"Man, I don't care. If I can just spend one night in the sack with that sleek little commando, my life will be complete."

29

Evan Hatcher's name had begun to appear in all the tabloids from the West Coast to New York. The young Australian rock star had cut out a massive audience among teenagers and musically stunted adults from twenty-one to sixty. The blatant sexuality of his act had just begun to dominate the supermarket rags.

On this particular day, the same photograph appeared in virtually every newspaper in America that dared to follow the exploits of the rising phenomenon. The young star, about to make his official American debut in an exclusive new supper club opening in Redondo Beach, had been photographed during a private party in the Hollywood Hills. The limits of good or bad taste had apparently been violated to the point at which he was now recognized as the ultimate rebel among the vast and growing number of entertainers whose crotches were more familiar to their fans than their faces.

The controversial photograph had shown the handsome young idol lying prone "in the missionary position" over his giant guitar, with which he had "fornicated with unabated zeal for over twenty minutes," according to the newspaper account. His backup guitarist, an anorexic blonde named Dizzy Dot, had her foot on his rump and kept up the beat while Evan Hatcher wailed the song during his guitar lovefest.

The tabloid went on to say that though it did not show up very well in the photograph, there was some "restrictive flesh-colored clothing between Hatcher and the recipient guitar" and that "no actual sexual congress had taken place."

Ordinarily the spectacle would have brought a smile to the sober face of Lolly Penrose. But as she perused the articles that lay spread out over her coffee table, she began to question the wisdom of her publicist, who had arranged for Hatcher to escort her to the grand opening of the Black Lamp on Friday. The young man—older woman thing had caught fire among some of her more famous contemporaries, who had benefitted from the endless publicity surrounding such relationships. Her agent and publicist had assured her that the suggested "romance" would rekindle the public awareness of a Lolly Penrose who refused to grow old with the rest of the world.

But the photo of Evan Hatcher making love to his guitar did nothing to build Lolly Penrose's confidence. To her he looked like a perfect idiot, a man she wouldn't have spat on in her heyday. And why didn't Evan Hatcher have a zany name like all the other rockers?

Lolly went to the liquor cabinet and produced an unopened bottle of scotch. Not to worry, she thought. On Friday night she would ask the young fool herself.

Onyx Lu had been genuinely thrilled when Lolly had called. She was especially excited at the prospect of Evan Hatcher's escorting Lolly to the opening of the Black Lamp.

Onyx certainly knew all about Evan Hatcher. Lolly at one point wondered if Onyx might have had something to do with the arrangements made by her publicist.

"Honey, you don't know how thrilled I am about having such a hot couple at my opening," Onyx had said. "Imagine the publicity! The great beautiful Pennyrose out on the town with the young stud who screws his guitar. Everybody will want to come to Black Lamp. Hey, Pennyrose, maybe you can teach that hunk not to waste all that time with his guitar."

The scotch made Lolly feel warm inside. She decided she would have one more before dressing for the day.

30

"**W**hat do you think, Caleb?" Ginny put the question to Willy as Coley Doctor vanished, pedaling behind a stand of pine a mile away. Supposedly he was headed toward the airstrip at Eureka to pick up the "company jet" for L.A.

Willy scrutinized Ginny's handsome face. Her loyalty, her persistence and her unbounded love always left him feeling strangely proud, but more than a little bit puzzled. He wondered at times if he would back her up with such unrestricted support if the wild scheme were hers.

When he had had his children with his wife years ago, there had been love, but no two-way street like this. Jennifer, his wife, had always been slavishly devoted to his commercial success, but he'd never mustered a reciprocal attitude. If Jennifer had had any agenda of her own, he had never known about it. From early on in their marriage, her chief concerns had seemed to revolve around which hairstylist to use and which gown to wear at their next social affair. Physically she had been a knockout. But it hadn't mattered. His random infidelity after their first year of marriage was inexcusable. He knew that. Those episodes brought back shame. No wife really deserved that kind of abuse and dishonesty.

But that part of his life was forever gone. The two beautiful children who had come from the marriage justified the time spent.

"Caleb, I asked you a question. Not that you have to answer it, but I would like to know what you think about Coley now. How can we trust a man like that? Our lives are in his hands."

"I'm sorry, Ginny. My mind was miles away. Coley Doctor might be our messiah or our executioner. I'd feel better if he didn't have the hots for some babe named Beryl. That seems to be his first interest. I think we are number two on his list, just before Logan Phipps, who pays Coley a thousand dollars a day. I may be naive, but I really don't think money would buy Coley's loyalty."

"You're more sure of that than I am. A thousand dollars a day is big money, Caleb. How can you be so sure of a character who was caught in a big drug bust himself?"

"He was exonerated, you know."

"Yes, and so was Onyx Lu."

"You have a way of putting your finger on the great absolute truth, my love. So was Onyx! As I see it, we have only two choices."

"Are you going to tell me?"

"Of course. We can trust Coley to help us devise a plan to jail Onyx, or we can set a course for the South Pacific and stay on the run for the rest of our lives. Now that may sound idyllic, but I've got a feeling you might get tired of me if you had to share my company twenty-four hours a day for the rest of your life."

"I suppose we should trust Coley for a while longer, though the thought of him shooting buckets with Beryl doesn't exactly inspire confidence."

"Spoken like a true female, Ginny. We can't run forever. Someday we would turn around and see Onyx. And, as you would probably agree, Reinard does deserve his book for all the trouble I've caused him."

31

The opening of the Black Lamp was now three days away. Onyx had decided to run the place as a legitimate restaurant and cabaret for the first month. A careful screening of the guests during that period would provide a list of genuine party people and swingers for the private affairs later. It was important that the Black Lamp be absolutely jammed from the beginning, with long lines out front so that an imperious maître d' could decide which couples could or could not enter. Exclusivity for the restaurant downstairs and the cabaret upstairs would be the objective for the opening month.

Onyx had designed similar cocaine super-marts twice in the past. She still maintained a list of her most affluent customers and had tried to keep track of as many as she could. Of course many of them had succumbed to the great white dragon. But there were still plenty of drug-tolerant, insatiable human beings with constitutions of steel who seemed to go on and on. Onyx's reputation for being able to produce high-quality product in a relatively safe manner meant a lot.

Onyx's new customers found that the ecstasy of sex and cocaine combined to lure them to her freewheeling parties every week. Creating the setting for the ultimate fantasy and then opening the door to let it become a real-life experience developed long-term customers, especially after the boost from the white powder exceeded the thrill of the sexual high.

Onyx had decided that on opening night she would cull out the real players from the merely curious and escort the select group to the cabaret atop the restaurant. There they would witness the screen legend Lolly Penrose in wild abandon as a practical substitute for Evan Hatcher's guitar.

Rumors would spread like wildfire in the bars and bedrooms of Southern California. Onyx's videotape would ensure repeat performances by the aging star.

Onyx lay spread-eagled on the massive bed in the master bedroom in Palos Verdes. Her fingers persisted in a feather touch across her lower abdomen. She closed her eyes and arched her back. She imagined the full moist lips of Lolly Penrose replacing the intimate attention of her hand.

That goddamn Wong, she cursed. Whenever she really needed him he seemed to be away. Right now he was in Oregon. After studying the charts carefully they had decided that Astoria would be an appropriate landfall for the *Tashtego*. Wong's mission was really very simple. He was to arrange a plausible accident that would remove Ginny Du Bois from the face of the earth forever. Logan Phipps would not know that her demise was not an accident. After all, people have been falling off boats and disappearing into the sea since the beginning of time. Willy would know, though. Willy Hanson would ache forever, bearing the responsibility for the death of Ginny Du Bois.

Phipps would not have approved of her ploy. The unfinished business with Willy Hanson was beginning to drive her to distraction. She was tortured by the memory of the derisive, grinning Willy Hanson as he left her bound and beaten in her own boat over a year ago. The killing of Ginny Du Bois was just the first step in the long slow revenge she had planned for him.

She moaned aloud as the now firm movement of her fingers brought the release she had sought.

The fact that Lolly Penrose was Willy's ex-girlfriend gave Onyx great pleasure. Though Hanson had nothing to do with Lolly anymore, he would assuredly be distressed to hear of the faltering star's becoming a cheap public relations stunt for the Black Lamp.

The telephone on her night table rang softly but persistently, rousing her from her pleasant reverie.

"Yes?"

"Eh! That's what I like, babes what say yes before they've heard the question. Evan Hatcher here, darlin'!" The voice was a crisp baritone, and very Australian.

"Ah, you are quite prompt. This is Onyx Lu. Are you checked in?"

"You betcha, darlin'. I'm at the Rancho Wilshire. Some digs I got here. I got a big satin circle for a pad that just don't stop. Care to have a look-see, doll?"

"Mr. Hatcher. Believe me, I'm not your darlin' or your doll. But from what I have been reading in the papers, you will not have any trouble filling that big satin circle. We've got to talk about Saturday night, when you will amuse the customers of the Black Lamp."

"Darlin', I'm all yours for the next two weeks. At your service, madam! Your pleasure is my pleasure."

"Let us hope so, Evan. I would like to meet you in one hour, at the Rancho Wilshire. Get yourself decent and meet me in the lounge."

"Do you have a little something special for me, love?"

"Whatever could you mean?"

"A little something that might help a good buddy do a fancy gig on his guitar."

"Do you really fuck your guitar?"

"Hey, don't be a silly little tart! Nose candy, baby. Nose candy! It's a long way and a long time from Melbourne. A little treat will make everything neat and then we'll talk about what I diddly-fuck."

Evidently Evan Hatcher was every bit as crude as his act. For a moment Onyx had doubts that her importing of the Aussie idol had been a wise decision.

"Mr. Hatcher, we have some important things to discuss. I will see you in one hour. It is important that you pull yourself together and act like a gentleman, or, Mr. Hatcher, you can find your own fucking way back down under. Do you understand me, sir?"

"Never meant to offend you, ma'am. Just being a little comical. It's just a fucking crude act on my part. Actually I am a fine gentleman and a sterling character. It will be my great pleasure to join you for an elegant tête-à-tête in the sumptuous lounge in one hour. I'll be good. Just you wait and see!"

Onyx hung up the telephone. Hatcher was obviously hard up. His open plea for cocaine made it clear that he would become her personal puppet quickly enough.

When Onyx Lu arrived in the lounge of the Rancho Wilshire, she was amazed to find a totally civilized Evan Hatcher sitting at the bar.

He was well groomed and wearing a conservative business suit.

"G'day, darlin'. Zowie, you're a wee wisp of a thing, aren't you? I'm Evan Hatcher."

Onyx didn't say a word. Hatcher's eyes went through the exercise of ripping the flimsy white sheath dress from her sleek body.

"Cat got your tongue, cutie?"

"Put your eyes back in your head, pig. You are here because I paid your way. Try to remember that." Onyx strode on into the lounge and seated herself in a dimly lit booth, where it would be possible to converse quietly.

Hatcher shoved a bill at the bartender, picked up his glass and seated himself across from her.

"I'm sorry, Miss Onyx. It's kind of my style to be offensive, you know. Maybe it's a disease. I flirt with the ladies wherever I find them. Just once in a while you can mix a wee little bit of pleasure with business. You know what I mean?"

Onyx ignored his question. "The Black Lamp opens Friday. And on Friday, I want you to be on your best behavior. The press will be there. You will be charming and sensational. You will also tone down your act. From the second night on, you can start loosening up your act a little. The cabaret loft of the Black Lamp will be open to invited guests only. No one gets by the velvet rope without our security screening. Incidentally, I happen to know that you did actually remove your clothing and have a sexual experience with your guitar."

"Bullshit!"

"I have a friend who saw it. So don't lie to me again. Mr. Hatcher, I can protect you or I can ruin you. So let's be honest, okay?"

"Maybe you got a little package for me. You don't know how I'm sweatin' for it. It's been a long time from Melbourne. Couldn't risk it on the plane, you know."

"Jesus Christ! Are you going to hang together for a two-week gig?"

"Not without, I ain't. That's part of our deal. That's what your guy told me in Melbourne. Don't worry about me hangin' together. I'll take those customers of yours and charm their pants off."

Onyx observed the performer closely and decided that Hatcher would need a permanent chaperone. But that was out of the question. She made a decision right there to use him for the first weekend and then get him out of the way. She would let Carlos decide just how to handle the details.

"Evan, here is a little gift for you."

With that, Onyx took a small leather pouch from her purse and slid it across the table to Hatcher. It was the size of a small tobacco pouch and was embossed with a silver-white dragon that stood high on the black leather.

Hatcher opened the pouch enough to peek inside and see a generous number of small, gleaming white vials. A broad grin broke across the Aussie's face as he grasped Onyx's extended hand and lavished a kiss on her palm. He then excused himself to make the predictable trip to the men's room.

When he came back, he was beaming and obviously brimming with confidence.

"You are my kind of a lady, Miss Onyx. Don't you worry your pretty head about me, now. I won't ever forget how you helped old Hatcher when he needed it most. And say, I want to thank you personally for getting me out of Melbourne afore the roof caved in."

"Evan, I expect you Thursday evening for a dry run at the Black Lamp. One other thing. On Friday night you will escort Lolly Penrose to the opening. I know that you have heard about that already. She is a dear friend. Treat her like a lady. Press and all will be watching. You might even tell the press how sexy you find Pennyrose."

"She's twice my age. Young chickies turn me on, you know."

"Evan, you'll just have to adjust for the next few days. Pennyrose a party-party girl. You be nice to her and you won't be sorry when you get her alone. Believe me, I know."

Onyx gave him one of her lascivious smiles, the only one she had sent his way during the short meeting.

"Hey, she must be fifty years old!"

"I know how you feel about twenty-five-year-old scotch. There is nothing like vintage scotch." Onyx leaned close to Hatcher and whispered,

"Think of Lolly Penrose as vintage pussy. See you Thursday night."

Onyx Lu rose and walked to the door without even saying good-bye. Evan Hatcher watched the undulating white sheath until it had vanished from view.

32

The *Tashtego* moved out of Eureka in the twenty-knot offshore wind. Well within sight of land, Ginny pointed the big ketch southwest by west, a Hawaii course if there ever was one. This should certainly fool the FBI guy if he was still watching. It would confuse the hell out of Coley Doctor, whom they had promised to call from either Coos Bay or Astoria, both far north of them. As for the trawler, if it indeed was on their tail, this course just might escape detection.

The weather was ideal for sailing, and the big

ketch moved well beyond sight of land by night-fall. Willy and Ginny had actually decided to take the whole Oregon coast in one broad sweep. They would sail sixty to eighty miles to sea and then point in toward Astoria, the mouth of the Columbia River far to the north.

"You know, Ginny, I'm in no hurry to get to Astoria. Four or five days would be fine. We'll call Coley from there. By that time he should be able to bring us up to date on what Onyx is up to."

"And then what?"

"Then we do one of two things. We figure out a way to kill her and get away with it, or we catch her red-handed in some sort of a shenanigan that will put her behind bars for the rest of her life. Of the two possibilities, I'd rather kill her."

"You're scary, Caleb. I suppose you'd then write your last chapter and send it off to Reinard and we would live happily ever after."

"Something like that, Ginny, something like that."

"What about Logan Phipps? You don't think for a minute that he would run like a scared rabbit back to Hong Kong, do you?"

"We can't take on the whole world, Ginny. Look upon this as a simple vendetta I have with Onyx for killing a couple of my friends. I really don't care about Logan Phipps. I don't even know him."

"Ah, but he knows you. And, my dear Caleb,

he is paying Coley Doctor a thousand dollars a day just to keep track of you."

"Coley is on our side. He likes us."

"But a thousand dollars a day, Caleb. Does he like us a thousand dollars a day worth? That's a lot of money for a basketball player who isn't good enough to make the NBA."

"Ginny, sweet lips, I have been a salesman all my life. Do you know what a salesman is best at? Do you know what life has taught him more than any other thing?"

"I'm afraid to ask, Caleb. I suspect it has something to do with female genitals." Ginny laughed.

"Ginny, that is strictly number two on the salesman's list. Number one is reading people. I have read Coley Doctor and decided that he is our friend. If I didn't think so I'd recommend staying right on this tack for the mid-Pacific."

"We would wind up off Midway Island, and I would wager that Logan Phipps would be waiting right there for us with a rocket launcher or something worse. I agree with you about Coley, much as my common sense should tell me not to. But I also think that Logan Phipps is not going to go away. He is dogging you just as tenaciously as you are going after Onyx."

Willy stood to spell Ginny at the wheel. The *Tashtego* was flying.

By the end of the day they were sixty miles from the California coast. They came about just as the sun dipped into the Pacific and took dead aim on Astoria, some four hundred miles north-northeast. Somewhere out there was a trawler, a mysterious guy in a blue Malibu, and Coley Doctor, perhaps on a bicycle. There were probably others. And Willy was going to have to outsmart them all.

33

It was ten in the morning when Coley Doctor pulled up in front of the Black Lamp in Redondo Beach. To his surprise, it was wide open. The massive doors were propped ajar with wooden blocks and workmen were carrying ladders, tools and bits of lumber to a truck parked curbside. He brushed past a workman and promptly came face to face with a swarthy, muscular man dressed in a dark silk business suit. The jacket bulged suspiciously as if he might be carrying a sizable piece.

"Sorry, we are not open yet," the man said with a definite Hispanic accent. He stood in the entranceway squarely in front of the towering Coley Doctor. "Perhaps you would enjoy coming back next week when we will be serving lunch and dinner."

"I am looking for a Miss Onyx Lu. I was told I could find her here."

The swarthy man studied Coley carefully as if sizing him up for a fight.

"That person is not here. It would not be necessary for you to see her anyway. I handle her affairs." The man's eyes came to rest on Coley's left armpit, where the hilt of the Glock he was carrying protruded against his scruffy old sports jacket. He decided to play his ace and get it over with.

"Logan Phipps suggested that I could find Onyx Lu here. I have business to discuss with her."

"I will see. You wait here." The man's demeanor changed slightly as he walked over to the maître d's podium to use the telephone. His eyes turned back to Coley as he waited for the call to go through. The conversation lasted only a few seconds.

"Onyx will be here momentarily."

That said, the man seated himself at a remote table where he could keep his eye on Coley and the workmen who were still cleaning up around the room.

"You must be Coley Doctor."

Coley was startled to hear a woman's voice directly behind him. He had expected her to emerge from inside the building. He spun around to confront a tiny woman, obviously of Asian extraction. She was strikingly beautiful, he thought at first glance. Exotic was probably a better description, he decided.

"I am Onyx," she said quietly. She bore a sharp resemblance to Beryl, but there was something much more intense and serious about this woman.

"You must already know why I am here," Coley said. "Is there someplace we can talk without Scarface over there listening in?" Coley nodded toward the man in the corner, who still had not taken his eyes off him.

"That is Carlos. He is doing his job. He keeps track of everything around the Black Lamp. But come, we'll go upstairs."

Coley followed Onyx out to the sidewalk, and they went into a small vestibule that hid the entrance to an elevator. The elevator moved silently to a third level, where it opened on a small but ornate lobby. A panel slid back, revealing the spectacular showroom of the Black Lamp. Onyx turned on the lights and they both stared at the artsy details of the large chamber.

"Nice place," Coley offered coolly.

"Very exclusive, Mr. Doctor. Entrance to this cabaret will be by invitation only. The general public will know only of the restaurant downstairs. Of course that isn't too shabby either. Now sit down and we'll talk. I will call you Coley. That okay?"

"It is." He still couldn't get over her striking resemblance to the much younger Beryl.

"Dear Logan told me that you would be in touch with me. He say I may give you some information that will help you find that bastard Hanson. Tell me, Coley, what do you know about him so far?"

"I was brought up to date by a file that Phipps had in his office. The man is wanted by the Feds on a number of counts."

Coley had to be very careful about what he said. It wouldn't do to get everything he knew about Willy mixed up with the file information. His peculiar role as double agent was being put to the test for the first time.

"Logan and I want you to find him as quickly as possible so we may speak to him privately. He is sailing in a small ketch named the *Tashtego* somewhere off the coast of California. I could give you a physical description and tell you some of his old hangouts. Perhaps that may help you find him."

Something was wrong, Coley thought. She made it sound as if Willy might be anywhere, perhaps right off Redondo itself. She was obviously trying to lead him on the wrong track.

"I want you to call me first when you find him. I don't like to pester Logan with these things. He is wrapped up in our new restaurant. I like to take as many details off his mind as I can."

"Onyx, you can bet that I will be in touch with you whenever I need more information." Logan Phipps was evidently not keeping Onyx up to date at all. Coley had told Phipps late yesterday that he'd sighted the *Tashtego* south of Eureka.

"Are you all work and no play, Mr. Doctor?"

"Private investigation is rather new to me and I find it a challenge. I find no time to relax. I do shoot a few buckets down at the schoolyard or at the gym once in a while."

"Really? I would like to do that with you sometime."

Coley tried to show no surprise that Onyx should share Beryl's interest in hoops. "You're pretty short for a basketball player, aren't you?"

"Yes, but I am accurate and very fast. I leave it to you to judge."

"Okay, we'll do it sometime."

"Tell me, Coley, do you consider screwing a sport?"

He turned to find her eyeing his six-foot-six frame with curiosity.

"A sport? Well, no. I have never really considered it a sport. I don't find it competitive."

"You are certainly wrong about that, Coley. Sometime very soon I will prove to you that you are wrong. Screwing is a competitive sport, and I am the world champion."

Neither smiling nor frowning, she walked directly to the elevator. He followed. On the elevator, she wrapped her arms around him and nuzzled close to his chest. She could feel his nine-millimeter pressing against her forehead.

As Coley stepped off the elevator and walked toward the sidewalk, Onyx spoke again. "Happy hunting, big guy. Remember to call me anytime."

34

Captain Alexandros had the *New Territories* pulling the giant seines a full seventy miles west of Eureka when he received a communication from Logan Phipps that the *Tashtego* had left the Eureka area. Phipps told him he should put the ketch under surveillance again and be very careful not to become visible to it. It was an educated guess that the ketch would head toward Puget Sound. Within minutes Alexandros was amazed to pick up what might be the ketch on his powerful radar, coming due west, right at the *New Territories*. The *Tashtego* was perhaps fifteen miles off his starboard beam.

He maneuvered the stern of the big trawler toward the speck in the far distance and put the setting sun between the *New Territories* and the *Tashtego*. Under those conditions it would be impossible for the *Tashtego* to identify him. It would be hard to see him at all.

Standing on the bridge, Alexandros put a powerful scope on what was indeed the *Tashtego*. In just a few minutes the ketch came about and pointed northeastward on a sustained course that would eventually put it somewhat south of the Columbia River delta. It might be that they were still headed for Puget Sound and they just wanted to tuck in closer to shore. Or they could be headed for the river mouth and perhaps Astoria. This information was encoded and relayed to Phipps via radiophone.

Alexandros hauled his nets and proceeded to parallel the course of the *Tashtego* northeastward. He was becoming impatient. Following the slower craft was tedious, especially when he had no inkling why he was doing it. In dense fog he had had several opportunities to ram the smaller vessel and get away with it. But the answer to his suggestion was always no. His whole assignment seemed such a waste of the resources of the *New Territories*. He would be glad when he could return to the serious business of bringing in shipments of cocaine from Baja.

It was the last communication of the day from Phipps that made him think the peculiar assignment would soon end. Phipps told him to be prepared to take a female passenger aboard on three hours' notice. From this point on he was never to be more than three hours away from the *Tashtego*.

"Finally," he said to himself on the bridge. "Finally something is going to happen."

He still didn't like it, of course. Phipps knew how he hated to have women aboard. He had to put up with Miss Beryl occasionally, but she was the boss's private stock.

Next time Phipps called he would offer again to arrange an accident. A landlubber could easily fall into a fish tank and smother, or just slip overboard and be gone forever. He thought back over the years and reckoned that he couldn't count the times he had done the boss a favor by arranging such shenanigans.

35

Logan Phipps was livid. After entering the Palos Verdes estate quietly, he had burst into the living quarters that he himself had provided for Onyx Lu, only to find her erotically entangled with Rafael, the houseboy. They were sprawled on the floor in front of the crackling fire in the huge stone fireplace.

"Rutting sow!" he screamed. "You belong in a bordello in Bangkok!"

The houseboy, terrified, bounded naked through a patio door to the garden.

Onyx, sitting cross-legged on the floor, was

amazingly composed. "Lo, I didn't know you were master of my fun and games too. I would welcome that. Come sit with me here and let's talk about it."

"Onyx! I don't give a damn about your free time. Your Macau whore behavior is your own business. How many men do you have in a day, for God's sake? Did you ever hear of AIDS?"

"Of course, Lo. I am very careful." Onyx grinned and opened her legs in front of Phipps. "Usually, and almost always, there is Wong. You know that, Lo."

The confident, seductive sophistication vanished momentarily from Onyx's face.

Phipps beamed at her discomfort.

"Yes, Onyx. Wong. Where is Wong? I wonder why some silly Macau slut would send him to Oregon."

"Oh, Lo! I meant to tell you." Her voice faltered. "I didn't want to bother you with such trifles. I want him to get rid of Willy before he causes us any more problems. It is my vendetta, Lo."

"No! I put Carlos in charge of security because he is a security specialist. Wong is a bumbling lackey whose only purpose is to occupy all your free time, and keep you from making a fool of yourself. Your business talents in general are tremendous, Onyx. But you have made a mistake with Wong. I will give you one last chance to prove yourself worthy of your position here."

"I am sorry, Lo. I had wanted to do you the favor—"

"Let me tell you something, Onyx. We can't get rid of the bastard as long as he is aboard the *Tashtego*. He is being watched by us, by the U.S. coast guard, the FBI, and yet other people we still haven't identified. If we make a move, that spotlight will be on us too! The FBI would love for us to make a mistake. That is why I have professionals like Captain Alexandros, Beryl, and Coley Doctor working on the problem. When the time is ripe, we will strike. But not until then."

Onyx rose and walked slowly toward Phipps. Though nude, she looked like a small child who had just been scolded. She raised her arms as if to embrace him.

"Don't touch me, Onyx! You smell like a whorehouse bedsheet. What in the hell were you doing with that poor lad? Take a cold shower, Onyx, and if you reach Wong before I do, tell him to get back to the Black Lamp. He is not to leave your sight, Onyx. If he fails at his assigned task, we might have to arrange a little accident for him."

"Thank you, Lo, for giving Onyx another chance. I think of only what can benefit you, Lo. I remember the old days in Macau and I owe it all to you, my master, for rescuing me. I will make you proud of me yet, Lo."

Phipps saw tears spill from the corner of Onyx's eye. Unbelievable, he thought. The little bitch actually has some real feeling buried within her. Or is she the world's best actress?

"Onyx. Take your shower. Then I want to talk to you a little bit about the opening of the Black Lamp. We may as well go over your plans as long as we are both here. I won't be able to show up for your dry run tomorrow evening."

36

Pelican Landing near Astoria, Oregon, had seen its best times during the early Northwest logging days. Then it was a bustling inn for fishermen, logging foremen and wealthy tourists who proceeded south along Highway 101 exploring the territory's scenic wonders. Now it was little more than a bait shop and short-order grill for locals and a few tourists who stopped for breakfast on their way south toward Seaside and Tillamook.

On this Thursday morning, a muscular Chinese man pulled his small rented Ford Escort into the gravel parking area of Pelican Landing. Instead of going right into the roadside café, he paused to walk among an assortment of dories and fishing skiffs offered for rent adjacent to the parking lot. He seemed to give an open twenty-footer a lot of scrutiny. The small open boat appeared to be in far better condition than the others and was equipped with an eighty-horse Chrysler outboard that was obviously a late model. He gave none of the other boats serious inspection.

Inside the roadhouse, Roberta mopped the coffee stains at the counter. She knew just about all her customers by their first names. It was unusual for anyone to stop by other than her regulars and an occasional tourist. The powerfully built man looking at the rental boats outside didn't look like either.

She rang up the cash register for the two regulars who exited just as the Chinese man entered the café.

"Who in charge of renting boats outside?"

"That would be Lester," Roberta said. "He's not here now but should be back in a half hour or so. He took a cord of split firewood to some folks at Seaside. Can I help you with coffee or breakfast?"

"I have tea."

The man spoke in a deep voice, louder than necessary. Roberta noticed that he left out words when he spoke, yet she had no difficulty understanding him. He was dressed in what could best be described as hunting clothes that looked new, as if he was wearing them for the first time. The light hip-length jacket was cinched tightly around his waist.

"Sure. I got teabags right here on the shelf. Folks around here don't take much tea. Going fishing, are you?"

"I take lemon with tea," he said, ignoring her question.

"Got no lemon. I have milk and sugar."

"That okay." The man sat quietly dunking his teabag, ignoring the milk and sugar. He eyed the woman intently, never seeming to blink.

Roberta felt uneasy, and hoped that another customer would come in soon or that Lester would return from Seaside.

"What are you going to fish for?" she asked. "The salmon aren't running now."

"I no fish. I just look around. I just need boat to look around."

"Well, you'll have to talk to Lester. Are you going out alone? Lester don't like that."

The man paused, glanced at his tea and then spoke.

"I wait for girlfriend. She coming over from Portland soon. She like take pictures. Scenery, camera. You know all like that."

"Well, I suppose that will be all right. But you'll have to talk to Lester. Not many customers for boats at this time of year. He's pretty particular about the twenty-footer you were looking at. If you really know boats, he'll let you have her, though."

"I know all about boats. He see."

The man turned his passive stare out the window to the open channel beyond the bridge. He sipped his tea and squinted toward the horizon. Far out, perhaps ten miles, a big trawler moved steadily north. The water was flattening out, and hardly anything was left of the early-morning on-shore breeze.

It was almost an hour before a battered old Ford pickup finally rattled into the gravel driveway. The driver seemed content to sit inside the cab and read his newspaper.

"Lester! Man here wants to rent a boat." Roberta called out the door. The strapping Chinese man brushed past her and walked out to the pickup.

"I rent twenty-footer with eighty house."

"What do you know about boats?"

"I know all about boats."

"You do, do you. Well, we'll just see about that."

The two of them walked over to the twenty-footer and talked for about ten minutes before they turned and came back to the café.

"Roberta, our friend here knows more about boats than I do. Let's draw up a contract so he can get out there and take some pictures as soon as his girlfriend gets here."

She drew up the contract. The man, a Mr. Wong Lee from Dana Point, California, forked over a $500 cash deposit, a credit card imprint and the keys to the rented Ford Escort.

"You'll have to bring her in afore the sun sets,"

Lester told him. "The race out there is no place for a stranger after dark."

"Yes sir. I try her out a little bit before my friend get here."

With that comment, Wong walked slowly back to the Ford and took a long duffel bag out of the backseat. He was careful to keep the laced end of the bag away from the view of those in the café as he loaded it onto the boat. The butt of a powerful Marlin hunting rifle protruded about two inches out of the bag.

Wong started the engine, let it run for a minute and then loosened the lines to the dock. Slowly he putted away from the café, fanning a soft wake to his stern as he headed under the bridge that was Highway 101. The broad neck of water that extended before him led to the Pacific Ocean. With a little luck he might meet the *Tashtego*.

He removed the big Marlin from the duffel bag, made sure the clip was in place and then put it in the portside keep, where he could pick it up on a moment's notice.

Onyx had been so insistent that he come back to L.A. at once when he had called her that morning. She didn't realize how close he was to the kill. If the *Tashtego* was indeed headed for Astoria, he would be sighting it any moment. Of course they might have put in at some small marina right off the channel. In that case he would soon know about it.

Onyx was a peculiar person, he thought. She

had sent him out for the kill, then tried to call him off when he had them practically in his gunsight. He had promised her he would fly home from Portland today. But he thrilled to imagine her great surprise, and his reward, when she learned of his success.

There it was! Down a small inlet to starboard he saw the oversized spreaders extending from the tall mast. It was the *Tashtego*. The last time Wong had seen it was two thousand miles away in Long Beach Harbor the night before it had disappeared. It stirred unpleasant memories. He had lied to Onyx.

The marina at the end of the small cove was tiny. There were two sailboats smaller than the *Tashtego* and several motor sailers of the sort used to cruise the Northwestern Coast. The marina was evidently a convenience and fuel stop for boats that didn't want to make the long haul into Astoria or even Portland for supplies.

Wong decided the place was too small for him to go ashore. Willy would surely recognize him from the old days when Onyx's parties had drawn Willy and Lolly Penrose. Wong would have to wait until the *Tashtego* left and confront them alone somewhere as he had originally planned. Reluctantly he turned the small motorboat back toward the 101 bridge, carefully noting places where he might conceal himself if he decided to ambush the *Tashtego* when it left the small inlet.

To hell with flying back today, he thought. His

exhilaration at seeing the *Tashtego* was too great. He decided to return to the marina and tell Lester he would be staying the night with friends anchored near Chinook on the Washington State side, where he had seen the *Tashtego*.

Onyx would be so proud of him tomorrow.

37

"**B**e on your guard, chum." Coley's message got right to the point. "Onyx has sent Wong north with a new Marlin long-range job. We're trying to call him back but so far we haven't succeeded. He tells Onyx he's flying home from Portland today. But I don't believe him or her. Leave a number where I can reach you today, Thursday. I figured out a way to nail Onyx cold. How about that! I wish you guys would hustle your ass to Seattle so we can get on with the show. Logan and I are becoming good buddies. Boy, you know, he is talking about giving me a raise already.

Use my voice mail to answer, unless, of course you are dead already. Bye now!"

"Damn! Voice mail is for the birds when your guts are really on the line."

Willy and Ginny walked together back to the *Tashtego*.

"What is the Marlin long-range job?"

"Oh, it could be a lot worse. He could be coming at us with an Uzi." Willy paused and shook his head. It's a long-range hunting rifle easily capable of ending all of our misery. Frankly, I think Wong is over his head. He was always known as a class-C bartender with an incurable case of satyriasis. I think that's what Onyx finds irresistible in him. One scenario we could hope for is that they would fornicate each other to death."

After they returned to the ketch Ginny sat down on the transom. Willy doused the cockpit lights and they both sat looking south to where the inlet met the channel. Ginny broke into a big grin.

"Guess what! I just don't want to think about it any more right now!"

Willy was glad to see her relax, ready himself for some escape. He slid to the floor of the cockpit and began to lavish kisses on her slim, suntanned ankles. "I like it here in the cove. It's quiet," he was mumbling between kisses. "Since . . . we have absolutely nothing to do until the morning fog lifts . . . we are going to find out once and for all which of us is the most insatiable."

"Are there any rules in this contest?"

"Absolutely not. You can do anything you want anytime you want to, and so can I."

"Maybe we ought to go below in the cabin," Ginny said, her passion beginning to interfere with clear speech. "A neighbor might drop by for a cup of sugar or something."

They both stood and briefly looked up the hazy channel.

"That guy deserves a medal," Willy mumbled. "He has to be the most tenacious fisherman I've ever seen. He hasn't moved in hours."

The fisherman slumped low on the deck of a small motorboat, the hood of a heavy parka hiding his face. He was too far away to make out an anchor line, but he was evidently anchored fast. A deep-sea rod extended from the stern.

"Fishermen are crazy, Ginny. He probably has a wife who makes him feel inadequate, or unsatiated," Willy said. Then he led her below to continue their adventure.

By the next morning, the coastal fog enveloped the small marina. When Willy went topside he discovered that one of the small sailboats was preparing to leave. He casually saluted a man in foul-weather gear who was freeing the lines about fifty yards farther down the channel. The man nodded and then bent over to tinker with the choke on an outboard kicker. The small engine roared to life and the man quickly tuned the choke until it purred in a soft, smooth idle. As soon as he was under way, the man turned toward the *Tashtego* and gave a thumbs-up sign.

"Did your brother ever find you?" the man

called over as the small sail slipped by the *Tashtego*.

Perplexed, Willy shrugged. "I don't understand. I don't have a brother."

"Yesterday, up the channel near Chinook, a stocky chap in a motorboat, an eighteen- or twenty-footer, was asking whether or not I had seen the *Tashtego*. He described your boat. He said he was your brother."

"Must be some mistake," Willy told the man. Even as he spoke he could feel the hair rise on the nape of his neck.

Ginny's head poked out of the cabin hatch as the single-hander made a small circle to approach the *Tashtego* again.

"I'm sorry I didn't tell you about this last night. But later in the evening I saw the same small motorboat fishing up there near the end of the channel. You were looking right at him so I figured you must have found each other."

"That's okay, pal, I guess we weren't paying attention." Willy took the cup of coffee Ginny offered. "He must have been looking for a similar vessel."

The skipper of the small singlehander waved good-bye and putted off up the channel. The haze was lifting rapidly and the channel was clear now almost all the way to where the inlet joined the Columbia.

Ginny sat down next to Willy on the transom as they watched the small sloop proceed up the channel.

"What do you think, Willy? It must have been Wong."

Willy put his arm around her shoulders and brushed his fingers lightly through her hair.

"Last night was one of the most beautiful nights of my life." Willy hugged her close and buried kisses in the small of her neck.

"Me too, Willy, me too."

They watched the small sloop blend into the mist, perhaps a half mile away.

"We've got to assume that it was Wong and that he's still out there waiting for us with that damn Marlin." Willy studied the inlet carefully and then turned to survey the land in back of them up the slope from the marina. Every now and then they could hear the sound of an automobile from some hidden road behind the trees.

"There are cars moving up there in the trees somewhere. We're sitting ducks if we stay here. If that was Wong he could be ashore. He could be anywhere."

"We've got to get out of here and do it fast. We'll make the run to Seattle. Five minutes, Ginny. Five minutes."

Ginny flipped the blower switch to clear the engine chamber of fumes while Willy scrambled to secure all loose gear and make ready for the sail. The diesel rumbled and Ginny unsheathed the mainsail so it could be raised quickly down the channel.

"What are we going to do when we see Wong

and his motorboat, Willy?" Ginny's thoughts were racing right along with Willy's.

"We have one thing working in our favor. Wong doesn't know that we know who he is, and he has no reason to deal with us until we get very close to him. Look at the water now. That small chop will be rougher when we hit the channel. That will be a tough platform for a sniper with a scope. We're relatively safe until we get close."

Ginny took over the wheel as Willy freed the dock lines. The big ketch split the channel, pointing toward the Columbia River a half mile ahead.

Ginny saw him first. "There he is, Willy!"

The outline of the motorboat became clearer by the second. The parka-clad figure of Wong sat upright in the stern. There was no movement at all in the motorboat for several seconds. Then Wong turned to the engine, and the outboard roared.

"Full speed, Ginny! We still have time. He has to pull the anchor. Give it all she's got." Willy realized that once the motorboat was under way, the hull speed of the ketch would be no match for it.

"We've got to ram him, Ginny! Full speed. Try to hit him somewhere between midship and stern!"

Ahead they saw Wong moving swiftly to the bow, struggling to get the small anchor aboard. They had only a few seconds until he would return aft to open up the throttle on the Chrysler.

They were less than fifty yards away when Wong freed the anchor and pulled the small Danforth aboard. Racing toward the stern, he stopped midship to pick up the rifle. For a second he turned to point the Marlin toward the *Tashtego*. Ginny and Willy were hidden from him, crouched as they were in the cockpit of the ketch. A single wild shot hit the cabin porthole near the bow. Wong then tossed the heavy gun aside and stumbled aft to reach for the throttle. But the second he had paused to squeeze off one shot had cost him dearly.

The heavy hull of the *Tashtego* rammed into the small craft almost dead center. Wong went flying over the stern, narrowly missing the flashing prop of the Chrysler engine. They could feel the motorboat rake along the keel of the *Tashtego*, sinking almost immediately. Wong thrashed wildly in the water as the *Tashtego* forged ahead and away from the sinking boat.

Now maybe a hundred yards away, Ginny throttled back on the ketch to allow Willy to hoist the main. A stiff morning breeze caught the tall sail and the *Tashtego* leaped ahead toward the wide river mouth.

Far in the distance they could see Wong wading from the choppy water onto the shore. Now a quarter mile away, they could see him raise his fist skyward and shake it until he was but a speck on the beach.

"Damn it!" exclaimed Willy. "I was hoping he wouldn't make it."

"Stop it, Willy! We're not killers. That poor bumbling fool is the least of our problems."

"If Wong had any brains, he would have pulled up on shore and found a firm platform for his Marlin. He could have knocked us both off in a couple of seconds as we went up the channel."

"Thanks for painting a vivid picture of me," Ginny said, smiling.

As the day wore on they put the *Tashtego* about thirty miles off the Washington coast. They let the big jib fly, and the ketch heeled over and pointed due north, toward Puget Sound.

"I have some bad news, Caleb," Ginny said later. For the past hour or so she had switched the diesel on and off several times.

"What? What's wrong?"

"We're heating up. When the engine is on for a few minutes, the internal temperature builds up abnormally. Also I hear a low rumble that I don't like. I think when we ran over that powerboat we might have snagged the screw for a time, and maybe bent the drive shaft. That's all I can figure."

Willy listened attentively and agreed that there was an abnormal vibration when the engine was revved up.

"I think we had better use it sparingly until we get to the sound. We're going to have to have it looked at, Willy. I think over a long haul it might break down."

Willy worked his way forward above the cabin. A chunk had been knocked out of the polished teak and a six-inch porthole had been shattered by the shot Wong had squeezed off.

"Willy, today's been a bitch, but last night was wonderful."

"You told me that already."

"I know. I will probably mention it again too."

38

It was Friday night. The publicists for the Black Lamp had done their job well. The newspaper ads had declared simply that Hatcher was opening in Redondo. But judging from the crowd lined up behind the velvet rope, almost everyone in the world had figured out the necessary details.

The code words had all gotten to the prospective customers as if by magic. It was as if Onyx were operating at the peak of a giant pyramid. She and her staff had probably called five hundred people, with Onyx personally handling over half of them. Each recipient of a call was urged to invite any friends who would appreciate an evening of "terminally decadent behavior." She assured them that a new, outrageous standard had been set for the amusement of the human species. Cryptically, the ads and the publicity referred to the black stone that was being polished to a new luster nightly. Guests were urged to observe a dress code that hovered somewhere between baring a little skin and wearing almost nothing.

Several prominent members of the entertainment community were repeatedly linked to the potential five-star restaurant. The gossip columns in the dailies had picked that up beautifully. The chef of the Black Lamp had been stolen away from the Oriental Hotel in Bangkok. He would be a lure the most discriminating gourmets would be unable to resist, for he was widely known to have a clientele that would cross oceans to taste his delicacies.

Nevertheless, the restaurant was just a front that legitimized the exclusive club two floors above for its nefarious backers.

Onyx Lu, Carlos and their star guests for the night sat at a corner table, elevated slightly so that they could observe all the patrons of the restaurant. A dark-glass window next to this VIP table looked out on the line still forming behind the velvet rope outside. It was only nine o'clock. The cabaret upstairs would not open until ten. Two tuxedo-clad former football players would serve as hosts and bouncers at the entrance leading to the elevator for the cabaret. It would be their job to sort out the somebodies from the nobodies.

Even Hatcher was right in the corner between Lolly Penrose and Onyx Lu. Hatcher cradled Lolly's shoulders with one arm while the other hand disappeared under Lolly's flared skirt, quietly exploring the vintage stuff that Onyx had assured him he would like so well.

Lolly was well into her second three fingers neat of scotch. This did not escape the attention of Onyx Lu, who called the waiter aside to give him specific instructions regarding what Lolly was to imbibe. It wouldn't do to have the guest of honor out of it before the evening started.

Completing the VIP table were supermodels Candy Bunton and Lamby Finch. Tiger Lawson, an ex-NFL nose guard, was escorting Bunton, and Finch was accompanied by former all-American basketballer Coley Doctor.

The opening of the Black Lamp progressed to a state of bedlam as the night wore on, just as Onyx had hoped. The chef threatened to resign on the spot several times. Onyx had to promise him Lamby Finch and a packet of cocaine. She already had her own more personal plans for Coley Doctor.

After dinner, the group bypassed the elevator and moved into a private stairwell that led to the cabaret on the third floor. Evan Hatcher disappeared into a dressing room, and the rest of the group made their way through a stage curtain into the showroom. Even Onyx gasped with amazement. The cabaret was already pulsating with action.

The light fixtures in the incredible room consisted of seven-foot-square brass cages suspended from the walls and ceiling. They were backlit with wavering, pulsing tones of warm-colored lights that revealed live performers in each cage who were frozen in blatantly sexual tableaus. They would change their erotic postures when the accompanying beat and the variable lighting compelled them. The bodies were nude and flawless, a male and a female in each of three cages. The other cage contained three people of indeterminate sex, skillfully and minimally clothed. Behind the cages a lipstick-red neon scrawl periodically penciled itself across the wall, proclaiming the room La Sex Ménagerie.

The cocktail waitress, in fact all the service people, were decked out in bits of strings and ribbons that covered absolutely nothing. There were two dance floors, one elevated in a Plexiglas enclosed room for those prone to exhibitionism, and another virtually without light except for erratic strobe flashes.

Onyx Lu began to mingle with the crowd, hugging those special friends she had personally invited. Many of her big customers from the old days were there, and all of them congratulated her for winning her trial in San Francisco. They seemed to feel that the verdict had exonerated them as well, giving tacit approval to their use of cocaine.

The known, sure-pay customers were given

credit cards to the restaurant; the packets of cocaine that would be made available to them
would show up on their charge cards as a sumptuous dinner for four at the Black Lamp. The delivery system involved the use of a valet parking
attendant, Alfie, who had worked for Onyx for
many years, and personal messengers who were
sent out the next day.

Opening night, however, was not to be typical
of the nights ahead after the payment and delivery system was perfected. Opening night was the
time to greet old customers and carefully identify
possible new ones. They would obviously have to
be cautious. The publicity for the Black Lamp
had brought in a number of strangers, all willing
to revel in the latest hot spot in Southern California.

Onyx, in a skintight sheath that was fitted to
her flawless body from turtleneck to ankles, surveyed the crowd with flashing eyes that could
not conceal her excitement. The Black Lamp cabaret was to be a prototype for a similar drug
marketing operations coast to coast for a covert
subsidiary of the Sino-American Trading Company. It was her hope that the venture would be
so successful that she would be called on to su-
pervise openings all over America. Such special
rank would give her condos on Maui and her be-
loved Cheung Chau. Logan Phipps's superwhore
from Macau would have the flashy and addicted
among the jet set as her personal toys for amusement and profit.

Onyx stood up and tugged at Lolly Penrose to

come with her. "Pennyrose, darling, I want you to meet a friend of mine who may be your best fan. She see all your pictures many times."

As they made their way across the room, it was Onyx who drew attention. The black body sheath was little more than gauze, and every supple sinew rippled erotically with each step.

"Beryl, love. I didn't expect you. You are very much a delicious bon-bon tonight. Meet my good friend, Lolly Penrose. She knockout, no?"

Beryl stepped forward to receive a peck on the cheek from Lolly. Onyx's eyes met Lolly's for just a moment, long enough for her to see that Lolly was higher than a kite. Lolly wavered.

Onyx hugged Beryl and buried a kiss in the hollow of her neck. Onyx lingered there, her hands subtly caressing the body of her young look-alike. But when Beryl stepped back she confronted Onyx with an icy stare. Onyx again thrust Lolly at Beryl, actually pushing the unsteady actress as if she were an inanimate object.

"You two get to know each other. I have a few people to meet and then we'll watch Evan Hatcher do whatever it is he does with his guitar."

Beryl spent only a few seconds with Lolly before asking her if she felt well enough to stay awhile. She had spotted the symptoms very quickly. Scotch and cocaine didn't mix too well. Beryl wondered if a drunken scene might not bring the Black Lamp too much notoriety on opening night.

"Miss Penrose, please sit here with me until Evan Hatcher finishes with his act." Beryl's eyes scanned the features of the slumping actress carefully, and then she eased her into a leather booth in a dimly lit part of the lounge. "We will stay here together for a while. Sip some Perrier with me and then we'll get you home. Tell me about your last picture. How long has it been since *The Long Chase?*"

Lolly turned and stared dizzily at Beryl.

"Who, who the fuck are you?" Lolly blinked rapidly, trying to focus on Beryl. "Where in the hell is Onyx?"

Then she lurched sideways into Beryl's lap and passed out.

Coley Doctor had watched all of this from a distance. Lolly's collapse had gone otherwise unnoticed in the madness of the cabaret.

"Let me take care of her, Beryl. I'll put her in one of the dressing rooms."

Beryl nodded her quick assent. "She is to have nothing more to drink. Nothing at all."

"I understand, but I think Onyx has plans for her." Coley propped the motionless star on her feet and began to make his way through the crowd to the dressing room. So many guests were so high that his trek to the backstage area went largely unobserved.

Beryl followed Coley into the dressing room and helped make her comfortable on the couch.

"I want her sent home as soon as she can walk out of here without attracting attention. I will settle things with Onyx. Headlines like this the

Black Lamp does not need. Mr. Phipps would not like this situation. She is loaded with coke. Where did she get it?"

"I would guess from Onyx or perhaps Hatcher. He's flying too. I just saw him backstage."

The tempo in the Black Lamp quickened. The wild beat and exploding lights made it seem as if the guests were inside a giant fireworks display.

The sexual tableau in each cage of La Ménagerie seemed to become more graphic, more authentic as the evening passed. Lovers in dark corners began to sink to the plush carpet and soft leather couches, mimicking the performances going on above them.

A voice broke out above the crowd, "Hey, they're really doing it up there."

The zombies and nonparticipants in the audience began to crowd near the cages suspended overhead.

"They can't be doing it. It's illegal in public, you know!" said one well-dressed young man who seemed to be alone.

He immediately caught the sharp eyes of Onyx Lu. There were only a handful of singles in the crowd, and she did not recognize this one.

"Who says so!" Onyx shouted over the din.

"I say so." The young man turned tipsily to confront the grinning Onyx. "Hey, wow! That's some dress."

"You like? Maybe I get you one for your lady friend. Where is she?" Onyx pushed up against the man, aggressively fondling his crotch.

The man grinned down at the small woman. "I betcha what you are doing now is illegal too."

"You no like? Then I stop and do something else. Where your girlfriend?"

"Oh, she's over there. I think she's had a little too much to drink." They turned to watch a very young woman slumped on a couch. She was in the midst of receiving intimate attention from an older couple who were evidently trying to duplicate the threesome in the cage above.

Onyx grinned appreciatively at the young man. "Hey, she real sport. You better rescue her, young fella, before she do something illegal."

Onyx shoved the tipsy man toward the threesome, satisfied now that he was not a solo. She moved on to work her way through the reveling crowd, making certain that she had greeted all her old customers and a few new ones who looked promising.

Suddenly, the tableaus of La Ménagerie darkened and the roar of the disco music ceased. The lights went out and total darkness consumed the room. There were a few squeals and screams and then silence.

A thin circle of light about seven feet in diameter was etched on the ceiling. The raspy high-pitched voice of Evan Hatcher pierced the room. The sound of his guitar blasted out through the amplifiers as the round slab of the performers' stage descended slowly from the ceiling suspended from four gleaming circular rods.

The crowd roared its deafening approval at the spectacular appearance of the Aussie rock star.

Almost everyone in the packed audience stood motionless on the dance floor or stopped the intimate revels in the nooks and crannies of the Black Lamp. At Onyx's table, Beryl squeezed in past the models to sit between Onyx and Coley Doctor.

The wild-eyed Hatcher was mesmerizing the crowd with the pounding and swinging of his giant golden guitar and with his voice, wailing lyrics in a raspy, almost inhuman tone.

"Hey man, what the hell is that?" It was Coley Doctor who asked the question first. He was taller than the others and was the first to see the woman lying on the floor of the descending stage. The circular stage came to a halt five or six feet above the dance floor.

A woman wearing nothing but black silk stockings and a black mask was sprawled on the stage with her head on a large pink satin pillow. Her long black hair fanned out over the satin pillow in all directions. Evan Hatcher dropped to his knees to simulate intercourse with his guitar while he continued to wail unintelligible lyrics.

The disco music started again. This time it was the piercing sound of a flute shrilly launching into Ravel's "Bolero."

Now Evan Hatcher placed the guitar behind his back and moved to straddle the woman on the satin pillow. The screeching rendition of "Bolero" was suddenly drowned out by the cheers of encouragement from the crowd.

Paramount among the shouts was "Lolly Penrose, Lolly Penrose."

Coley Doctor studied the partly masked face on the pillow. "My God! They're right. That's Lolly Penrose!"

Beryl, her eyes seething with fire, glared at Onyx, then with lightning speed slapped her across the face. She then streaked toward the stairwell and burst into the stage control room to confront Carlos.

"Stop it! Stop it! Lights out and stage up!"

Carlos screamed at the technician. It took just a few seconds to hit the right switches and start the platform's ascent.

Meanwhile the now raucous crowd pressed near the stage and stood up on couches and tables to watch the ascending tableau as long as they could.

"Was that really Lolly Penrose?"

"Hell yes, I'd know her anywhere."

"Nah, she was just some bimbo made up to look like her."

"You're nuts. That was Lolly Penrose. I saw her downstairs earlier this evening."

Soon a voice came on to announce that they had seen the only performance Evan Hatcher would give that evening. He went on to say, "I hope you have all enjoyed the simulated erotic tableaus presented by our company of talented mimes." He placed emphasis on the word "simulated."

One man with a voice that could be heard above the din called out, "Simulated, my ass! Hatcher and that babe were getting it on. Hell, I ain't blind!"

Onyx Lu sat alone now in the corner of the Black Lamp, a stream of blood trickling from the corner of her mouth where Beryl had struck her. The disco music droned on more quietly now. The crowd began to thin out, but many chose to stay to dance the night away.

Onyx spoke aloud to herself. "Now, Pennyrose, you slut, you belong to me. I will make you like it."

39

The run of the *Tashtego* from Chinook north to the broad mouth of the San Juan de Fuca Strait was accomplished quickly. The broad strait separating Vancouver Island, Canada, from Washington State would take them to the Port of Seattle, some hundred miles inland.

The big ketch had behaved beautifully. Winds had been accommodating, so even now as the *Tashtego* came about to enter the channel eastward to Puget Sound, they could do so without the diesel. They would not need to test the troubled drive shaft until they were well into the waters of the sound and seeking dockage.

The majesty of the soaring Olympic peaks ranged south of them in full view. Even with the problems lying ahead, Ginny and Willy took time to exult in the marvelous and seemingly endless natural beauty that surrounded them.

The elusive trawler that had seemed to dog their course all the way to Chinook vanished. Perhaps they were just paranoid about the vessel or just paranoid in general. They both missed contact with Coley and were anxious to bring themselves up to date on what was happening in Los Angeles. They had succeeded in buying the time they had wanted, and Willy had managed to finish all but the last chapter of his book.

It was a fascinating story. The obvious miscarriage of justice and the failure to convict Onyx Lu would be proved, and another blow would be struck for judicial reform.

Now, though, it seemed like a mere introduction to a much bigger story, just touching the tip of the massive iceberg that constituted the Sino-Americo Trading Company.

Ginny had been below for some time, studying the charts for the waters ahead of them toward Seattle. The area promised to be a navigational challenge for her; she remembered making the passage only once before. The route was strewn with islands and passages that had to be carefully identified. The project was further complicated by the hazy weather they could expect.

When she emerged from the cabin the *Tashtego* was already fifteen miles into the strait.

"Captain Caleb. Do you have any idea where you are?"

"Absolutely not, lady. You've got me confused with someone else. I'm merely an aspiring first mate. The captain of this vessel is a navigator beyond reproach. She'd never, for instance, get caught up by a pile of rocks, like those just over there."

"Have no fear, matey, I have been studying what's ahead and have decided that it would be more prudent to veer north, closer to the Canadian side of the channel, even though it may tack on a small amount of time."

"Why?" Willy's chief concern now was getting to their destination as quickly as possible.

"I hate to bring up a perfectly dismal subject. But I have been thinking of our dubious friend out there, the trawler. Of course he may just not be out there at all anymore. But maybe he is."

"What makes you think it's safer on the Canadian side?"

"If we keep to this course, by evening we will be tucked in close to Port Angeles. Say the trawler is waiting for us like we think he did at the Golden Gate. Port Angeles is a perfectly logical place for a trawler to hole up and be able to survey everything that goes on in the strait. If the weather turns sour, he could cruise the channel. I think we stand a much better chance of avoiding detection if we stay near Vancouver Island. If we're lucky enough to get the usual haze we could easily slip by Port Angeles. If there is any weather at all you just can't see across the channel, much less spot the *Tashtego*."

"What about radar?"

"I think that would be very difficult. This piece of water is much too busy. All the boats might be detected, but they would be hard to identify in a nice fog."

"Okay, let's do it. If all goes well we would be near Seattle in the morning either way. What is our precise destination? If we have problems with the drive shaft, we'd better know where we're going. By the way, do you suppose it could be a damaged prop that's causing the vibration? In that case we might find a quick fix."

"I really don't know, Caleb. Either way the vibration will eventually lead to big problems. Maybe we'll get lucky. I do have a spare prop aboard. My plan is to put in at a small boatyard on Shilshole Bay just north of Seattle. Believe it or not, I have friends who keep a stinkpot there."

Willy scowled and shook his head. "We can't identify ourselves to anybody we know. You know that. We could get your friends drawn into this and maybe even killed."

"Don't worry, Willy. I'll call them on the phone and plead a lack of time for getting to see them. I'll promise them a rain check if they insist on seeing us. A girlfriend of mine married this old codger who has been around boats all his life. They actually live south of Tacoma. It's quite a distance, so I don't think they would dart right up to see us if I don't invite them."

"You're the skipper, Ginny. But for God's sake don't do anything that would put them at risk. What is a young girlfriend of yours doing marrying an old codger?"

"You wouldn't believe what she told me. And I can't tell you either. If you ever met them it would be embarrassing for me if you knew."

"Don't worry, my imagination is probably better than the real story anyway. Whatever it is, I betcha the old codger's got the bucks running out of his ears."

"That too, lover. But the other reason is wild."

"It sounds like something you should tell me sometime when we're snuggled up in the sack."

Ginny beamed a warm smile toward Willy as she gave the wheel a big spin to come about. They were pointed toward the coast of Vancouver Island, directly across from Port Angeles, Washington, to the south.

Evening was approaching now, and the big orange sun was poised just over the sea on the western horizon behind the *Tashtego*. The breathtaking panorama of the Olympic peaks still loomed in the southern sky. At this moment it was starkly clear, a rare day in this Northwestern paradise.

And right on the water, on the Washington coast, pinpoints of auto headlights moved at water's edge.

Ginny pointed southward. "That would be Highway One Twelve out to Neah Bay, where we first came about to enter the strait. It would be

216

fun to pack a lunch and drive out there some-time. Oh, Willy, do you think we'll ever have the chance to do normal things like that someday?"

"Maybe not until I get to be an old codger, like your friend's pal. Jesus! I hope we both live that long."

40

Captain Alexandros still looked like a sea captain standing beside the rented Buick. It was getting dark and the *Tashtego* was rapidly fading into the backdrop of Vancouver Island far to the north. He steadied the powerful glasses against the top of the Buick, trying to keep the ketch in sight. They had followed it all the way from Neah Bay. It had taken them an eternity, it seemed, to make the few miles tucked in along the Washington coast.

"The silly bastards are using sail. Sailboat people are idiots. I should have rammed the bastards off California when I had the chance."

The two seamen he had with him nodded their complete agreement. They were tough and muscular, with hands permanently scarred from errant hooks and lines back in the days before they had been lucky enough to be hired aboard the cream puff of a trawler, the *New Territories*. They had been hired in Hong Kong where the *New Territories* had been built, and had stayed aboard ever since.

One of the men grunted something in Portuguese and pointed toward the distant *Tashtego*, which he could evidently still see with his naked eye.

"Yes, damn it, I see. I see. They're tacking north instead of toward Port Angeles. They could be headed for Victoria or even Vancouver."

The *New Territories* had been holed up in Port Angeles for two days awaiting the *Tashtego*. Now the ketch appeared to be slipping away to the north. Logan Phipps's operatives on land had been so sure that their destination was Seattle. Somebody must have screwed up an assignment, probably that crazy Wong, Alexandros reasoned. Anyone who could get himself rammed by a sailboat when he had eighty horses strapped on the back of a motor hull must be a real fuckup.

Phipps had told him the whole story, topping it off with the news that Wong had been instructed to report aboard the *New Territories* this very afternoon. "Custody!" Phipps had said in his morning communiqué. "Keep him in custody with no shore leave. He is to remain a prisoner aboard the *New Territories*. He must never get back to Los Angeles alive!"

Wong would probably be there when they returned to Port Angeles. Well, it was a simple enough assignment. Alexandros would just have KoKo bust his head and knock him into the fish locker.

The three kept their eyes on the *Tashtego* until it melded with the haze along the Canadian coast.

"Oh well," Alexandros said aloud to the two hands, "they're probably heading for some little cove along the Canadian coast, a cozy place for them to hide for the night. Let's get back to the *New Territories*. We have a new hand coming aboard. KoKo, I want you to bide your time and then beat the piss out of him. I want you to show him where he stands."

KoKo grinned and flexed his massive shoulders. He hadn't broken any bones for a long time.

41

Logan Phipps had decided to call a strategy meeting in Newport Beach. He had asked Coley Doctor to delay his flight back to Seattle for one day so that he could help concoct a final solution to what he considered the WOW problem. WOW was shorthand for Willy-Onyx-Wong. Phipps, Beryl and Coley were to meet in Phipps's office at the Sino-Americo Trading Company.

It was a perfect time for Coley and Beryl to get together to shoot a few buckets. He made a date to pick her up at her apartment in Newport and then take her to the Gold Coast Gym and Court Club for a few laps and some hoops, though he still wasn't convinced that the diminutive Beryl would be able to get the ball up to the net.

Beryl's apartment turned out to be a waterside layout within walking distance of Sundowners, one of Coley's favorite restaurants, famous for coconut-batter shrimp. He parked the aging Mercedes he had picked up at a federal auction a couple of years back and rang the doorbell. He could vaguely hear a melodious chord of chimes within.

The door opened in a couple of seconds, and there stood a stark-naked Beryl in the process of snapping on a bra. Coley tried to collect his thoughts quickly.

"Can I help you with that? Or maybe I should come back in a few minutes. What the hell are you doing standing there like that?"

There was a trace of a smile on Beryl's lips. She was obviously pleased by Coley's reaction.

"Please come in. Sit down and amuse yourself. I will be ready in five minutes. Just going to slip into some sweats and sneakers. You are fifteen minutes early, you know."

"Me? I'm sorry."

"No, you aren't, Mr. Doctor. You are having a ball right now. I might as well let you see me naked. I remember when Logan was talking to us in his office, you spent the entire time undressing me with your eyes. I will be all covered up with sweats in a minute or so. But all this will still be under the sweats and you will be thinking about it, won't you?"

"As a matter of fact, I will. I confess I am just a curious kind of guy."

Coley noticed that Beryl was making no move to get into her sweats. In fact, she sat on the arm of a sofa as she spoke.

"The truth of the matter is that you really don't want to shoot baskets with me, do you?" she said with brazen confidence.

"I guess I really don't."

"I'll tell you what, Coley, I don't either. It is not that I can't. But right now I don't want to."

"What's on your mind, sweet flower?"

"We have two hours. Strip down, Coley, and we'll see how crazy we can make each other."

Coley rose to pull the sweatshirt over his head. This really couldn't be happening. He must be dreaming.

"Coley, you have to answer one question for me. I am very practical. You will find that out. As of a week ago when I filed your company physical exam, you were one hundred percent okay. Now the question. You been fooling around? How about Onyx?"

"No. Now you have to answer one question for me."

Beryl was on her knees, beginning to massage the balls of his feet. "Fire away, hero."

"Would Logan Phipps kill me if he found out about this?"

"I really don't know. If Logan gets upset with someone, he has many punishments worse than death. I'm not going to tell him, are you?"

"Hell no."

"Maybe I better ask you one more question." Her massage had now worked up to his hamstrings.

"Shoot."

"Is there anything at all about you that Logan and I don't know as it pertains to your work?" Beryl stopped her massage abruptly and looked up at Coley, staring unblinkingly into his eyes, lips parted, awaiting his reply.

He broke into a sweat. Of course in his position almost any man would. He thought about Ginny and Willy, out there on the boat. He was probably their only hope. He couldn't help wondering why Beryl had asked the question. Did she know about his dual employment? Was she testing him? He really didn't know whether he was about to get laid or die.

"Hell no, sweet flower. I can't think of a thing."

"I'm glad you said that, Coley. Now if you don't mind, let's both shut up. We have an hour and fifty-one minutes. I'm going to start right here where I left off and work my way up to your nose. Then I am going to turn around and work my way back down, head first. Do you have all that clear in your mind?"

"Yes."

"Then shut up!"

An hour and fifty-eight minutes later they were speeding in Beryl's Jaguar up MacArthur Boulevard toward Logan Phipps's corporate office.

"Logan expects punctuality, Mr. Doctor. There

is never a valid excuse for being late other than national cataclysm. Even if we are extremely fortunate, we will still be four minutes late." Beryl seemed entirely serious, but nevertheless allowed Coley to periodically stroke her inner thigh as they neared the Sino-Americo complex.

"Say, don't you think you know me well enough to call me by my first name, or does Phipps have some rule about that too? To my way of thinking a cataclysmic orgasm is a perfectly valid reason for being late."

Beryl's face remained icily immobile as she pressed harder on the accelerator to race through a yellow light. She still did not bother to file a complaint about Coley's wandering hand.

"Mr. Doctor, the time is here for you to think about the WOW problem. Logan is going to want some advice about how to proceed. Onyx is getting neurotic about Willy Hanson. You saw her erratic behavior in the Black Lamp."

Coley lifted his errant hand and turned toward her in his seat.

"Hey, little flower, I would rather see just what Phipps is thinking about before I start suggesting anything. I'm really not getting paid to think, you know. I'm paid to keep my eye on people and report."

Coley's stomach gave a little flip. He had made the same comment to Willy and Ginny. Both of his employers obviously expected him to offer advice and opinions.

Beryl sped into the parking area in front of the Sino-Americo Trading Company exactly on time.

She stretched back in her seat for about thirty seconds as Coley continued his idle caresses. She then lifted his hand from her thigh and brushed a light kiss on his fingers.

"Hey, we are already a minute late. What happened to your punctuality all of a sudden?"

For just a fraction of a second, Beryl shot him a barely perceptible flicker of a smile.

"Thanks for shooting buckets with me, Coley. Maybe we'll do it again sometime."

Beryl and Coley were ushered into Logan Phipps's expansive office. On a massive rosewood table stood a crude but appealing hand-carved totem pole. The only other object on the table was a single manila file folder set before Phipps's chair.

Coley Doctor couldn't restrain a smile. He had sent the totem pole to Phipps after purchasing it in Astoria for fourteen dollars. At the time he had thought it was kind of neat, but now, sitting in the artsy splendor of Phipps's office, it appeared crude indeed.

Coley and Beryl sat in adjacent chairs at the table. Beryl stared at the totem, but her expression revealed nothing of her inner thoughts.

Phipps entered the room and sat down at once behind the manila folder.

"Mr. Doctor, I like that." He waved his hand at the crudely crafted totem pole. "You certainly earned your first week's pay with that. You have very good taste, Mr. Doctor."

Coley shrugged and smiled, not knowing

226

whether he was being made fun of or being complimented.

"I'm glad you like it. I'll try to do even better next time."

"I would like two hundred more just like that one. We will lacquer them and fit them with teak bases. Then we will sell them at a handsome profit to Japanese tourists in Alaska and Maui. You see, there are many ways to make money if you can fit the product to the customer. Can you get two hundred more of them quickly?"

Coley stared at the totem pole, which seemed to take on a tinge of authenticity as Phipps talked about it.

"I am sure I can get more of them. If you really want them I will find them somewhere, even if I have to make them myself."

"That's the attitude I like, Coley. But please don't dare do it yourself. In his crudeness, the artist is actually quite talented. I would prefer his work, not yours."

"You got it, boss." Coley was quickly getting impatient with the conversation. They had been called in for what apparently was an important meeting, and Phipps was going on and on about the carving. The man was hard to figure.

"I've heard it rumored about that one can purchase cocaine at the cabaret above the Black Lamp. This rumor comes to me via a source unconnected to our staff. Such a gross untruth could turn a spotlight on us and result in the closing of the Black Lamp." Phipps's tone remained matter-of-fact.

He opened the manila folder before him and read through a couple of printed pages before continuing his monologue.

"The Black Lamp is a prototype for a restaurant and cabaret chain that will have counterparts in over twenty-five American cities. To have such rumors start while our plans are still in the embryo stage bodes disaster. I want to stop all such rumors. I want both of you to go to the Black Lamp often and to drop in unexpectedly on La Sex Ménagerie. If anything clandestine is observed you are to get back to me immediately. If cocaine is being sold at the cabaret it is important that this activity not be traceable to the management of the Black Lamp."

In other words, Coley Doctor surmised, the world was supposed to believe that the setup in Redondo was a legitimate business.

Phipps spoke again, chosing his words carefully. "One other thing. The Macau whore is becoming careless. I have heard rumors that a blatant exhibition of oral sex involving a well-known movie personality occurred onstage. Of course we all realize that this did not occur, but yet the rumor persists. I have already spoken to Onyx. I want you both to keep your eyes open as well. The thrust of public image for the Black Lamp is always to be on the cutting edge of trendiness and sensationalism, but never to cross over the line into what might be considered public corruption."

Coley wondered if Phipps was backing away from the whole drug marketing scheme. At the least, he seemed eager to dissociate himself from it until all the wrinkles were ironed out.

Phipps cleared his throat, obviously preparing to say something else.

"The next item on our agenda today demands immediate attention. Onyx has sent that crazy fool Wong north to Washington State to pursue Willy Hanson and Ginny Du Bois. She persists in believing that they are out to get her, even though twelve jurors proclaimed her totally innocent of trumped-up drug charges. Our Macau whore is not rational about this matter, and we are going to have to take it out of her hands. You must direct your efforts to locating Wong so he can be placed in the hands of people who will dispose of him."

Just like that! Dispose of him!

Phipps turned another page in the small folder and picked up two Air Alaska tickets. He slid them across the polished rosewood to Coley and Beryl.

"I want you on this flight at seven P.M. this evening. You should be in Seattle by ten o'clock. You will be met at the airport by a man who will identify himself as KoKo. He will take you to the *New Territories*, where further details of our plans will be related to you."

"What in the hell is the *New Territories*?" asked Coley.

"Ah yes, you don't know, do you?" Phipps eyed Beryl for a moment and then proceeded.

"The *New Territories* is a vessel that we command. It is a fishing trawler that will provide you with very nice accommodations and spare you the necessity of finding a hotel. You will find Captain Alexandros a perfect host."

Coley's thoughts raced back to Willy and Ginny and the trawler he had spotted from the cliffs above Eureka.

"Mr. Doctor, Wong is a loose cannon. The FBI knows of him and must have a substantial file on his activities. In fact, they probably have him under surveillance right now. It will be your job to find him and inform KoKo of his whereabouts. KoKo will take over from that point."

Phipps began to amble around the circumference of his office as he spoke. "After that detail is taken care of, we will get down to the real business at hand. You will be assigned as many persons as you need by Captain Alexandros."

Phipps hesitated and stood before the floor-to-ceiling window that overlooked Newport Harbor.

"Our plan is to separate Willy Hanson and Ginny Du Bois. I must inform you now that you will be an integral part of this plan, an overt participant rather than just a tool of surveillance. Once we begin, there can be no turning back, Mr. Doctor. You will not leave our employ until Beryl is satisfied that the project is completed."

"You are suggesting a kidnapping?"

"Kidnapping? That is a harsh word. Perhaps it should be explained to her that a temporary detention aboard the *New Territories* would ensure that her playmate, Willy Hanson, would have an opportunity to stay among the living."

"What would we gain by this?"

"A commitment, Mr. Doctor. A commitment that Hanson will turn over to you all the research and material he has accumulated, even the figments of his own imagination. I refer to all the material collected to support the fraudulent exposé of Onyx Lu which he has promised his publisher."

"He won't do that. How could we ever be sure of him anyway?" Coley heard himself sounding like a genuine cohort of Phipps.

"He will accept our offer, Mr. Doctor. Then we will be able to trust him because then he will work for us."

"Why would he do that?"

"To stay alive, Mr. Doctor. To stay alive."

"What about Ginny Du Bois?"

This time it was Beryl who spoke up. "She will have an accident. Obviously there is no other way."

Phipps smiled a broad grin for the first time. "Our Beryl is quite pragmatic, isn't she, Coley?"

42

It was one of those days on Puget Sound when the sky melded with the water. In the total absence of wind the *Tashtego* rumbled ahead, its drive chain obviously damaged. A trail of exhaust lay low along the wake, lending an acrid odor to the still air. Ginny kept her eyes fixed on the engine heat gauge, trying to adjust the RPM's to an optimum level.

The bad visibility demanded that they constantly refer to the charts and identify each channel marker as they passed. They both felt strangely secure about the passage. It was hard to imagine that anyone was keeping track of them now. As the day progressed the *Tashtego* limped badly. To keep the engine cool enough to continue meant keeping it at a crawl. At this rate it would take most of the day to make Shilshole Bay.

At one point a giant container ship moved well to their port side, lumbering along at five or six knots. In its wake trailed a train of smaller vessels, willing to let the big ship point the way into Puget Sound. The *Tashtego* could not keep up with the parade.

It was well into the afternoon when Ginny piped up with a shout of glee.

"There it is!" She pointed to a big red buoy. "We'll hang a ninety-degree port change here. This should put us in the marina at Shilshole Bay in less than an hour."

No sooner had they made their port course correction than a vaguely familiar rumbling resonated off their stern. A giant fishing trawler, its silhouette barely visible in the soupy haze, lumbered by and proceeded south into the sound.

Willy and Ginny stared at the passage.

"Ginny, we can't get hyper over every goddamn fishing boat we see. These waters are alive with trawlers just like that one."

"I know. It will be just great to get ashore. I know a perfect place where we can lose ourselves for a couple of days while they fix up the *Tashtego*."

All at once in the thinning haze, as they began to approach the shore, they saw an endless stretch of coastline with masts of all configurations as far as they could see. A long dock holding the harbormaster's office lay dead ahead.

Ginny put the controls gently into reverse as they carefully approached the long dock. A hand came out to help tend lines; then an elderly, salty-looking man appeared in a ratty old cap with worn and crushed gold braid.

Ginny quickly explained the trouble with the prop; dropping the names of her friends who were long-term tenants of the marina. At the instruction of the old salt, a muscled young fellow scrambled aboard and pointed the way to the far north end of the marina. A slip wide enough to accommodate a much larger vessel was unoccupied. A giant crane stood ready to lift the *Tashtego* from the water. Ginny nimbly maneuvered the ketch into position.

Willy vaulted onto the dock to oversee. A surge of confidence swept through him. The *Tashtego* would be less noticeable in dry dock sitting between a number of boats that were even larger. He gave Ginny a thumbs-up sign. What a skipper! The last several hundred miles with the malfunctioning drive shaft couldn't have been handled any better by an engineer.

"You did it, baby! You could sail this thing right through the gates of hell and I would go along for the joy ride."

"Don't be silly, Caleb. Nobody could singlehand the *Tashtego*. When we head back south, you're going to be skipper."

One of the workmen propped a ladder up to the cockpit and Ginny climbed down. She immediately crouched behind the stern to take stock of the screw. One section of the prop had about half of its surface chopped away. This had no doubt resulted from the encounter with Wong's boat.

"Oho! I think that's the problem," she said as she continued to inspect the keel just back of the screw. "At least let's hope so."

It was impossible to determine whether or not there was any further damage to the drive chain. It would take a mechanic to find out if a new prop would take care of the problem.

"Okay! We get to hang around for a day or two." Ginny was exuberant. "I think you'll love my little hideaway. The first thing I'm going to do is take an endless shower and then try to sleep around the clock. Do you want to join me?"

"Need you ask? But we have to call Coley first."

Ginny grimaced. She realized Willy was right. They had been out of touch for a long time.

"Okay, Caleb. For just a fleeting moment I got the exhilarating feeling that we were just normal cruising bums out for a good time." She paused to look at the majestic *Tashtego*, now slung in a giant cradle.

43

Lolly Penrose stared at the *Times* headline in disbelief.

EVAN HATCHER DEAD AT 29

Aussie Rock Phenom Plunges Off Cliff of Rugged Torrey Pines Coast in New Corvette.

"Ain't nobody here but us," he had said. She clearly remembered the huge circular black satin mattress, the pink satin pillow in the middle, and then the gentle urging. There was Evan Hatcher's face high above her as his golden boots straddled her. "Ain't nobody here but us, honey. Nobody here but us."

Then all of a sudden there was the cheering of a crowd and laser and strobe lights flashing from below. "Hey, he's really doing it." Over and over again, "Doing it . . . doing it . . . doing it."

Then, mercifully, the lights faded away and the cheering crowd seemed far below. And that was all she could remember.

"You son of a bitch!" she screamed as she convulsed, stumbling to the liquor cabinet. A bottle of scotch stood like a god offering her solace for a humiliation too bitter to recall.

She nursed the bottle like a baby's pacifier until she fell whimpering to sleep.

44

The Water's Edge was a quaint hotel built on a small pier overlooking Puget Sound. The bustling Port of Seattle surrounded it. Willy and Ginny's cozy accommodations were right on the water. Floor-to-ceiling windows provided a spectacular mural in motion, especially spellbinding at night as the harbor traffic silently lit the shimmering waters of the sprawling harbor. Rainier in all its snow-topped splendor lay to the south of them. To the north the coast bent just where the Shilshole Bay Marina held the *Tashtego*.

Neither Ginny nor Willy had realized the extent of their exhaustion. In a matter of minutes their entwined bodies were motionless in deep slumber.

They had gone to bed while it was still daylight with the intention of napping and then going out to dinner. Exhaustion had overcome them in the beginning of lovemaking, and now, freeing himself gently from Ginny's entangling limbs, Willy crouched under the covers to read the glowing hands of his wristwatch: 2:45 A.M. He propped himself up on an elbow to stare out the windows. In the distance a giant ferry, lit up like an isolated city, scudded across the flat reflecting waters of the sound.

Ginny stirred slightly and extended an arm far enough to touch him, then once again dropped off into a deep sleep. He looked at the woman who had persisted in following him every step of the way in his unpredictable mission. She had skippered the *Tashtego* the entire length of the Pacific Coast in their dangerous adventure. A definition of love had always eluded him. But as he gently held Ginny's extended fingers he knew he had found it.

In the semidarkness of the room, he swung his legs off the bed to sit where he could reach the telephone. He decided he would try one more time to reach Coley Doctor. Carefully he punched the numbers that would get him into Coley's voice mailbox in Los Angeles. His body tensed and his mind snapped fully alert. There was a new message for him.

"Hey, old pal. You remember the bimbo I told

you about with the five miles of legs hangin' from her earlobes. Man, it was like dropping a three-pointer from twenty-five feet. I guess it was even better. Things are starting to pop fast. I'll be seeing you a lot quicker than you think."

There was a pause in the message. Coley seemed to be trying to find words.

"I can't tell you too much. You might get yourself killed. Whatever happens, I repeat, old pal, whatever happens, keep your cool and remember that old Coley's in charge. If you don't remember anything else about this message, remember that old Coley's in charge. Oh yeah, one other thing, just in case the Good Lord intervenes and makes old Coley eat a bullet, you are on your own. So carry that popgun thirty-eight you got and keep it loaded at all times. And one other thing. I guess that makes two other things, don't it? Our pal Wong is still running loose with a Marlin. Logan Phipps and everybody else in the world is trying to kill him, and I expect they will succeed. However, keep on the lookout until the dirty deed is done. Try to call in every four hours. One other thing—that makes three other things. I ain't makin' enough money. Think about that. Have a nice day. By the way, ain't the weather great here in Seattle? Surprise!"

"Holy Christ! What a jerk!" Willy couldn't help muttering just loud enough for Ginny to hear. He felt her stirring beside him.

"What did Coley say?" she mumbled from somewhere under the pillow.

"Here, you better listen to this." Willy redialed

the voice mailbox and put the telephone in her hand. She listened to the end with her eyes closed, then handed him the phone to hang up.

"Sounds like old Coley is getting laid."

"Is that all you've got to say? The son of a bitch is here in Seattle and he didn't even tell us where."

"Maybe he's hung out a Do Not Disturb sign. I bet you would do the same thing if you could find some bimbo with five miles of legs."

"How can you be so goddamn relaxed?"

"Caleb, come on down here under the covers with me. I want to show you something."

"Show me something? Isn't it awfully dark down there?"

"Caleb, there's a glow down here, I'm so hot."

"Hey, I've got to see that!"

"I'm glad, Caleb. I'm really glad."

Rapt in their energetic, mindless erotic explorations under the covers, they were oblivious to the stark drama now building on Puget Sound just outside the big glass sliding doors.

It was a moonless night on the water. A small runabout with running lights doused was putting alongside the Water's Edge Inn. The lone occupant of the runabout carefully counted the glass doors facing the water. Then the Oriental burst into a broad grin as he satisfied himself that he had correctly enumerated each door to match the numbers on the doors along the hall inside the hotel.

Carefully noting the placement of an antenna on the roof of the hotel, the boatman maneuvered the runabout to a point about fifty yards away and closed the throttle down to an idle. There was virtually no current on the flat surface of the water, which was broken only occasionally by fishing birds. In the darkness he unsheathed the big Marlin that he had retrieved from the waters of Juan de Fuca Strait just two days before. He had cleaned and oiled the soaked weapon carefully and was satisfied that it was ready to do its job. The Marlin made him feel powerful as he crouched in the boat and planned the next few moments. Onyx would be proud of him, he thought. Planning a perfect revenge and showing his superior wits by getting away with it would endear him to her once and for all.

For a moment he looked nervously to the north. His escape would have to be accomplished at high speed to a point onshore about four miles up. The rental car was already parked and waiting for him. He figured the four miles would take him about eight minutes. Then he would abandon the boat, hop in the car and proceed to the airport.

He putted a little closer to the Water's Edge and the glass doors he had marked for assault. Anchoring his knees firmly, he positioned the stern of his small vessel directly in line with the targeted room. The sights of the Marlin were carefully aimed about two feet from the base of the sliding doors. His plan was to empty the magazine across the door at that level, wreaking devastation on any occupants of the room who were either standing or in bed.

The firing of the Marlin cannonaded into the night air. In a matter of seconds it was all over and the powerful outboard roared to life.

Inside, Willy leaped to his feet and instinctively groped for the .38 he had left on the night table. Standing at the glass door, he could make out the wake and dark hull of the motorboat already a couple of hundred yards to the north. Along the ceiling near where he stood, a single bullet had bored through the glass and traversed the room. To the left he heard the crash of falling glass.

Ginny sprang to the window to huddle against Willy, who cursed with frustration as the speedboat vanished into the dark.

Lights began to flicker on in the hotel. They could hear shouting and heavy footsteps in the hallway. There was a pounding at the door.

"Everyone all right in there?"

Willy scrambled to put on his trousers as Ginny buried herself under the sheets. Opening the door, Willy was confronted by two men in some kind of security uniform.

"We're okay. Just a small hole in the door. What in the hell is going on?"

"Some idiot playing with guns out there on the water." The guards were especially wide-eyed, obviously not at all used to this kind of excitement at the Water's Edge.

"You can be thankful you didn't get the room next door," one blurted out. "It's all shot to hell!"

Willy closed the door and put the chain in place.

In the background they could hear the approaching sirens of police cars.

Willy squeezed Ginny close to him.

"I'm sorry, honey. We're going to have to get the hell out of here fast. There'll be a lot of questioning that I would rather miss. It'll be a while before Wong knows that he missed, and we might as well put some distance between us and the Water's Edge while we've got the chance."

"Oh, Willy, that was too close." Ginny trembled and held him tight before getting her things together.

By the time they passed the front desk, the Seattle police were swarming past them down the hallway. The desk clerk was trying to ignore the whole thing.

"How did you folks enjoy your stay?"

Willy smiled. "That was some hell of a wakeup call." Willy couldn't resist pushing him a little bit.

A man who could have been the night manager came to the rescue of the desk clerk. "I am very sorry for all the disturbance. This is a new experience for the Water's Edge. People do sometimes get drunk and do crazy things in their boats, but this is a new extreme. I'm sorry."

The desk clerk handed Willy a receipt.

"Now don't forget to take one of our fresh Washington State apples with you," he urged, waving upward the full basket of plump apples on the registration desk.

Willy obliged by jamming a couple of them into his pockets before pushing through the doors with Ginny to make his way toward a taxicab line across the parking lot. He had the .38 in the side pocket of his jacket, finger on the trigger all the time. As they piled into the cab, Willy suddenly realized that it probably wouldn't be a good idea to go straight back to the *Tashtego*.

"Give the driver the name of a big downtown hotel," he whispered to Ginny.

"Take us to the Seattle Hilton."

The cabdriver nodded with a scowl. At this hour of the morning he would have much preferred a fare to SeaTac Airport rather than the few blocks to the Hilton. He threaded his way between the police cars still jamming the parking lot.

"What the hell is going on in there?" Now committed to the short fare, the driver suddenly felt the urge to make the most of things.

"Big wild party going on. A lot of broken glass. Some guy got caught trying to fornicate with an orangutan." Ginny cut Willy short with a sharp jolt to the ribs.

"An orangutan! Boy! I'd like to see how the cops handle that one!"

"You'll have to forgive my husband, he's had too much to drink," Ginny offered.

"Hell, lady, I would drink too if there was guys running around doing stuff like that to monkeys."

At the Seattle Hilton, Willy shoved a ten-dollar bill at the driver and thanked him for the short haul.

"No problem, pal. I'm going back to the Water's Edge and see if they caught the monkey."

The door slammed and the taxi took off into the predawn darkness. Ginny couldn't resist laughing.

Hand still on the trigger of the .38, Willy silenced her with a probing kiss.

They embraced for a long moment while Willy took stock of things.

"I know one thing," he whispered. "We can't stay here at the Hilton. If anyone questions the cabdriver, we're cooked. I think the police will be very curious about why we abandoned the room so quickly. We did have a bullet hole in our door."

They started walking briskly around the block, all alone on the streets of Seattle. The barest hint of dawn was beginning to light up the sky in the far northeast. Finally, they passed the big glass tower of the Washington Sheraton and turned into the almost empty lobby.

Willy produced his Caleb Jones credit card and registered for a room. It was the first time he had used his new identity and he wondered how smart it was. He certainly didn't want to leave a paper trail. Reinard back in New York knew of his Caleb Jones bank account, and now the Sheraton knew of his credit card.

The room was hardly as romantic as the one at the Water's Edge. Strangely enough, from their vantage point in the Sheraton, they could look almost due west and actually see the Water's Edge down on Alaska Way. Two Seattle police cars were still parked out front.

"What if we go to a pay phone and call the Seattle police?" Willy said to Ginny. "We put the finger on Wong. We describe him in detail and even describe the Marlin he totes around. When you stop and think about it, the ruckus he caused at the Water's Edge was pretty serious. If that room had been occupied, people could have been killed. In fact one of us could have been killed by the bullet that came through our door. I would think that the police would consider it a priority to nail the guy."

Ginny nodded. "Well, of course I agree it's a good idea. But why now, Willy? You've always blown your stack when I suggest going to the authorities. And Seattle is full of men who look like Wong. How are you going to pinpoint him for the police?"

"We can pinpoint the Shilshole Marina, and tell them to look around there. The Marlin must be nearby. Once they find that and run ballistics, he's in big trouble."

"Give it a try, Willy. But maybe we should bounce it off Coley first. After all, how do we know it was Wong at the Water's Edge? How did he find us so easily? The last time we saw him he was wading around in the water near Chinook, with his boat sunk."

"You think the hotel manager might have been right? People just get drunk and do crazy things on the water?"

"Willy, I don't really believe it, but it is possible."

Willy stared at the Water's Edge far below. Another police car had just joined the two parked in the lot.

"First of all, Wong is as good with boats as anyone you could find. I can easily imagine that he got a hold of another small boat and actually found us somewhere in the Juan de Fuca Strait and followed us right into our dry dock. Knowing Wong's capabilities around water, that is very possible. In fact, how else would he have found the *Tashtego*? He had to find the *Tashtego* and then follow us to the Water's Edge."

"Lover, bounce it off Coley."

"I will, right now, if I can get the bastard."

Ginny joined him at the window and stared off into the distance toward the Water's Edge.

"So you've come around to trusting Coley one hundred percent?" Willy asked.

"No. Maybe ninety nine and forty-four one-hundredths, like Ivory Soap, but not one hundred percent."

"Well, I'm glad to hear that, but I'll call him anyway. You only live once, honey!"

Willy picked up the phone to dial the voice mailbox in Los Angeles while Ginny sprawled out on the king-sized bed.

There were no new messages. Then Willy took a hell of a chance. He left a message giving Coley their new number at the Sheraton and instructed him to call. When he hung up the telephone, he wished he hadn't done it.

He took his clothes off and laid the .38 on the night table next to him pointing right at the chain-locked door. He turned out the lamp and snuggled next to Ginny, who turned to face him in the darkness.

"I hope you remember that we have some unfinished business to take care of," Willy said. "We were kind of interrupted this morning."

"Caleb, tell me you will never go away."

"Hey! No fair talking serious. In fact, no fair talking."

45

Lolly Penrose's telephone rang at 10 A.M. in her Bel Air condo. She stared at it, afraid to move for fear of reactivating the pulsating headache that was just about to subside. She decided to wait until the caller left a message.

"Hello, sweet Pennyrose. I'll bet you are there. Your devoted Onyx needs you. Everyone at Black Lamp is asking about Pennyrose. Shame, shame on Evan Hatcher. God fix him plenty good for messing around with my Pennyrose. Everyone knows it was all an act up there. Everyone knows but Evan and he can't tell nobody."

"Onyx! Okay, I'm here. What happened to

Hatcher? Not that I care about that son of a bitch. How did it happen?"

"Onyx tell you all about it, Pennyrose. You no worry. Not many people see what really happen in La Sex Ménagerie. The lighting was bad and you were actually too high over most of their heads. They think Evan was just making like he was doing it. They all have lotsa fun. They think it phony tableau like on other stages. I tell you all about it, Pennyrose. That why I call. Let's do lunch. Okeydokey?"

"Onyx, I'd like to see you today. The goddamn studio has been calling all day long. I don't know what to tell them. I had just turned the volume back on on my telephone a little while before you called. You've got to tell me what happened."

"You no worry so much. Meet me down on the pier at Tony's in couple hour. We talk. I have something to show you. Then we do lunch. Hey, how about that! Pennyrose, we do lunch, then I do you! That okeydokey with Pennyrose?"

"Onyx, I'll meet you at one o'clock. I look terrible. I'll be wearing a coverup of some kind. I've got to know about everything that happened. Okay?"

"Oh, you'll know, baby, you'll know."

With that, Onyx clicked off the line, leaving Lolly feeling very uncertain about their meeting.

She went to the wet bar out of habit, but did not break the seal on a fresh bottle of scotch. The experience with Evan Hatcher was all she could think about. A tête-à-tête with Onyx Lu was hardly what she wanted, but she needed answers and Onyx was the only one she knew to turn to.

Lolly slid open the door to the deck and stepped outside. The day was a dazzlingly rare one for Los Angeles. The smog had blown away and the San Gabriel Mountains to the north stood in sharp relief. She couldn't recall the last time they had been visible. The Palos Verdes loomed high in the south, and the Pacific was etched as a dark gray line on the horizon beyond Redondo Beach, where she would meet Onyx.

She strolled back inside and let the cleansing fresh breeze blow through the open doors. The lust for the scotch returned, but she fought it off, knowing she would have cocktails with Onyx.

Lolly turned on the answering machine to listen to the accumulated messages. Five brief calls had come from the studio, the last one a voice she did not recognize, asking if she was okay, and if she had read a script that had been forwarded to her. There was also a call from Reinard Gossman in New York, Willy Hanson's friend whom she'd had a fling with once upon a time. Too much of a prude for her. But not in the sack, she reflected, as the memories brought a smile to her face. He was coming to California on business, he said, and maybe they could meet for dinner. And then what, Reinard?

The next call was a real jolt. The crisp Aussie voice of Evan Hatcher crackled from the recorder.

"Hey, lovey! We're some team, eh! We are on our way to San Diego for a friggin' fishin' trip.

We stopped here in Laguna to do a line or two. That bloody dyke Onyx is really pissed. She'll cool off. The two of us will have to give her a spin someday! Just kiddin', love. G'day, sweet lips."

Lolly started to tremble. She had never got a phone call from the dead before. His voice was so clear it sounded as if he were in the room with her. Who in the hell had been with him?

She went to the coffee table and reread the newspaper account. The *Times* stated flat out that Hatcher had been alone in the vehicle. He had driven onto the Torrey Pines golf course north of San Diego and devastated a couple of greens before plunging into a ravine to the edge of Pacific. The car had narrowly missed two surf fishermen casting along the beach below, and they had reported the accident.

Lolly walked to the answering machine and replayed Hatcher's message, then walked back to the bar and stripped the seal from the new bottle of scotch. She decided she would have just one three fingers neat before meeting Onyx Lu for lunch. That had always been Willy Hanson's way to cure a hangover.

The pier at Redondo Beach offered everything from fried-fish shanties to upscale eateries with extensive menus. They were meeting at Tony's, about halfway out on the pier, where diners could watch the procession of breakers cresting and then pounding onto the narrow beach below. To Lolly, there had always been something very therapeutic about watching this ceaseless pounding of the coast.

As she parked her car in the underground garage adjacent to the pier, she thought of the many times Willy Hanson and she had done this same thing. They had timed their cavorting around Southern California to arrive at Tony's just in time to watch the orange sun plunge into the ocean. Willy Hanson. The son of a bitch was on her mind.

Onyx Lu was already seated at a remote window table in the corner. As usual, she looked perfectly beautiful and serene. Lolly was envious. She knew they were both about the same age, but for Lolly, looking good was round-the-clock hard work.

"Pennyrose, you look so chic. In fact you look chic hot. And I have so much time to enjoy you."

Onyx rose to press a kiss onto her lips, prolonging it just a little beyond what would usually be considered appropriate.

"Look! The sea otters have come to play and amuse us." As Onyx spoke, a pair of the playful mammals arched to the surface of the water, then swirled out of sight beneath a large breaker.

Lolly stared at the cavorting creatures. "Yes, Onyx, they put on a good show. And after it is over they still have their self-respect."

"Ah, Pennyrose is sad. That makes me sad. Those bastards with their cheap talk and their rumors. That is what makes Pennyrose sad. As I say, sweet flower, only Evan Hatcher knows for sure what happen. And he is dead. Only uncertain mindless rumors are alive."

"Rumors, hell! I know what happened. I am alive and I have to live with it all. Evan may have been a fool, but now he's dead, and I find it very difficult to behave as if nothing happened."

She swallowed her venom for a few moments while the cocktail waitress took their order. Lolly requested Perrier just to nettle Onyx.

"By the way, Onyx, who was with Evan when he died?"

Onyx wore an expressionless stare. A great actress, Lolly thought.

"I read newspaper account like you. Hatcher was alone. He was alone and damn fool was joyriding on Torrey Pines golf course. He was drunk and full of cocaine. That is why he is dead."

"You are dead wrong, Onyx. He was with someone. He called me from Laguna Beach. He was going fishing with someone."

"That not true. You find time to look at police blotter and you will see that not true." Onyx grinned and went on. "You no worry, 'cause that not true."

"I saw the embroidered leather pouch in Evan's dressing room. You should stop giving those to people, Onyx. They are becoming a trademark. Hatcher might have had it on him when he died."

"My rose petal, you worry too much about that. You can buy them by the hundreds from street peddlers in Macau. Anybody can. Besides, he make slut out of Pennyrose. I very glad he die."

Onyx slid a small envelope across the table to

Lolly, who opened it to find a single small photograph inside. It must have been taken from a camera in the ceiling of La Sex Ménagerie. Lolly Penrose lay spread-eagled on the tufted black satin. A fiery-red satin pillow gave exotic contrast to the fan of her jet black hair spread across it. The photograph confirmed conclusively the penetration of the star. The ceiling vantage point of the camera rendered Hatcher unidentifiable.

Lolly sat tall in the chair, looked up, then stared off into the distance where the otters cavorted merrily. Tears stained her cheeks. The worst of her fears were now realized.

Onyx waited for an explosion as Lolly fingered the photograph pensively.

"So it comes to this. I've spent twenty-five years building a reputation in this crazy town and all of a sudden, as you so well put it, he makes a slut out of me. Lolly Penrose goes X-rated. Maybe we can send this one out with my updated bio. A lot of people would say, 'See, I told you so. I always knew she was a slut.' "

Lolly was running on in a nonstop monologue.

"Goddamn you! Goddamn Willy, goddamn Reinard, goddamn booze. Goddamn my stupid husband, Karl. Goddamn you and your cocaine . . . I want to die, die, die!"

"Stop it, Pennyrose. All is okay. Nobody know but us two chicks. I have only picture and negative. Here, you take picture and tear it up."

"There must have been two hundred people in that room. They all . . ."

"Saw nothing, my sweet rose petal. You were way up in air. They cannot see through stage. Only a few people far back think they see something. And their fucking minds are crazy on cocaine. Onyx not stupid, my sweet Pennyrose. They not incriminate themselves. Rumor is just rumor. Nobody believe it without picture."

Lolly gaped silently at the diminutive Oriental who was whispering her remarks. She fingered the salacious photograph thoughtfully. She saw no reason to question its validity, although she supposed that such a thing could be trumped up. Hatcher was not identifiable at all.

Lolly dabbed at the corners of her eyes with a napkin. The proud, beautiful face that had become familiar to moviegoers was ashen and streaked with makeup. She took one last look at the disgusting photograph before ripping it into tiny shreds, putting them back in the envelope and then into her purse.

"And the negative?"

Lolly extended her open hand, only to have it grasped by Onyx, who lavished a lingering kiss on her palm.

"I have it in safe place." Onyx grinned at the sober-faced star. "I get it for you sometime. As they say . . . not to worry!"

Lolly decided not to have lunch and ordered another Perrier.

"So why are we here, Onyx? If some sort of blackmail is what you intend, you could have accomplished that on the telephone. I was there! I didn't need to see the stupid photograph. What is it you want from me, Onyx?"

"I worry about Pennyrose. You drink too much. You are sick, Pennyrose, or you would have never let Hatcher do what he did. I want to help you. Lolly Penrose is very big name. People come from all over to see Lolly Penrose. I want you to have small share in Black Lamp. We want to call it 'Lolly Penrose's Black Lamp.' "

"Who is the other half of the 'we'?"

"The money people. They live in Hong Kong. They plan to build chain of chic cabarets all across this country. We hire marketing people who say we need celebrity imprint. You are just perfect, Pennyrose. All you have to do is show up once in a while with your famous friends. We do everything else. We draw up a use of name contract and you get percentage from restaurant."

Lolly certainly hadn't expected this. Luckily she was sober and knew that this decision was beyond her.

"You'll have to talk to my business manager. She once suggested that I market my name. Maybe we can do that, but you'll have to talk to her."

"That's the way to go! Pennyrose, I will have the papers drawn up so she can go over them. We will be able to make the Black Lamp one of the world's great restaurants."

"Onyx, you must know that I would want no part of the cabaret upstairs. I really don't care if I never see that place again."

"Of course. I would guess that you will change your mind about that, but suit yourself."

"And what about the negative?"

"Oh, you still worry about that. That is stupid. It is in safe place, but I get it and give it to you. Okeydokey?"

Lolly nodded, deciding that for the moment it was better to have Onyx as a partner than not. Reinard Gossman was coming out in a couple of days. Now there was a businessman she could at least trust. She would ask him what he thought.

"Onyx, I really must go now. All this rigamarole makes me very poor company. Draw up the papers on the deal and I will show them to my manager."

When Lolly stood up, Onyx rose to give her a hug.

"Hey, now we partners. That just about like being married. Maybe you come to my house and we celebrate. Onyx make you feel real good."

"Onyx, we will talk soon . . . and don't forget that negative."

Onyx let Lolly walk out of the restaurant alone. She decided she liked Lolly better when she was oiled up with scotch.

46

Logan Phipps had spread a detailed street map of Seattle over his massive rosewood desk. He had circled several locations with a marker: Sea-Tac Airport, the Water's Edge Inn, a Shilshole Bay marina and the closed cannery where the *New Territories* had received a permit to dock.

Onyx had finally heard from that fool Wong, who had pinpointed the location of the *Tashtego*. According to Wong the vessel was high and dry in a boatyard on Shilshole Bay. Strange that the bumbling Wong would find the *Tashtego* first. He had followed the ketch all the way down the Juan de Fuca Strait into the sound.

Since the *Tashtego* was now on land, there was all the more reason for Wong to follow his original instructions to be taken off the chase. Logan had given Onyx the location of the *New Territories* to pass along to Wong with the insistence that he turn himself over to Captain Alexandros for further assignment. Onyx was beginning to be a problem. If she didn't produce Wong quickly, he would have to have a showdown with her. The fact that Wong had located the *Tashtego* for them had given him a life, at least until he turned himself over to Alexandros. Onyx's vendetta was tying up too much of their time and effort.

"People damn well better start following instructions," Phipps said aloud as he stood back to look at the map spread before him.

Coley Doctor was beginning to irritate him. It was important to separate Willy Hanson from Ginny Du Bois before the *Tashtego* put out to sea again. He had sent Beryl north with Coley because she had Coley's complete attention, and she never failed in anything she was asked to do. She was a remarkable woman. Someday he would have to take her to Hong Kong on the *New Territories*. But his thoughts were interrupted by an urgent telephone call from Onyx Lu.

"Lo, I have, as they say, good news and bad news."

"Onyx, I am in no mood for games. Obviously, you have something very distressing to tell me. Why don't we get that over with first?"

"It's Wong. He in big trouble in Seattle. He was involved in some kind of shooting in a hotel in Seattle. Seattle police have him in jail. They catch him with hunting rifle, which they have confiscated. Believe me, Lo, he was on his way back to Los Angeles when they caught him. He need bail."

"Onyx, this is your mistake. You will pay for this one. I warned you. I'll get him a lawyer to protect our interests. It sounds like this is going to take some time. Wong must go!"

"Remember, he find *Tashtego* for us. Wong do many good things."

"You and I have finished talking about Wong forever. Understood, Onyx?"

"Onyx understand, Lo."

"Now that we have that over with, what is your good news?"

"Lolly Penrose has agreed to be our partner in Black Lamp for almost nothing. She will show business manager papers. She will make perfect front, Lo."

"I'll bet she wanted the negative."

"Yes, I tell her not to worry. I have it in safe place. I tell her someday, Lo."

"Oh hell, make a few prints and give her the negative. There is no use opening the door to blackmail."

"Very smart. She be very happy."

"Onyx, the Seattle problem will soon be over. There will be no need for a vendetta any longer. From this time on, you are to devote all your energy to making a success of the cabaret. Do you understand that?"

"Yes. Lo, do you trust that big tall Coley fellow?"

"That's a strange question. Shouldn't I?"

"You know I have very good instinct. I have very good instinct about man-woman hot stuff."

"Onyx, you have the basic instinct of the Macau whore that you were."

"I just thought I better tell you."

"Don't you think I have eyes?"

"Yes, and so does Beryl. I saw her looking all gaga at that big fellow."

"Beryl has her motives, just like you do, Onyx. She knows how to get next to people and find out what makes them tick. I am sure you know exactly what I am talking about. Good night, Onyx."

Phipps hung up the phone before she could respond. Coley Doctor certainly was not an open book. He hadn't yet been put to the test, but that was coming soon. It would soon be his responsibility to send Willy Hanson and Ginny Du Bois off to their ancestors. Meanwhile Beryl would dig into Coley Doctor's mind and learn more about him than he knew about himself before they both got back from Seattle.

Yes, Beryl was something special. Someday perhaps she would join him on the board of the Sino-Americo Trading Company.

47

After the conference with Logan Phipps, Onyx had decided that the time had come for a talk with Carlos. With Wong evidently out of circulation in a Seattle jail, it would be necessary to make Carlos a closer ally. She had decided to invite him to the Palos Verdes house.

She felt isolated. Phipps was beginning to worry her. It was becoming increasingly obvious that the villas on Maui and back in Cheung Chau would never be hers. She was destined to be the operator of La Sex Ménagerie indefinitely. As Logan had put it, cash flow was not up to snuff, and it was time to start making the millions of dollars that this great free land of America was offering the agile minds of the Hong Kong–Baja coalition.

That bitch Beryl was getting to be a problem too. And now she was up north handling the Willy Hanson mess. She was a sharp cookie, no doubt about that. She had accomplished something that Onyx herself had never been able to do: find the way into the sharply creased trousers of Logan Phipps.

Now Carlos was late. As chief of security for Phipps, he was intolerant of interruptions in his routine. He hung on to his turf with the same pride he took in his ingenious ability to carry out his executions with no loose ends and no backlash.

She finally heard the chimes indicating that the front gate had been activated. A few seconds later Carlos's nondescript car came up the driveway. Carlos bought cars that would draw little or no attention to him. They were always the most popular Ford or Chevrolet of any given year. In fact, everything Carlos did in life was calculated to focus attention on anyone but Carlos, the consummate hit man.

A morning fog was still rolling along the coast, and the sun had not yet burned its way through the blinding haze. Carlos had paused after parking and was crouching to inspect one of his tires. Onyx decided to go outside and perhaps have her talk with him while strolling through the garden.

"Carlos, O great warrior. You never come to

see Onyx. That was nice. I have been thinking about you."

Carlos joined her and started walking toward the garden. On the way, they passed the greenhouse. A quick glance inside confirmed that the green tarp which he had placed over the kegs of cocaine several weeks ago was still in place. He wondered if anyone other than he and Onyx knew exactly where the shipment was. For just an instant, he had a flashback of the exploding van that reminded him of the execution.

Carlos didn't like reminders. When a job was done, it was done forever. Recollections served no purpose. Onyx had paused nearby where they could both see the green tarp. That bitch, he thought. She is bringing back memories on purpose. She wants to remind me that she knows what I did. She wants me to fear her.

"Lo and I have been discussing the fine job you have been doing. You make the opening of the Black Lamp easy. We have had no trouble."

Carlos looked quizzically at Onyx, wondering just what her definition of trouble must be. He thought of the wild ride with Evan Hatcher down the coast. Trying to get the crazed fool to drive himself off the cliff at Torrey Pines had been big trouble. Evan Hatcher had thought he was having great fun. Carlos shuddered. The risk to his own well-being had been entirely too high. He decided to say something to Onyx.

"The Hatcher thing, it wasn't easy at all. There could have been trouble. If he hadn't driven off the cliff, he might have died of overdose anyway. They will investigate, you know. He was loaded and they will try to find out where he got the cocaine."

Onyx grinned at Carlos.

"Maybe he get it from some movie star."

"Maybe, Onyx, maybe." Carlos shrugged, his dark brow furrowed in a frown. He moved farther down the path, away from the greenhouse and the green tarp.

"Carlos, my brave Carlos," began Onyx.

Carlos winced. He did not relish her possessiveness.

Onyx went on, "I know that you have a most difficult job. If you have trouble, you keep it to yourself. It never comes back to Lo or myself. We apppreciate your efficiency. You are not like that crazy Wong, who is brave but a bungler."

Carlos looked at Onyx in surprise. It was not like her to cast aspersions on Wong.

"Wong is being held by the police in Seattle. Nothing really serious, but until he is able to return, I am going to have to rely more on you. How much money do we pay you now, Carlos?"

It was a silly question; she already knew the answer.

"I make a thousand a week, and special bonuses of ten thousand for Hatcher-like events. I thought you knew that, Onyx."

"Lo and I would like to double that, Carlos. Does this please you?"

"Of course."

"And what are you going to do with all that money?"

"I'll probably buy a ranch and breed Angus down in Jalisco." Actually the property he envisioned was not in Jalisco at all, but that was not any business of Onyx's.

"For you and your Luisa Maria, I bet."

Carlos remained silent, infuriated that she would bring Luisa Maria's name into it.

Onyx persisted. "I think you should bring Luisa Maria to Redondo Beach. Wine and dine her at the Black Lamp. She would be very proud of the important job you have there."

"Luisa Maria would not like that. It would interrupt her studies." Carlos looked right at Onyx with a sullen gaze and tapped the nine-millimeter that bulged under his left armpit.

"You are no fool, Onyx. You know this is not a business that a religious young woman like Luisa Maria would approve of. You know that, Onyx. And so you know that there is nothing that should cause you ever to speak her name again. That is the way it must be."

Onyx turned and walked toward the greenhouse. She opened the glass door, entered and then sat down on the tarp that covered the kilos of cocaine. Carlos followed but stopped at the open door of the greenhouse. Onyx crossed her legs provocatively, then lay back on the kegs. She slid the flimsy silk wrap she wore down to her hips.

"Don't be such a fool, Carlos. You commit the ultimate sin. You murder. Why not give in to the other sins that are much less volatile and so much more pleasurable? You can have the best of all possible worlds, Carlos, and your sainted Luisa Maria need never know."

"I have heard you referred to as a Macau whore. You are that, Onyx. And I do not pleasure whores."

With that Carlos turned on his heel and strode back to his Ford, eager to get off the Palos Verdes property before he put the nine-millimeter to use.

He looked at his wristwatch. He was supposed to have called Coley Doctor's voice mailbox a full fifteen minutes ago. Instinctively he felt that Doctor was a man he had to keep his eye on. Somehow he was different from all the others.

48

It was the early morning after their second night in the Sheraton.

Their high perch in the hotel gave Ginny and Willy a feeling of security, and for the first time in many days they had slept long after sunup. Both were in deep sleep when the telephone awakened them with a high-pitched ring. Willy jerked to a sitting position; his hand slapped onto the nightstand instinctively to grip the .38 still pointed at the door.

Ginny rose to her feet to peer out the window to the Water's Edge. A single police car was still parked out front.

The telephone gave a fourth strident ring.

"Willy, darling, that has to be Coley answering your call. You better pick it up."

"If it isn't Coley, we're in trouble for sure." Willy lifted the phone from its cradle.

"Okay, I'm awake. Who the hell are you?"

"Jesus! Is that any way to answer the phone? I'm your old buddy, the point guard from Watts."

Willy breathed a sigh of relief. Ginny sat down next to him to share the earpiece.

"Coley, we've got to figure out a more efficient way of communicating. What the hell time is it?"

"It's Thursday morning, pal. I'm sorry I didn't call you last night, but I couldn't do that from my new digs aboard the *New Territories*. Been working some plans for my boss, Logan Phipps."

"Coley, please translate that. We are about ready to jump out of our skin here. The *Tashtego* will be ready tomorrow and we don't know whether it's safe for us to go aboard."

"Things are breaking pretty fast but I can't go into detail until the same time tomorrow morning. But at least you don't have to worry about Wong and his Marlin anymore.'

"Why is that?"

"He was picked up by the Seattle police for some crazy shooting spree down at some waterfront hotel."

Ginny couldn't suppress a squeal of satisfaction. Their call to the Seattle police had worked.

"That's great. What is this *New Territories* thing?"

"Believe it or not, the *New Territories* is that

fishing trawler that has been on your ass all the way from San Francisco. As far as I have been able to find out, you have had three spectators following you around, the trawler, the FBI and Wong. Four if you count me."

"Didn't you say you had your digs aboard the *New Territories*? What the hell is that all about?"

"Remember the classy little quiff, name of Beryl, who wanted to shoot buckets with me? Well, I guess Logan Phipps is a frugal man. He's putting us up in adjoining staterooms aboard the *New Territories*. Saves hotel bills and builds up company morale."

"Sounds to me like he's trying to have big sister keep an eye on you. I hope you don't talk in your sleep, Coley."

"By the way, your old pal Lolly Penrose is hitting the stuff big-time. Put on a nasty show for the folks in Onyx's new joint. I think Onyx would give up one boob and one leg just to get her into the sack."

Ginny stood up again to stare out the window at the police car in front of the Water's Edge.

Willy kept talking to Coley. "How close are you to finding a way to nail Onyx so that we can all get back to a normal life?"

"Very close. Very, very, close. By the way, don't count on getting back on the *Tashtego* quite yet. I may need both of you in L.A. within a week. Old Coley may have to ask you to fly. We will all know in a day or so."

"Ginny and I are going out on the town tonight. I want you to join us, Coley."

"Sorry, Caleb, that just doesn't fit my plans. My thousand-dollar-a-day job calls to me to be front and center this P.M. But soon, man. Soon. Where you guys going?"

"To Schooners Notch, overlooking Lake Union. You ought to come see us. Give your low-end clients a break. Dinner at eight."

"I gotta get back to the trawler tonight. Sorry. Keep the thirty-eight loaded and enjoy yourself. What's the name of that place?"

"Schooners Notch."

"Thanks, I'll put that on my list. Check my voice mail a little more often, okay?"

"Sure, Coley."

"And by the way . . ." There was a long pause. "No matter what happens, trust me. Got that? Trust me." And then Coley hung up.

Willy felt uneasy. Coley had wanted to tell him something but wouldn't. He wished he hadn't told him they were going to Schooners Notch and considered changing plans. But now there was a slim chance that Coley would show up. Willy heaved a sigh and decided to stick to his original plan.

They took a taxicab from the Sheraton to the restaurant, where an attendant opened the door and welcomed them. The view from high above Lake Union was spectacular. The evening had turned clear, and the thousands of lights that ringed the lake stood out like a huge sparkling necklace.

Inside, they were seated in an alcove that gave them some privacy and a dazzling view of Seattle. Across the room a pianist played effortlessly, creating a soft, romantic atmosphere. Willy surveyed the room while he clasped Ginny's hands in his own.

"This is not bad. I feel like I've got everything I want right now. But you know, honey, I feel that same way all day long no matter where we are, as long as we're together."

"Thanks, Caleb." Ginny smiled in a way that warmed his soul.

"Believe me, Ginny, I have no desire to spend the rest of my life on the run. Our lives can be exciting without being in constant jeopardy. I've wondered a million times why you put up with it."

The waiter approached their table.

"Hey, let's start with a couple of those fruity rum drinks that drive you crazy."

"Caleb, I want a Mai Tai. I want to drink to the trans-Pacific we haven't made yet."

"Sounds great. Make that two Mai Tais."

The Schooners Notch was very nearly at capacity. It wasn't until after a few people left that Willy became aware of a party of three on the far side of the same lower level they were on. Two were thickset Oriental men in finely tailored silk suits. The other was a woman sitting with her back to Willy and Ginny. She had long blond hair that fell almost to her waist. Once in a while he caught a quick glimpse of her profile and was able to tell that, despite the blond hair, she too was Oriental.

Willy and Ginny were getting into their main courses when the blond woman stood up and started to walk in their direction. Willy stared intently at her youthful face when she passed by, apparently on the way to the powder room.

That vague gnawing in the pit of his stomach returned.

"What is the matter, Willy?" Ginny extended her hand to grasp his. "Who is she?"

"I guess I'm just jumpy. That woman, except for the blond hair, is a mirror image of Onyx Lu. She is a much younger woman, though. I guess I was startled, that's all."

"But she isn't Onyx? You're sure."

"Absolutely."

"She is wearing a wig. I could tell."

"It makes no difference. She's not Onyx. I'm sorry, Ginny. I don't want to spoil your dinner. I'm being paranoid. Let's do something special for dessert, since we only get to dine like this once in a blue moon."

"Marvelous suggestion. I'll have bananas Foster, and a Grand Marnier."

"I think we'll just make that two."

As he spoke, the two men who had been sitting with the blond woman arose and stood at the window by their table. One of them was pointing to something out on the water below. Willy was struck by the ruggedness of the two men. The fine silk suits only emphasized their muscled physiques.

The bananas Foster came along with the Grand Marnier. The cocktails and the fine Cabernet they had enjoyed with their dinner had already made both Ginny and Willy slightly high. The fabulous evening had been unlike any they had known recently.

"You know what?" Willy had moved his chair closer to Ginny's so that he could put his arm around her waist as they sipped the Grand Marnier. "I am the luckiest man on the face of the earth." Willy slurred his words slightly, and then went on, "I think Lou Gehrig said that."

"Who?"

"Lou Gehrig. He played for the Yankees. You wouldn't know about him. In fact, I can barely remember."

Ginny smiled. "Willy, do you think that we, using all of our remaining wits, can find our way back to the Sheraton?"

"Of course. We'll just tell a cabdriver to take us there. We'll tell him to drive slowly. We're in no hurry."

There were just a handful of patrons left in Schooners Notch when Ginny excused herself to go to the rest room. Willy leaned back, totally relaxed. He looked at his watch. It was 11:15. They had spent more than three hours together without discussing their mutual problems, other than his foolish apprehension over the Oriental trio.

Just as he thought about that, the trio rose to exit the dining room, passing near Willy on the way. One of the men glanced quickly, almost furtively, at Willy as he passed.

Willy stared at him, hoping to catch his eye again. But it didn't happen and he felt greatly relieved when the three passed the piano bar and disappeared from view.

The maître d' stopped by Willy's table, and they chatted briefly about the excellent Washington State Cabernet.

Willy looked at his watch again. It was almost 11:30. He tried to remember when last he had looked at his watch, and realized that it had been a long time. He rose and decided to take care of the check up front and then wait for Ginny in the vestibule. Glancing about, he could see that save one other couple they were the last patrons in the restaurant.

Willy paused at the piano bar to stuff a ten-dollar bill into a brandy snifter atop the black-lacquered baby grand. The pianist nodded his thanks and continued to play. Willy paused to watch him for a few moments, wishing that somewhere along the road of life he had learned to play the piano. The man played effortlessly and obviously drew a lot of enjoyment from it.

Willy looked at his watch again. It was 11:35. He wondered what was delaying Ginny. He was sure now that she had gone to the rest room more than fifteen minutes ago. Maybe she had become ill, although she had shown no signs of it when she had left the table. Maybe all the alcohol had been too much for her.

He looked out over the restaurant from the vestibule. The last couple left in the dining room was preparing to leave. Something had to be wrong. He decided to seek help from a passing waitress.

"Miss, my companion went to the powder room quite some time ago. I wonder if you would mind going in there and seeing if she is okay? I would appreciate that very much."

The woman smiled and nodded. "Yes, sir, I will go check."

She was in the rest room only several seconds before she emerged shrugging, her palms extended skyward.

"There's no one in there, sir. You may look for yourself if you like.'

Willy's pulse must have jumped a hundred beats as he flung open the door.

"Ginny! Ginny!" He shouted her name but it was obvious that the small room was empty.

Willy exited to confront the waitress again. The maître d' was now standing near her.

"This is impossible! Is there another rest room here?"

"No, sir, there is not. I believe that the young lady left with some other people some time ago."

"That's impossible!" Willy shouted.

He was rapidly losing control. He began popping his fist in his hand in desperation. The maître d' was eyeing him suspiciously. The two remaining customers passed by on the way out, craning their necks, trying to determine what all the commotion was about. It must have seemed pretty obvious to all that he had just been dumped by his companion.

Willy made his way to the maître d's podium. He was fumbling around for money to pay the check, trying to stay as calm as he could, not wanting anyone to become alarmed and call the police. He pushed two hundred-dollar bills at the waitress, now also standing at the podium, and told her to keep the change.

The maître d' approached Willy at that point and said, "Are you Willy Hanson?"

Willy nodded, amazed and terrified that anyone there could possibly know his name. The maître d', stern-faced, began to fish around in a small drawer in the podium. He withdrew a small scrap of paper.

"I wrote this down, sir. I insisted on doing so. I didn't want to confuse the young lady's message."

"What young lady?" Willy was still shouting, though he stood only inches away from the maître d'.

"Beautiful young lady. Slender with long blond hair." The manager tried to smile pleasantly.

Willy's mind flashed instantly to the sleek Oriental woman. He remembered that the Orientals had left just moments before Ginny had gone to the rest room. He broke into a sweat. His hand slid instinctively to the .38 now jammed into his jacket pocket.

The maître d' was trying to decipher his own scribble on the scrap of paper.

"The young lady told me to pass along this message to Willy Hanson when he leaves. She did not want to disturb you while you were dining with your lady." The maître d' looked directly at Willy, wondering what sort of a situation he had become a part of.

"Get on with it. What is the message?" Willy

was now speaking in abnormally modulated, clipped tones.

"The young blond woman said to tell you that Onyx sends you her warmest regards."

"Onyx!" Willy screamed the name aloud as if it were a curse. It was all crystal clear. If he had only listened to his instincts!

The blond woman had worn a wig. He remembered the dark glasses. Even more clearly, he remembered the way the woman walked. Somehow she had been made up to appear much younger. But it had been Onyx. He was sure of that now.

Ginny had been kidnapped! She was out there somewhere in the Seattle night with Onyx and her two goons.

49

Captain Alexandros poured a liberal quantity of Courvoisier into a large snifter and seated himself comfortably in the elevated helmsman's chair aboard the *New Territories*. He deeply inhaled the aroma of the fine brandy as he doused the lights on the bridge of the trawler. It was approaching midnight, and with the lights down he could see more clearly up and down a stretch of Alaska Way. Sometime soon he should see Beryl, Coley, KoKo and Leyte coming along with their "guest."

The captain didn't like that son of a bitch Coley. He had been pumping at Beryl all day long in that fancy aft stateroom. He couldn't wait to tell Logan Phipps about that. He felt certain Phipps would order KoKo to drop all six foot six of him into the fish locker.

A long time ago Alexandros had reasoned that most of the people who lived on land were nuts. Three-fourths of this globe was water, and to him that made water man's natural habitat. Aboard a vessel a man could have what he wanted for his own self. A vessel was a world closed to the outside, free of any contamination the captain did not want aboard.

He leaned back and swirled a mouthful of the fine brandy and felt it warm his insides right down to his stomach. The only trouble he ever had aboard the *New Territories* was when Phipps insisted that his crew mix in with landlubbers. Like right now. Why in hell couldn't they be on time? The traffic was beginning to thin out on Alaska Way but the black, shiny Town Car Beryl had leased was nowhere in sight.

He wondered whether they would have to knock the woman senseless before getting her aboard the *New Territories*. Land people never failed to upset life on a vessel. If there was any ultimate truth, that was one for sure.

Alexandros swigged another mouthful of brandy and propped his legs up on the chart table. He hoped this Ginny Du Bois would be one ugly split tail, otherwise KoKo and Leyte would want to take turns on her for a while before dropping her in the fish locker. He had told

Logan Phipps a hundred times that a woman turns any ship into a hell ship.

Less than three miles away, Coley Doctor was having his own problems. His rented Lincoln Town Car careened down a steep driveway concealed by dense shrubbery and adjacent buildings, leading away from Schooners Notch. The vehicle screeched into a hairpin right turn that sent him the wrong way down a one-way street. Coley had planned it all ahead of time and prayed that they would meet no other car for a couple of hundred feet until he could pull into a driveway and douse the lights.

Ginny was scratching and clawing at him like a crazed animal. She had been uncontrollable since the Lincoln had started down the driveway. She had seen him and gone straight to him, thinking he would accompany her to their table. Instead he had taken her arm, gently at first, but insisting that he had "big news for her to tell Willy." He was insistent, and Ginny was feeling the effects of the drinking. She reluctantly followed him outside.

Coley shoved her into the open door of the Lincoln and piled in behind her, pushing her roughly into the passenger seat. As he roared down the driveway she caught a glance of the blond woman and her two companions exiting the restaurant. Desperately she fumbled with buttons, trying to open the window or door to shout for help.

One of the men motioned toward their car. It

wasn't a wave, however, it was a thumbs-up gesture. The man was signaling to Coley! They were obviously participants in her abduction.

She went right for Coley's crotch with one hand and his eyes with another. Coley let fly with his massive right arm, trying to fend her off as he screeched into oncoming traffic. Steering with his left hand, he missed the intended driveway and finally bumped over a curb about a quarter of a mile down the road. He then managed to steer the car up against shrubbery to help conceal them. He quickly doused the lights and then turned to grab Ginny by both arms. She already had her teeth deep in his right wrist. In the rearview mirror he saw the other Lincoln exit the driveway and make the obligatory left turn, no doubt confusing the taillights of the traffic up ahead as his. Coley, now in severe pain, held Ginny firmly by both wrists and heaved a sigh of relief.

"Relax, goddamn it! Relax! We're safe for a while."

Coley looked Ginny right in the eye and then slackened his grip somewhat. She was at him like a shot, ripping a gash across his brow.

"Now stop it. Everything will be all right. I can explain all of this." He once again got a tight grip on her.

Ginny struggled away as far as she could against the door. Once again Coley relaxed his grip.

"Coley, Willy's going to kill you for this."

"Here, you can save him the trouble." With

that Coley removed the nine-millimeter Glock from his holster and laid it in Ginny's lap.

Ginny grasped the gun with both hands, careful not to put her fingers anywhere the trigger.

"Open the door, Coley."

He fumbled in the dark until he found the right button and then opened the door. Ginny got out and stood at the side of the car, still holding the gun. Calmly she got back into the car and slammed the door. She laid the Glock on the seat between them.

"Okay, Coley. Willy must be going nuts back there."

"Now don't sell Willy short. I told him not to worry."

"Coley, I don't think he expected your simple assurance to cover kidnapping. By the way, who are those people, the blond and the two guys?"

"The blond is Beryl with a wig. She's Logan Phipps's right arm. The two other guys were KoKo and Leyte. They are the kind of dudes who would enjoy ripping the livers out of live polar bears."

Coley extended his hand as if to console her, but she would have no part of it.

"Look, Ginny, we have no time to spare. Those guys could come back. I'll drop you off at the Washington Sheraton. We can talk on the way."

"For Christ's sakes, why, Coley? Why?"

"Ginny, they were going to kidnap you and hold you aboard the *New Territories*. There was no stopping them. I managed to convince them that I should handle the job for them. Kidnapping you had heavy risk attached to it. Beryl was more than willing to let me try. This was a way of proving my total loyalty to them. Beryl still has reservations about me."

"How do you know that?"

"It's the way she acts in bed sometimes. She will ask me the damnedest questions right in the middle of a big hot rush. Like she's trying to trip me up."

"Okay, Coley, spare me the details."

Coley was pushing the speed light. The tower of the Sheraton loomed in the distance. He stopped at a gas station where he'd spotted a pay phone. Taking Ginny by the hand, he led her to the phone and called his voice mailbox, insisting that she say a few words.

With the call completed, he assured her that things would be all right. "When Willy comes to his senses he'll call the voice mail. Come on, let's get going. Willy might beat us back to the hotel."

"I don't even know that he will go back there. There's no telling what he might do. He might even get the Seattle police to search the *New Territories*." Ginny shook her head. "What did they want with me, anyway?"

"It's part of Onyx's vendetta. She's out to punish Willy for what he did to her. The syndicate, my boss, also wants you both dead."

"What are they all going to say when you turn up without me?"

"I'm going to have a car accident, baby. It's going to be a spectacular son of a bitch, right where they can see it. They're going to assume for the moment that you're dead. Later on, they **may** suspect you got **away**."

"Are you going back?"

"Hell yes, Willy and I are going to bring **down** the curtain on all those bastards. I can't **wait to** get started."

Ginny looked at Coley Doctor in wonderment. She hadn't been sure of that until this **moment**.

"How are you going to explain that I'm **sup-** posed to be dead while you're still alive and well?"

"You've already solved that problem for me. Take a good look at me, doll."

Coley had a huge gash on his forehead, **and** the stream of blood had soaked his shirt **collar.** Blood was also oozing from the corner of his mouth where he had caught one of her elbows. He began ripping and tearing at his clothes.

"When I get out of the car next time, I'll find a mud puddle and roll around in it. You know, you're a regular wildcat. I was wondering how I was going to make myself look like I had been in an accident. But I wish you could have taken it a little easier on my crotch. I think you may have done some damage down there."

Ginny smiled. "I'm sorry, Coley. I would **have** killed you if I could have figured out a way."

They had reached the Sheraton. Ginny **quickly** got out of the car to enter the hotel. **Realizing** that she too must look a horrible mess, **she** quickly ducked into an elevator.

She walked down the long hall while **she** fished the room key out of the depths of **her** purse. She turned the key slowly in the lock and opened the door, flipping on the light switch as she did.

There in the corner of the room sat Willy Hanson pointing the .38 straight at her head. She flipped off the light, walked across the room and fell sobbing into his arms. They sat clutching each other in the darkness. Neither of them could find words for a long time.

50

Downtown Seattle can be a maze of one-way streets. Sometimes, especially when you're pressed for time, it seems as if you just can't get anyplace from where you are. Coley maneuvered the big Lincoln, trying to find the exact location he had discovered earlier in the day.

Alaska Way was the broad street alongside the water, a very busy thoroughfare, alive with the business of the Port of Seattle. The trawler *New Territories* was pulled up by a dock adjacent to an old fish cannery. The bridge of the trawler pointed north. The Seattle Space Needle spired skyward in all its night-lit brilliance on a high hill just to the northeast.

Earlier in the day Coley had picked a spot where a city street came to a dead end at a bluff in full view of the *New Territories*. There was a flimsy guard rail at the dead end of the steep road and a small area where he had turned around. From there he had trained his binoculars on the *New Territories* earlier in the day.

Beyond the guard rail was a sheer incline of perhaps a hundred feet that ended in a parking area adjacent to Alaska Way.

There it was! He looked down the steep incline and saw the *New Territories* just ahead, probably less than two hundred yards from the guard rail.

He parked the Lincoln, got out and trained his binoculars on the gangway of the *New Territories*, where there seemed to be some activity. Beryl, KoKo and Leyte were standing at the top of the gangway. Evidently they had given up their search for him.

Coley studied the group on the bow, all but their heads now hidden by the high structure of the solid bow rail that surrounded the foredeck of the *New Territories*. The bearded Captain Alexandros joined them. They were all in Coley's full view, while the darkness of the night and the two-hundred-yard distance hid him.

Right now was the time! There would never be a better moment for carrying out his plan. Coley walked slowly up Battery Street about a hundred feet to where he had parked the Lincoln just around the corner. Fortunately at this late hour there wasn't another soul stirring on the dead-end street.

He splashed a full gallon of gasoline all over the back seat. Then, sitting on the passenger side with the door ajar, he turned the ignition key on, and then the lights. He steered around the corner and pointed the Lincoln down the steep incline toward the flimsy guard rail. He jammed his left foot down on the accelerator for a split second and managed to fling himself out the door an instant before the car hit the rail.

All eyes on the bridge of the *New Territories* were riveted to the crash on the cliff above them. The careening Lincoln burst through the rail and became airborne for a second before plunging down the cliff end over end. It smashed into the parking lot below with a loud roar and was engulfed by flames almost at once. Moments later, the full gasoline tank exploded in a boiling fiery column.

Coley hd been terrified as he rolled along the ground. He had not realized that getting out of the moving car would be such a struggle. His momentum had been stopped by what remained of the guard rail.

He began to move his limbs one by one, and decided nothing was broken. He slowly got to his knees and crouched back from the rim of the cliff, afraid he would be made visible by the brilliant light of the fire below.

At the cross street above him, he could see half a dozen spectators. Still bending his tall frame into a crouch, he walked a short distance up the incline and then plunged into an alleyway that led to his left.

"What a hell of a show," he murmured. "What a hell of a show."

A full block from the scene he came to another street and turned to work his way down toward Alaska Way and the *New Territories*. He caught a view of himself in the window of a store front. He hadn't noticed that the shoulder and sleeve of his jacket had been ripped off by his tumbling fall. He lifted a trouser leg and found an ugly gash on his calf that would probably need stitches. He wouldn't need to fake looking as if he had been in an accident.

The noise of fire trucks and other emergency vehicles filled the night air. By the time he got to Alaska Way on the waterfront, several police cars and ambulances were assembled in the parking lot. The flames were still boiling skyward.

He crossed Alaska Way and stood for a few moments in the midst of a small crowd that had gathered to watch the excitement. Emergency medical personnel were standing by with stretchers and radio scanners awaiting the call from firefighters should they locate survivors.

Coley began to walk down the now crowded sidewalk toward the pier where the *New Territories* was docked. It was now time to face the music.

He stopped for a moment to examine the throbbing injury to his calf. He ripped a piece from his shirt and wrapped it over the area as tightly as he could. The blood seemed to have stopped flowing, but the wound needed attention soon. He limped quickly on toward the *New Territories.*

"Coley!"

A gruff voice came to him from somewhere out of the crowd. Coley turned around to see a husky man in a dark sweater and watch cap striding rapidly toward him.

"Coley!" The man's pronunciation was peculiar. He said his name as if it were Coleeee.

As the man emerged from the crowd and approached Coley in the darkness, Coley realized it was KoKo. The man looked back over his shoulder to make sure they were alone.

"Coley, girl burn up in that car?"

"I am afraid so, KoKo. I've looked all around the place for her. I'm sure she is dead."

"Too bad. We see her at restaurant. She beautiful woman. Leyte and I wanted to fuck her before we kill her. Maybe captain would let us keep her around for a few days. But now she dead."

"Yes, KoKo, I'm sorry." Coley shuddered thinking about the risk he had taken in the kidnapping. If he had screwed up, Ginny would now be in the hands of these animals.

"Oh well, that okay. We were going to kill her anyway. Captain will be happy. He no like women aboard *New Territories.* Captain be very happy."

The two of them started walking toward the *New Territories.* KoKo was eyeing him carefully as they walked. Coley was exaggerating his limp.

"How you get out of car?"

Coley had expected the question and knew he had to be careful about how he answered it. He would have to tell the same story to all the others.

"At the top of the cliff, there was this barricade right across the road. The woman was clawing at me before I noticed it. I thought the street went on down to Alaska Way. When we hit the barricade, my door flew open and I got thrown out. She went on over the cliff with the car."

"You are lucky man. Nothing left of Town Car."

"KoKo, do you know that baby had only a hundred and twelve miles on it?"

KoKo grinned. "Car died fast. Just like woman die. Oh well. It don't matter. She probably lousy fuck anyway."

The two of them walked toward the pier, Coley lagging slightly behind the compactly built KoKo. He estimated that KoKo was only about five feet eight, but he had massive shoulders and arms. The man was probably two hundred pounds of raw muscle. Coley doubted he would be able to handle him in a fight, considering the condition he was in right now.

"You drive awful fast," KoKo said after standing still for a moment to let him catch up.

"What's that, KoKo?"

"You drive awful fast from Schooners Notch with woman. By the time we get on road you are far away. Why did you do that?"

"The woman started to go nuts when she realized I was making her go with me. She fought like a wild cat before I slugged her. I just wanted to get out of there as quick as I could."

"We were going eighty. You must have been going a hundred. That stupid. It lucky you didn't attract police. How come you take so long to get back to boat? We were there for long time."

"I just plain got lost. All those one-way streets downtown are a bitch to get used to."

"You right, I get lost too. I get lost too if I with sexy woman with ass like that. I bet you have nice fuck before she die."

KoKo looked him right in the eye and smiled broadly. Coley decided right there that the lewdly grinning KoKo was a species all alone, somewhere beneath the scum of the earth.

Coley returned a grin of his own. He just didn't have it in him to put any response into words.

By the time they had reached the gangway of the *New Territories*, he was really hurting. He no longer had to feign a gimpy leg.

Beryl stood at the top of the gangway eyeing Coley as he laboriously climbed aboard. Her face was as inscrutable as always. It was as if she were watching a total stranger board the trawler. Captain Alexandros stood nearby with Leyte.

Alexandros extended a hand to KoKo without saying a word and they walked together to a point near the bow pulpit where they were beyond the hearing of all the others. Coley knew everything he had told KoKo was probably being repeated to Alexandros.

Beryl walked up to him and brushed her hand across his bloody brow. The hint of a smile crossed her face.

"Coley, you are a mess. I take it that Ginny Du Bois is dead."

"You got that right." Coley nodded toward the dwindling column of smoke in the distance. Now it was mostly whitish steam that rose from the wreck as the firefighters continued to pour on water. For the first time he could see that several other vehicles were involved. Evidently the Lincoln had fallen on at least two other cars in the parking lot. They likewise had been gutted with fire and lay shriveled and twisted from the intense heat. No doubt their exploding gas tanks accounted for the extra flareups that had puzzled him as he had watched the spectacle.

Coley watched the waning blaze and prayed that there had been no people in the other vehicles.

Captain Alexandros abandoned his conversation with KoKo in the bow and strode toward them.

"KoKo says that the woman you took from Schooners Notch is dead. This will no doubt please Phipps. Please come to my quarters and we will call him from there. He may have some questions for us."

"Sure, why not?" replied Coley. "I would like to get that over with and then clean myself up."

"Do you need a doctor?" Alexandros ran his eyes up and down Coley's tall frame and shook his head in seeming concern.

"I don't really think so," Coley answered. "I think I can take care of it myself. You must have a first-aid kit aboard."

"We can do better than that," replied Alexandros. We have an ex-Navy corpsman aboard who can give you proper attention. At sea he has even set bones for us."

Captain Alexandros turned toward Leyte, who had observed everything that had happened so far. "Leyte, go below and fetch Fallon. Tell him to take his antiseptic kit and report to Mr. Doctor's cabin right away."

Alexandros then turned toward Coley. "As soon as Fallon has finished, you come on up to the bridge and we'll call Phipps."

Beryl walked toward the aft cabins with Coley.

"Tell me about it, Coley. You look a mess, but it must have been exciting. I'll bet it was a lot more fun than shooting buckets in the gym." She looked up at him with a dazzling smile.

Coley felt proud of himself thus far. Everyone seemed to believe him.

Fallon, the ex-corpsman, was waiting at the door of Coley's cabin by the time they arrived. Beryl stayed while Coley stripped down to his shorts. Fallon bathed the ugly wounds and within minutes had packed up his kit and left.

Beryl called Alexandros on the intercom and advised him that it was too late to bother Logan Phipps. It was approaching 3 A.M.

"Now, Coley, I want you to tell me everything that happened since we saw you leave Schooners Notch. Oh, Coley, it is so exciting. From now on, you are going to lay back on the bunk and relax. You will talk and tell me the whole story while I make your aching body feel good." With that Beryl lowered her shoulder strap and let the only clothing she wore drop to the floor.

She crouched on the bunk and began to massage the unwounded calf of Coley's right leg.

"Coley, you are not talking." She looked up at him with a provocative smile much in tune with her massaging fingers.

"Coley, you are not keeping your part of our bargain. Start talking, Coley. Tell me all about it."

51

Lolly Penrose kept having this dream. It was really more like a nightmare because of the way it always ended. She was in a small flaming-red sportscar. There were only two seats. She was sitting on Evan Hatcher's lap as they drove recklessly up and down some of the coastal canyons near Malibu. Hatcher persisted in a sexual onslaught as they raced along the canyon road.

"Sittin' on the old peg is better than a seat belt, baby!" In each dream she could hear him saying that over and over again in his Aussie twang.

The dream always ended with a burst of pain

deep in her groin, followed by her waking up alone in the garden near the pool of the condo. After each dream, she could not rid herself of the desire to get out of bed and take a shower that sometimes would last for an hour.

The dream this morning had been more intense than usual. For the first time, she had glimpsed the driver of the sportscar, though not clearly enough to identify him.

She wondered why in previous dreams she had never thought about who might have been driving the car. She supposed it had something to do with her wanting to block the whole evening out of her mind.

Now she was trying desperately to remember the details of her fiasco at La Sex Ménagerie and patch in some of the blanks. Though all of the newspapers had carried the original story, only a couple of the raunchiest tabloids had referred to hers and Hatcher's performance as a "live sex act." Even they had toned down their follow-up coverage quite a bit since her attorney had threatened trouble.

Today was the day she would meet with her business manager and Onyx at the Black Lamp for lunch. If all went well, the sign proclaiming the restaurant as Lolly Penrose's Black Lamp would go up in just a day or two. Onyx had already shown the sketches to Lolly, and they were tasteful and subdued, much in tune with the classy decor of the ground-level restaurant.

The only reference in the contracts to La Sex Ménagerie was an agreement that the Black

Lamp would do charge account billing for the upstairs facility for a small fee.

The lunch took place as planned, and the contract was signed without change. Lynn Southerland, Lolly's business manager, felt so comfortable about the arrangements, in fact, that she left the lunch as soon as the deal was closed.

"We are partners, darling!" Onyx was all smiles and extended her hand across the table to squeeze Lolly's tightly.

"Onyx, the Black Lamp is a lovely place. The menu is so incredible that I see it written about in the press every day. I feel very good about being part of it. I can certainly stand some good publicity, you know."

"See, love, I told you the bad publicity would blow over quickly. Nobody really cares to think of their Lolly Penrose as anything but wonderful and beautiful."

"Onyx, I have a question I must ask you, because you are probably the one who knows the answer. Who drove me back to my condo the night of the opening?"

Onyx hesitated for several seconds. Her face sobered as she looked directly into Lolly's eyes. Onyx recalled the night clearly. Lolly had been out like a light. Evan Hatcher had held her on his lap in the open sportscar as Carlos drove the short distance to Lolly's condo.

"Lolly, Evan Hatcher drove you home before he went to San Diego. He take you home. Why do you ask?"

"The whole night is a blank. I guess I'm ashamed of myself for getting into such a state. I keep having these nightmares about Evan attacking me in the car."

"That bastard! You mean he rape you while you were on the way home? That bastard! I glad that son-a-bitch is dead. Do you remember anything else?"

Onyx reached across the table to clasp both of Lolly's hands in her own.

"No, I don't. It's all a blank. Maybe my dreams will go away now that I've talked to you."

"Hey, guess what? I have the negative. It is yours to tear up and throw away. Maybe that will put an end to Evan Hatcher forever. I sorry I brought him over from Australia. Now he go home in coffin, and we can be very happy."

Onyx reached into her purse and produced an envelope, which she handed to Lolly. Lolly stuffed it into her purse without looking at it.

"I want you to come to Palos Verdes. We have a party, just you and me. You can relax there a few days around the pool. You forget all unpleasantness and let Onyx make you feel like new woman."

Lolly stared at Onyx, marveling at the feeling this exotic woman had for her.

"Really, Onyx, I couldn't do that. I have a script I must read. It's a good part and I have to get down to business and take it seriously."

"Bring it with you! I will personally see to it that you are not disturbed."

"Onyx, maybe. But I am getting hungry. Let's

see what our fabulous chef has on our menu to-day."

The chef outdid himself in preparing the entrees for Lolly and Onyx, personally delivering and describing each of the delicacies he had prepared.

Lolly was enjoying an exquisite chocolate mousse when Onyx noticed Carlos moving through the restaurant. He disappeared behind a paneled door at the rear of the restaurant, then emerged a few minutes later and walked directly to their table. He delivered an envelope to Onyx and started to walk away.

Onyx read the message and then stuffed it into her purse.

"Thank, Carlos." She paused for a moment and then called him back to the table.

"Carlos, I want you to meet Lolly Penrose. She is our new partner here in the Black Lamp. I want you to make sure that there is always a table reserved in her honor, and for her use." Then, turning to Lolly, she said, "Carlos oversees the management of this restaurant and also is in charge of all security. If you ever need help, you call Carlos."

Carlos looked steadily at Lolly with deep-set, steely eyes. If the man had any cordiality or humor in his soul, it was certainly invisible to Lolly Penrose.

"It is a pleasure meeting you," he said without animation. Then he touched his hand to his forehead and gave Lolly a quick, almost imperceptible nod before turning on his heels and walking again to the back of the restaurant.

"Carlos, as they say, is not a people person," Onyx said with a smile. "But he is very good at other things. He stays in the guest house in Palos Verdes and his presence there gives me a great feeling of security."

Lolly felt a queasiness coming over her, but was determined to keep her discomfort a secret. She stared out across the crowded restaurant without seeing it. What she saw instead was a red Corvette racing down the canyon road near Malibu. She was sitting on Evan Hatcher's lap. He was holding her viselike around her waist and forcing foul-smelling kisses into the hollow of her neck. All the while he kept trying to move her into position to penetrate her as they roared down the canyon road.

The driver of the red Corvette was no longer a mystery. From out of the depths of her semiconsciousness came a sudden vivid clarity.

The driver of the speeding Corvette paid no attention to the rape going on next to him. He kept his steely eyes ahead of him on the canyon road. Lolly could see it now clearly as if it were just happening. It was Carlos, the man who was now her own employee at the Black Lamp.

"Pennyrose, why you look so sad? Can I get you something?"

Lolly shook her head, afraid to reveal what was racing through her mind. That was Carlos in the Corvette, and it had probably been Carlos with Evan Hatcher just before he died.

Now they were all sharing this secret. Carlos must have been instructed to do away with Hatcher.

Lolly stood up from the table. "Onyx, I'm afraid I am not feeling well. Perhaps the meal was too rich. At any rate, I need to leave now."

"Pennyrose, you go home. Rest up and then bring that script to Palos Verdes. You won't be sorry.

Onyx watched Lolly walk out of the Black Lamp and then turned back to her cordial. Some day, she thought, she would get Lolly to Palos Verdes alone and she'd get her really oiled up on scotch, and turn some fantasies into long-awaited reality.

52

Luisa Maria Rodriguez was a name that commanded the attention of scores of young men all over Guadalajara. There were some who would spend hours standing around on the Avenida de las Pulgas, hoping for just a glimpse of her. The general's daughter was considered the prize catch in all of Jalisco.

When Carlos Alonzo Lopez came to Guadalajara he and Luisa Maria were inseparable. Luisa's mother approved. Once at El Bandilero he had drawn a pistol on a young man and told him, "If you think one more unpure thought about Luisa

Maria, I will put one of God's bullets through your head."

Carlos had frequent business in Los Angeles, and then the other admirers tried to win her for themselves. But try as they might, they were unable to get her to respond to their advances.

The letter for Luisa Maria that arrived from Los Angeles caused quite a stir. It said that Carlos had become general manager of a very unique and soon-to-be-famous restaurant in Redondo Beach. His success was so stunning, in fact, that his grateful employers were honoring him with a special event likely to be attended by many famous people. This included Lolly Penrose, the legendary actress who was a favorite among the film fans of Guadalajara.

In the letter, the owners of this fine establishment invited Luisa Maria to join them for the celebratory evening at the Black Lamp. The occasion was to be a surprise to Carlos. Airline tickets were enclosed and luxurious hotel accommodations described. The letter was signed by a Miss Onyx Lu, operator and owner of a place called Lolly Penrose's Black Lamp.

Luisa Maria of course wanted to go, but knew that her protective parents would probably not permit the visit. It was a great surprise, then, when the general insisted that she go.

The general knew little about this Carlos fellow, who was not from Guadalajara. He had always seemed aloof and secretive and seemed to intimidate the other young men. Luisa Maria was completely distracted by him and was refusing to see all other potential suitors. Now was the time. The general would see and learn much more about this Carlos through the eyes of her mother, who would accompany Luisa Maria to Los Angeles. They would be gone only one night, and he would send along his trusted lieutenant, Paco, to keep a watchful eye on both women. What could go wrong?

The woman extending the invitation, Onyx Lu, had offered to meet their plane, and none other than Lolly Penrose would accompany them to their hotel.

53

It was a crisp, dazzling clear day along the coast that shelters the sprawling marina on Shilshole Bay. The *Tashtego* was still tucked away snugly in a cradle near the south end of the marina. All work had been completed several days before, and the sleek ketch was awaiting only the order from its owner to put it back into the waters of the sound.

After some discussion it was decided that Willy would make the trip alone to the marina. It would be Ginny's job to play dead. They had agreed that the battered old Chevrolet Malibu held a solution to one of their problems. Coley had left no new messages for them in his voice mailbox since Ginny had last seen him. At worst, Coley might truly be dead.

The clincher had been the story carried on the television news early that morning. The photography had been spectacular. The parking lot at the base of the cliff at the end of Battery Street was a roaring inferno by the time the TV mobile unit had arrived. According to the story, a car had plunged off the cliff in a fiery crash that had set several other cars afire in the parking lot below. The newscast reported that the number of casualties resulting from the fire would be unknown until the wreckage cooled and investigators could search the area carefully.

Ginny had said immediately, "Coley told me there would be a big fire. My God! I hope he got out of that thing."

They had decided to proceed on the assumption that Coley was alive. The problem then would be later news reports that would reveal that Ginny had not died in the crash. How would Coley explain that fact to those scoundrels aboard the *New Territories*? The least they could do would be to give him some insurance if they could.

Now Willy exited the taxicab near a boat ramp at the north end of the marina and began to wend his way south through the busy parking lot. He found himself patting the handle of the .38 frequently. He spotted the dented old blue Malibu a full hundred yards from where the *Tashtego* sat in its cradle. He and Ginny had long ago concluded that the guy inside must be FBI looking for bigger fish than the two of them.

The tenacious occupant was now slumped behind the steering wheel, a newspaper propped in front of him.

Willy patted the .38 nervously to make sure it was snug and secure in his belt. He was seized by a spasm of fear as he approached the Malibu.

"Beautiful, isn't she. The *Tashtego* is a hell of a sailboat." Willy's voice sounded calm and collected, but he was about ready to jump out of his skin.

The man looked up. If he was surprised, he didn't show it. A hand holding a pencil was pressed against a *Seattle Times* crossword puzzle pinned against the steering wheel.

"A very nice boat. I envy you being able to sail her so often." The man's eyes dropped to the bulge at Willy's waistband. "Look, I don't mind continuing this conversation." His eyes moved swiftly to meet Willy's. "The first thing you have got to do is to keep both hands in full view. Then we can talk. I believe in a level playing field."

Willy relaxed his grip on the revolver and brought his hands into the open, shrugging slightly.

"When are you going to put her back in the water?" the man asked.

Willy shrugged again. "Are you FBI?"

The hint of a smile played around the man's face. "As a matter of fact, I am." The man reached into his jacket pocket and produced a folder carrying identification. He put it away without giving Willy more than a quick glance. "I guess Coley Doctor must have told you about me. I've run across him off and on ever since San Francisco."

"You know Coley!"

"Hell, everybody in my racket from here to Miami knows Coley Doctor."

Willy feared that might be bad news.

The man turned in his seat, slowly scanning the parking lot around them. Then he extended his hand out the window.

"I'm Mark Whitcomb, FBI. I wish you would keep your hands off that piece. It makes me nervous. You touch it again and I'll have to take it away from you." Whitcomb paused and broke into a faint smile. "You're in enough trouble already, you know. I could start by hauling you in for obstruction of justice at Onyx Lu's trial in San Francisco."

Willy was buoyed by the fact that Whitcomb didn't demand that he turn over the revolver. Obviously Whitcomb had an agenda that did not include nailing Willy Hanson right at the moment.

"Whitcomb, I need your help. I promise you all the help I can give you when this thing is over."

"So what can I do for you?"

"Did you hear about the big fire down on Alaska Way this morning?"

Whitcomb didn't expect this question at all. "Heard something about it on the radio. Car ran off an embankment at the end of Battery Street. Set fire to a lot of other cars in the parking lot below. Now how would that possibly concern you?"

"My lady friend was supposed to have been killed in that car. She wasn't. It would take the heat off her if Onyx Lu's bunch of thugs thought she was. It might also save Coley Doctor if he's still alive."

"Look, Hanson, you've been driving us crazy for a long time. Frankly, I don't think your life is worth two cents. When Logan Phipps wants to step on someone, he does just that. Squish! Like a cockroach on a pantry floor. That's what we're waiting for, Mr. Hanson. You are the roach on Phipps's pantry floor." Whitcomb slowly drew a nine-millimeter from his shoulder holster and laid it on the seat beside him.

Willy felt himself tense up. Directly behind Whitcomb's car about two rows back in the parking lot, a van had moved into an open space. Whitcomb had spotted it in his rearview mirror even before Willy had seen it, and had drawn the nine-millimeter just in case. Three people climbed out of the van and walked toward a row of slips in the marina.

"Mr. Hanson, you are asking me to manipulate the press, or the even the local police department. That is breaking the law, Mr. Hanson. I work for the FBI. Now what do you think I'll do? Put yourself in my shoes."

"I think you're going to do everything you can to protect a couple of innocent people."

"Coley Doctor? An innocent person? Please, Mr. Hanson." Whitcomb put the revolver back in its holster, then reached down to turn the key in the ignition. He leaned his head toward the window to speak.

"Mr. Hanson, let's just play like we never met."

With that, Agent Whitcomb backed the scarred old Malibu out of the parking spot. Willy watched him all the way to the street, where the car turned south toward downtown Seattle.

Glancing at the *Tashtego* in the distance, Willy decided to return to the hotel without going aboard. He was worried about leaving Ginny alone and anxious to know whether Coley had made contact yet. They had no way of knowing whether Coley had survived the car crash until they established phone contact.

Willy stopped in a large restaurant next to the marina parking lot. He told the hostess he was having car trouble and asked if she would call him a cab. That done, he proceeded to a telephone and called Coley's voice mailbox. Nothing new. He then called Ginny at the Sheraton. She sounded nervous as hell. She hadn't heard from Coley either.

The taxicab seemed to take forever getting back to the hotel. He thought about their predicament. He would give Coley only one more day to make contact. If they didn't hear from him, he might well be dead. He thought about the confrontation with Whitcomb. At least it was confirmed that he was FBI. Sadly for Whitcomb, Willy and Ginny would soon leave Seattle, and the FBI whiz would sit and stare at the *Tashtego* indefinitely.

Ginny and Willy spent a restless night. When morning finally arrived, Willy slipped out of bed, trying his best not to awaken her. He picked up the morning paper that had been shoved under his door, took it into the bathroom, shut the door quietly and turned on the light.

TWO KILLED IN FIERY PLUNGE OFF BATTERY STREET

The headline jolted him fully awake. Two killed? Willy hadn't expected to read that anyone was killed.

The article stated that the charred remains of two people were found inside an incinerated late-model Lincoln Town Car that had plunged through a barricade at the end of Battery Street into the parking lot below.

One body, a short heavyset male bound with chains, had been found inside the trunk of the vehicle. The other remains, found in the passenger area, were those of a woman, judging from charred jewelry and shoes.

Willy couldn't help smiling. Whitcomb had done the plant job he had requested on the woman.

But the guy chained in the trunk was a mystery. Willy didn't believe Coley could be labeled a "short heavy-set male."

"Ginny!" Willy said, sitting down next to her on the bed. "Whitcomb planted the story about a woman being in the car. This should buy time for Coley and take the heat off of us for a while." He stroked her hair.

Ginny rubbed her eyes and smiled as she read the newspaper carefully. "But Willy, who is the short fat guy in the trunk?"

"I don't know, but it can't be Coley. Maybe Whitcomb planted that information, too."

"Maybe. Or maybe the body was already in the trunk when I was in the car with Coley. He was headed straight for Battery Street. He wasn't wasting any time. I could tell that."

"Let's hang around here one more day and see if he calls. He might be stuck on the *New Territories* or, hell, he might be in the sack with Beryl."

"If that's the case we may not hear from him for a week."

54

It was eight o'clock sharp when Captain Alexandros summoned Coley Doctor to the bridge of the *New Territories*. Just for appearances, Coley left the quarters adjoining Beryl's through his own door. As he did it he realized that he hadn't fooled anyone.

"Mr. Doctor, did you sleep well?" If the captain suspected anything, he certainly didn't show it.

"As a matter of fact, I didn't, sir. I am afraid this gash on my leg is becoming infected. I would like to find a doctor ashore to check it out . . . or perhaps have one brought on board."

"No problem, Coley. We will not be leaving for

Los Angeles until morning. I'll have KoKo take you ashore this morning. Meanwhile I called you to the bridge to show you the morning paper." Alexandros had spread the newspaper out across the chart table.

"Thank you, Captain." Coley wondered why KoKo was to accompany him ashore. He would have to find a way to get to a telephone without KoKo's finding out. He turned to study the newspaper spread out before him.

The headline screamed TWO KILLED IN FIERY PLUNGE OFF BATTERY STREET. Coley's stomach gave a little bounce.

"Two? Captain, I don't understand. Was someone in one of the cars parked below the cliff?"

Alexandros smiled and waved his hand. "I suggest you read the whole article and then we will discuss it. First I want to congratulate you on a job well done, Coley. I had some mild doubts, I admit, about your story. I'm glad to learn that I was wrong."

Coley read the story with utter fascination. He had expected that the newspaper coverage would undermine his story, but this account actually verified it.

"But who in the hell was the guy chained in the trunk?"

The captain turned the pages of the *Seattle Times* until he got to page seven. His finger pointed to a small article headlined SUSPECT RELEASED IN HOTEL SHOOTING. The article went on in some detail to report that a Wong Lee had been released from custody because of lack of evidence of his alleged participation in a shooting incident at the Water's Edge Hotel. Wong Lee had been able to produce a witness who testified that the rifle found in his car and used at the shooting was found behind a warehouse at the end of Galer Street, where they had driven to watch the sunset. Coley turned to face Alexandros. "So how did he get in the trunk of the Lincoln?"

"I am afraid KoKo is responsible for that. You see, Wong refused to return to the *New Territories* after he was released. KoKo didn't mean to kill him when he hit him with the hammer. He gets a little overenthusiastic now and then."

Coley felt increasingly ill. These people were maniacs and he was tightly tied in with them.

"Captain, do you mind if I ask you one question? Frankly, it has been bugging me ever since I drove the Lincoln."

"Certainly, Coley. Any question you want. We will be working together and I want you to understand our end of this organization." The captain tapped his fingers lightly on the chart table.

"That car was a brand-new Lincoln rented from Avis. The Avis people have a hell of a computer. Aren't you afraid that you've left a paper trail?"

"I can see that you think things through, Mr. Doctor. Well, somewhere in our unofficial book of rules, there is one that says, 'Always let the dead man rent the car.' "

"You mean Wong rented the car."

"That would be following our rule, wouldn't it, Mr. Doctor?"

"That is brilliant, Captain. I'll tuck that away for future use."

Alexandros folded the newspaper and lifted it off·the chart table just as KoKo came to the bridge.

"KoKo, it won't be necessary for you to accompany Coley. I've made an appointment with a doctor I know up on Virginia Street." He handed Coley a piece of paper with the address on it. "If you just walk down the street to the Water's Edge Inn, there will be a bunch of cabs waiting outside."

Coley left the bridge immediately. Both Alexandros and KoKo watched him turn left on Alaska Way and walk toward the Water's Edge.

"Okay, KoKo. Keep your eye on him. Don't lay a hand on him. Just follow him everywhere he goes. Phipps wants him back in L.A. He killed the girl, so he must be okay. But there is something about him I don't like. You would think he would have more sense than to fuck around with the boss's private stock. Tell me, KoKo. Is that loyalty?"

KoKo grinned. "I think Phipps probably want him in L.A. so he can personally take care of him. Nobody like to have their sweetie fucked by somebody else. Coley do that all the time. I think Phipps find a way to kill him very slowly." KoKo grinned, left the bridge, hustled down the gangplank and climbed into an old, dirty pickup truck loaded with gardening tools. The driver of the pickup pulled away from the curb and let the approaching taxicab pass. Leyte, in a big, floppy straw hat, then pulled out behind the cab and kept several car lengths behind it.

Coley gave the driver the slip of paper with the address on Virginia Street. He knew he would have to be very careful. The captain knew the doctor, and he knew exactly how long it would take to get there. Alexandros might even have the doctor phone him when he left. He turned to look out the rear window of the cab as inconspicuously as possible. A couple of cars and an old pickup truck laden with gardening tools were behind him.

When they made the left turn, the vehicles behind him followed. Coley eyed the cabdriver closely. He had been first in line at the hotel. It seemed unreasonable that he could be a plant. He breathed a sigh of relief. Evidently Alexandros believed he had killed Ginny. After seeing the doctor, he would certainly have time to make the phone call. Coley asked himself the same question over and over again. Who in hell was the woman who had burned up in the accident? It had to be a pedestrian down in the parking lot. My God! Had he actually killed somebody?

Coley got out of the cab at the address on Virginia Street, paid the driver and walked into the building. It was an old building with no telephone booth anywhere. He found the number of the doctor's office and opened the door.

There was a small anteroom with a bench. The door to the office was slightly ajar.

"Hey, out there. I'll be right with you," came a voice from the other room.

Coley looked longingly at the telephone sitting on the small desk, but didn't have time to be tempted.

The doctor came out, leading a man with a heavily bandaged arm toward the door. "Come in and see me in about three days. I want to dress that wound again." Then he looked at Coley.

"Mr. Doctor, looking for a doctor. That has never happened to me before, Mr. Doctor." The man grinned at his little joke and led Coley into his office.

The doctor removed Coley's bandages and bathed the ugly wound.

"Whoever dressed this wound did a good job. I would probably have taken a couple of stitches, but it is starting to heal nicely, so we won't bother with that now. You will probably have quite a scar. Were you a beautiful young lady, I would suggest some cosmetic work later on."

Coley winced slightly as the doctor finished bathing the wound with some kind of antiseptic.

"Well, I sure ain't no kind of a beautiful young lady, so I'll just forget about that. Besides, women like scars on men."

"What?"

"I say women like scars. They like to think their man is a rough son of a bitch. See this scar right here?" Coley pointed to an old healed wound on his chest. "Knife wound. Got it in a fight in Watts when I was a kid. Do you know that lots of women like to kiss that ugly old scar?"

"Really. I can't imagine that. All the books you read seem to imply that women like gentler men."

"Only in bed, man. Only in bed."

"Well, I don't have any scars. Maybe that's why I have such bad luck with the ladies. It really doesn't matter much to me anymore."

"Then you must be dyin' or something."

The doctor smiled and then looked directly at Coley. "I guess you will be returning directly to the *New Territories.*"

"Yes, but I may walk a bit. I haven't been getting much exercise lately. I feel better just knowing my leg is going to be okay."

As Coley left the building, he took a quick glance down the street and saw the battered old pickup truck filled with rakes, hoes, hoses and wheelbarrows. His pulse quickened as the recognition came to him. He had seen the same vehicle behind him when he left the *New Territories.*

It was one of those old pickups with a small rear window, so he couldn't really see the occupants of the cab. He walked in the opposite direction and turned the corner. He paused just around the corner for a full thirty seconds and then carefully glanced back. The pickup was gone. He was being followed after all.

A pickup truck versus a man on foot was certainly no match, especially in Seattle with all the one-way streets. Coley smiled. He would shake them in no time and make that telephone call.

He had already ducked into a doorway when the pickup truck passed the intersection a block away. He retraced his steps up the hill and went into a luncheonette that had a row of telephone booths in the rear. He paused to purchase a package of the stinking cigars that so annoyed Ginny Du Bois. Then he went into one of the booths and dialed the number of the Washington Sheraton.

"Caleb Jones's room, please."

"Jones here." Willy answered on the second ring.

"Hey, did you see the big bonfire?"

"Coley, we had about given up on you. Are you here in Seattle?"

"Yep, just a few blocks away. But I can't risk seeing you. I have a couple of Phippsites on my tail. I gotta talk fast and get back to the *New Territories*. We're going to L.A. tomorrow, riding the trawler."

"Coley, who in the hell was in the trunk of the car? We thought it was you."

"Shame on you, I told you not to worry. Are you sitting down?"

"Yes."

"It was Wong. Phipps's fancy lawyer sprung him; then KoKo nailed him with a hammer. My buddies down on the boat are nasty, nasty, nasty. I didn't know he was in the trunk when I kidnapped Ginny. That was just one of their little surprises. Hey, I'm real sorry about the woman.

In fact I am all sick inside. She must have been walking down below the cliff."

"You know, Coley, we ought to let you sweat for a while. You could have got Ginny killed."

"Look, man, they were going to pull a snatch. If I hadn't volunteered, it would have been KoKo and Leyte. I stuck my neck out too, you know."

"Coley, there was no woman killed in the car wreck."

"But it's all over the papers."

"You can thank your friend Mark Whitcomb. He planted the article to save your ass."

"He ain't my friend. He's the FBI that nailed me in Miami."

"But you were exonerated."

"Yeah, but Whitcomb don't believe it. It was his conviction. That's like the Celts blowing it all in double overtime. I guess he was the blue Malibu."

"Yep, staking out the *Tashtego*."

"Well, he'll sit there and rot in that dumpy Malibu, because you guys got to fly back to L.A. and stay there till the *New Territories* comes steamin' up to your door. We're leaving in the A.M. I don't know whether I'll ever get ashore to use my voice mail, but keep trying it. Why don't you stay at the Porto Sol there in Redondo. It's a nice little spot for you and Ginny to cozy up in until I get there for the party next Friday night."

"What party?"

"There's a big party at La Sex Ménagerie, Onyx's new joint. One of your old girlfriends is a big star there. In fact they named the restaurant downstairs after her. Would you believe Lolly Penrose's Black Lamp?"

"Are you smoking something, Coley?"

"Yep, one of Ginny's favorite cigars. It's all coming together man, with 131 kilos of cocaine as evidence. There is just one problem."

"What's that?"

"Staying alive, pal, staying alive. Hey, by the way, you been doing any thinking about my raise?"

"Good-bye, Coley."

"Ta-ta, boss. And you too, Ginny. I know you're listening in. I can hear the heavy breathing."

"Be careful, Coley."

55

Lolly Penrose looked at the six bottles of scotch lined up on her bar. Not one seal was broken. Her liquor dealer had delivered them last Wednesday. Today was Wednesday again. Behind the bar was a plastic tote bag containing six more bottles of the famed single-malt. This was the standing order that was delivered every Wednesday, and it was miraculous that this week's order had come in before the last had run out.

Her reluctance to saturate herself with scotch had begun the afternoon she had lunched with Onyx Lu at the Black Lamp. It had something to do with her recognition of Carlos as the driver who had watched Evan Hatcher rape her. It had even more to do with the same Carlos apparently killing Hatcher in San Diego the next evening.

It had a lot to do with Onyx Lu too. Carlos was a hired killer, after all, who acted according to instructions.

Lolly Penrose looked at her nude form in the large mirror.

"I spend a lot of time looking after you, babe," she said to herself. She cocked her famous derriere to one side and decided it was still good. In fact, her whole reflection was more pleasing to her than it had been in quite a while. Maybe it was just because she could see herself more clearly now that she wasn't drunk all the time.

"You've been bad!" she said to herself in the mirror. She thought about the list she had compiled the day before: forty-one names of bed partners over the past couple of years. That did not include four women.

She turned her back to the mirror and peeked over her shoulder.

"Not bad at all," she murmured.

And then there was the cocaine. Lots of cocaine. She was certainly lucky there. Her tolerance was much greater than average.

Lolly slipped on a robe and walked outside to sit on her deck. Yellow smog hung ugly in the air. Usually days like this disgusted her, but today it didn't bother her at all.

She had been bad. She said it aloud. "I've been

bad." But she consoled herself that at least she had never tried to hurt anyone else.

Lolly walked over to the bar and cracked the seal on a fresh bottle of scotch. She loosened the cork but then pushed it back in the bottle. Then another thought came to her: I wonder how many other people Onyx and Carlos have killed. My God, I've been bad, but I've never been a killer. She put the full bottle back on the bar.

Reinard Gossman would be landing at LAX in about an hour. She hadn't seen him in more than a year. Their affair had lasted more than six months and had been a wild one. Reinard was still Willy Hanson's agent. Her mind drifted back to the Onyx Lu trial in San Francisco. She had actually cheered the acquittal one night when out for dinner with Reinard. That was the night he had threatened to slap her if she didn't shut up. That was the last real date she had had with Reinard.

Reinard had always been a good listener. Tonight she was going to tell him all she knew about Carlos and Onyx. She would even talk to him about Evan Hatcher. She had to talk to someone. Reinard's trip to the Coast was a godsend. He would listen, and he would know what to do.

Friday night Reinard would accompany her to the gala they were putting together at the Black Lamp. Lolly had already decided that the occasion would be her last visit to the restaurant that now bore her name.

Lolly's thoughts were interrupted by the telephone. Usually she waited for the answering machine to screen the call, but she picked up the receiver, certain it would be Reinard.

"Pennyrose, you sexy bitch. I been thinking about you. Someday I will tell you what I think about when you are on my mind. It is crazy, crazy, Pennyrose."

"Onyx, you are crazy, crazy. Can I help you with something? I am expecting company, so I can't talk long."

"Oh, I so sorry to hear you have company. I guess I am selfish. I see the smog in the hills. This would be good day to bring your script to Palos Verdes. I could help you by the pool. Good idea, eh, Pennyrose?"

"Impossible, Onyx. Impossible! I have company."

"That is so so bad. We will do it other time. Can I ask a favor of you?"

"What is it, Onyx."

"I have a friend coming from Guadalajara. She is eighteen-year-old girl from convent school there. She is coming with mother. They are such good friend from long ago. Their family is practically royalty in Mexico. I do not feel adequate to take her to shops in Beverly Hills. Could you do this for only a couple of hours on Saturday? She idolizes you and would have big story to tell her friends back in Guadalajara."

"Really, Onyx, I would rather not."

"Pennyrose, that not nice at all. Her father is a generalissimo, much good friend to the president of Mexico. Consider it tip-top promotion for Black Lamp."

"Onyx, I must hang up. I will talk to you tomorrow. Perhaps, perhaps is all I can say right now."

"Thanks, sweet dolly, I knew you would. Her name is Luisa Maria Rodriguez and she will meet you at Polo Lounge."

"Onyx!" But Onyx had already hung up. Oh well, an hour or two. What difference would it make?

56

Captain Alexandros invited Coley Doctor to the bridge to watch the big trawler cast off all lines to make its way up the sound. Coley watched Alexandros give the succession of orders that would put the trawler under way. The man was obviously very much at home on the sea, and under different circumstances Coley might have looked on the voyage to Los Angeles as a grand adventure.

"And how did you like my friend Dr. Gabrielli? He graduated from the University of Milan, you know."

Coley could feel the third degree coming for

taking so long to get back to the *New Territories*. The fact was he had seen Whitcomb and then wandered around for a couple of hours debating whether or not to ditch the *New Territories* and head south with Willy and Ginny.

But he finally concluded that if they were to succeed, he needed to stay in the good graces of the Sino-Americo Trading Company for a few more days.

"Dr. Gabrielli was great. Actually, other than cleaning up the wound a little bit, he had nothing to do. He said Fallon did a great job."

"Fallon is a U.S. Navy corpsman with much battle experience. I'd trust Fallon with almost anything." Alexandros paused. "I'm afraid you alarmed Miss Beryl somewhat yesterday when you took so long to return from Virginia Street. She worries about you. Of course, I guess that is her job, to worry about things and make sure everything goes right. Talking to her is exactly like talking to Phipps. But I suppose you know that."

"Beryl is brilliant. If I were Phipps, I would certainly want her working for me." "But she had no cause for worry. I felt so reassured by the doctor that I decided to walk back to the *New Territories*. It was almost all downhill. I went to Pike Market and bought a half dozen cannolis. You know, I ate the whole box."

"That is hardly a warrior's diet, Mr. Doctor. You know that we are all warriors."

"I suppose we are, Captain, I suppose we are."

"KoKo and Leyte, along with some of the other boys, do some regular exercises every afternoon.

They like to wrestle. Perhaps you would like to join them in a match or two."

"Hey, that sounds like fun!" Coley lied. He wondered whether or not KoKo's wrestling gear included the hammer he had nailed Wong with.

Soon they were on their way out of Puget Sound, pointing west by northwest into the Juan de Fuca Strait, which led to the Pacific. The captain called each marker off, identifying each on the chart as they made their way up the channel.

Alexandros insisted that Coley stay on the bridge with him during the morning hours, and Coley's stomach soon felt the effect of the experience. His discomfort became apparent to Alexandros.

"I'll tell Fallon to bring you some seasick pills to the bridge. Meanwhile, pick out a landmark far out on land. Keep your eyes on it and try not to look at anything else. I didn't have any idea you were such a landlubber, Coley. Maybe it's just all those cannolis you ate down on Pike Street."

Alexandros scowled when Coley turned to glance at him, and at first Coley thought the scowl was meant for him. But he was looking at Beryl, who had emerged from her cabin for the first time that day and was standing by the rail dressed in a bulky sweater and the shortest shorts imaginable. Across the bow KoKo poked at Leyte and then pointed to Beryl. Both hands stared at the exotic woman.

"Damn fool," grumbled Alexandros. "She is supposed to stay in her cabin and dress like one of the hands if she insists on roving about. Coley, would you mind speaking to her about that matter. A woman's flesh is nothing to be seen by working men at sea."

"I'll talk to her, Captain. Sometimes women are just plain stupid." And sometimes just plain beautiful, Coley added to himself.

Coley left the bridge to join Beryl at the rail. At least the distraction had taken his mind off his queasy stomach. Shooting some buckets with Beryl just might be the thing for his seasickness. Then all of a sudden he knew why he was ill. It wasn't seasickness at all.

He was embarking on a thousand-mile sea voyage with a bunch of killers who apparently all hated each other. No wonder he was nauseated.

"Miss Beryl, I have a message for you from the captain."

"Don't tell me, Coley. I bet I can guess exactly what it is."

"Okay, shoot!"

"The captain thinks that the flesh of a woman should not be visible to the other hands."

"Hey, that's pretty good. That is almost verbatim what the captain said."

"Do you agree with him, Coley?"

"I can't say as I do."

"Then fuck him."

"I really don't think the captain goes for that sort of thing. In fact I am not sure what the captain goes for. There is a certain amount of common sense to his advice, though. You've got some real rough-and-tumble guys in this crew. It just may not be wise to provoke them unnecessarily."

"Do you think Logan Phipps would permit such a thing?"

"Logan Phipps ain't here."

"Ah, but they know I am Logan Phipps's woman." Beryl spoke without emotion.

"I wonder what the crew is thinking about me. You know, the adjoining cabins, the thin walls and all that. What are they thinking about me shooting buckets with Logan Phipps's woman?"

A hint of a smile crossed Beryl's face. "I think they probably have a gambling pool, taking wagers on when Phipps will have KoKo split your head open with his hammer."

"Jesus! Do you really think so?"

"Yes, but don't worry about it. Nothing would really happen to you unless I expressed some displeasure to Logan. You have certainly given me no cause for that. So don't spoil our beautiful trip, Coley. We've gotten rid of Wong, and we've gotten rid of Ginny Du Bois. Logan will be very happy with both of us. In fact, perhaps we should go to the cabin and celebrate."

"Do you think so, Beryl? I think everyone aboard the *New Territories* is watching us."

"Coley, this sweater is getting very warm. I must take it off. I'll either take it off in the cabin or right here."

"Okay, you win," Coley conceded. "We'll go to your cabin and celebrate. We certainly don't want to start a goddamn riot!"

It was only a few paces to Beryl's stateroom.

Coley didn't even bother to use the entrance to his cabin.

Beryl had flipped the sweater over her head before the door was completely closed. It was pretty obvious to Coley that she was actually turned on by the peril of their situation. For Coley, it would take a little time.

"Coley, please sit down for a while and relax. Logan Phipps doesn't really give a damn what we do in here. I have a special favor to ask of you."

"I can't wait to hear." As he sat down in the spacious club chair he could feel the derringer he had sewn into his jacket lining only yesterday afternoon. It was wedged between his leg and the arm of the chair. He had gotten it from Agent Whitcomb at Pike Market.

They had both agreed that if trouble should arise on the *New Territories*, someone would probably relieve him of the nine-millimeter.

"So what is this special favor?"

"Two years ago in Bangkok, I met a prostitute whose specialty was pleasing tall men." Beryl, now wearing only the short shorts, produced a piece of paper that had been tucked inside a book. "At my insistence, she told me about her trade. Knowing that some day I might meet a tall, tall man, I asked her to draw a sketch. Here it is. Do you think we could do this, Coley?"

Beryl's eyes widened; her pupils dilated; her face was as inscrutable as always.

"Sure, princess. Ain't nothin' to it!"

Back on the bridge, Captain Alexandros studied the charts. The sun was now low in the western sky as the *New Territories* approached Astoria. If the ideal weather held up they would make Los Angeles in four days. They might even have time to spread a seine and take a few yellowtail. It seemed a pity that a great vessel like the *New Territories* spent all its time transporting kilos of white powder up and down the coast. Such a vessel deserved to exercise her birthright once in a while. Someday he would take her out and fill her to the gunwales with yellowtail. He would like to do that just once.

His eyes wandered to the curtained port of Beryl's cabin. A frown crossed the captain's weathered face as he spat a curse in that direction.

"What in the hell do they do in there for hour after hour? They're making a whorehouse out of this great ship, and they will pay!"

KoKo, now standing on the bridge with the captain, nodded his assent.

57

Onyx pressed hard on the accelerator of the slick black Jaguar and raced up MacArthur Boulevard from the Coast Highway near Newport Beach. The glass tower housing Sino-Americo was just ahead.

Never before had she dared to call unexpectedly on Logan Phipps, but the news from Carlos had been too shocking and infuriating for her to react any other way. Perhaps Carlos had the message mixed up. Carlos was getting too big for his britches anyway. What right did he have to deliver such an important communication? Phipps owed her an explanation.

Onyx steered the Jaguar into an open parking slot a full hundred feet from the lobby of the building. She sat quietly for a few moments, trying to organize her thoughts.

Her hand dropped from the gearshift to the small shoulder bag she had brought with her. She unsnapped the flap of the bag and slipped her hand inside to grasp the compact .22 automatic. Logan himself had given her the pearl-handled beauty. He had pointed out that all weapons had their purpose. While the small-caliber gun was hardly an assault weapon, it was easily concealable, and given the element of surprise would do the job if she "just kept pulling the trigger."

Looking across the parking area, she could make out the building's security guard, barely visible at his podium inside the darkened glass doors. She decided to take the .22 with her. How could she trust Logan? She knew he was an employee of Logan Phipps. The security of the building was such that no one could get past the guard if he or she was not expected, and Onyx knew she would have to deal with this immediately.

She slammed the door of the Jaguar and strode to the entrance of the building. She wore a bright turquoise Thai silk minidress with four-inch matching spike heels and absolutely nothing else. No doubt she would get the immediate attention of the young guard.

"Miss Lu to see Logan Phipps." The very short skirt was riding up under the heavy handbag.

Onyx did nothing to change that as the guard paused a moment to drink in the scenery.

"Is Mr. Phipps expecting you?"

"I afraid he may not be. I here as big surprise." Onyx gave the man a warm smile and tugged at the handbag, which hiked up her hem another inch. Every inch was critical at this point.

The guard was taking his time leafing through the building log to see whether any guests were expected.

"I don't believe Mr. Phipps is in yet today," he said, still openly scrutinizing the exotic guest.

"Oh yes! He in. I park my car right next to his." The guard looked out to bear witness to what he already knew. The twin Jaguars were parked side by side.

"I'll have to check and see if Mr. Phipps can see you today. That is our rule here, or rather his rule. I am sorry."

Onyx looked around the vacant lobby, then pulled the miniature .22 from her handbag and aimed it at the guard's midsection.

"Get Logan Phipps on the phone and hand the phone to me."

The guard turned ashen. He dialed the number and handed the telephone to Onyx. In a swift motion, Onyx lifted his revolver from its holster and slid it under the overhang on the podium.

"Logan, dear, I downstairs for surprise visit. Your cute young fella down here won't let me

341

come see you. Shame on him. He about to die right here and make big mess in lobby."

"Onyx, what in the living hell is going on? Come up here and leave that poor man alone. Have you gone crazy?"

"Thank you, Lo." With that she set the phone back in its cradle. She motioned with the gun toward the bank of elevators. "Come. Now! You are going up to Logan's floor with me."

"Why—"

In a lightning-fast move, she jabbed at the man's wrist with the automatic.

"Just do what you are told, or I send you to ancestors, you fool!" The intercom was already buzzing. It was no doubt Phipps trying to get the guard station.

Onyx could see that the guard was not really a person to fear physically. It was her estimation that he had no inclination to die for Logan Phipps.

When they entered the elevator the guard pushed the button for Phipps's floor, then stood across the elevator cab staring at the menacing weapon. Onyx tugged just a little more at the short skirt, hoisting it a bit above the point of critical anatomical exposure. The guard's eyes flitted rapidly to the tiny triangle of jet black and then just as quickly back to the barrel of the .22.

Onyx grinned at the man, who even in his fear was practically drooling.

"You fat policeman. You are fool. You should have been nice to Lo's friend. Goodies go only to those who are nice to Onyx. Now I have to tell

Logan that his creepy stupid security man look up Onyx's dress. He not like that. He make you pay." Onyx grinned at the uneasy man and just for a second considered humiliating him even more. But by then the elevator had reached Logan Phipps's floor.

Onyx prodded the guard in the back and forced him to lead the way across the anteroom to the door of Phipps's office. There stood Phipps with a gun in his hand very similar to the one Onyx held to the guard's back. Assessing the situation quickly, Phipps tossed his gun onto a couch.

"Henry, please return to the lobby and take your post. Miss Lu and I will be all right together. Please don't let anyone bother us."

"Yes sir!" The man needed no further urging to return to the elevator.

Onyx walked over to the couch and picked up Phipps's gun. She hefted it in her free hand for a moment and then tossed it back on the couch.

"Were you really going to shoot me, Lo? After all the many years and all the memories we share from the early days in Macau, were you really going to shoot me?"

"Of course not, Onyx, but how was I to know what sort of harebrained scheme you were up to? If you had let Henry do the talking on the intercom, I would have asked that you be sent right up. That was unstable, Onyx. You just can't fly off the handle like that."

"Somebody else fly off handle." Onyx emphasized each word with a thrust of the tiny revolver. "Somebody kill Wong. Wong find *Tashtego*. Wong

343

set up Beryl and Coley Doctor with that information. Then somebody kill Wong. Tell me, Lo, tell me exactly who kill Wong."

Onyx lowered the .22 so that the barrel pointed straight to Logan's abdomen. That was the spot where a volley of shots from the small weapon would probably do the most damage.

"Oh, for heaven's sake, Onyx. You are being stupid. I would have told you everything as soon as we met. I just haven't had a chance. I only found out myself late last evening." Logan backed away a couple of steps and sat on the edge of the big rosewood desk.

"Wong was a bumbling fool," he said. "The *Tashtego* ran over his open boat and left him floundering in the water. The idiot tried to terminate Hanson and his girlfriend by shooting up a hotel in downtown Seattle. We thought about letting him rot in jail but we had to spring him because of all the things he knew."

Onyx was eyeing Phipps carefully.

"Still, everything would have been all right if he hadn't gotten into a scuffle with KoKo aboard the *New Territories*," he went on. "KoKo and Wong are two of a kind. When people like that fight, there is no winner and no loser. There is merely a live person and a dead person. I am afraid that KoKo hit him with a hammer."

"Then it is true. Wong is dead. I was hoping that Carlos had it wrong, but Wong is dead and KoKo killed him."

Onyx felt warm tears stream down her cheeks.

She knew Phipps would be shocked to see her display such genuine grief.

"Lo, get off the desk and get down on your knees." Onyx brandished the automatic nervously, still dripping tears.

"What!" Logan Phipps moved slowly.

"Quickly, Lo! Get down on your knees." She made another sharp gesture with the automatic.

Phipps did so very slowly, his mind laboring to find a way to avoid the classic stance of a renegade about to be executed.

"Are you insane? Wong did idolize you, it's true. But I am the one who truly loves you."

Onyx now held the automatic with both hands. She moved forward to a point just a few inches from where Phipps knelt. Both fingers were on the trigger. Any sudden motion would send the bullets flying.

"Kiss me, Lo."

"What!"

"Kiss me just like Wong used to do when he came home from one of your wars. Lo, I am going to count three. One . . . two . . ."

She could see the death in his eyes. He knew she would do it. He kissed her beneath the skirt. She kept her eyes open.

"Thank you, Lo. I think that is quite enough. We are even now." Onyx backed away, still leveling the shiny automatic at the kneeling Phipps. "You know, it would be nice if you would come to the Black Lamp Saturday night. You would probably find it fascinating. Come incognito. You will have fun seeing how your money is spent. It is a special party for Carlos."

Onyx backed away and pressed the elevator button. As she stepped in, she said, "Tell your security desk to let me pass."

The elevator opened in the lobby. Henry tensed as the diminutive Onyx passed by giving him a big smile and a quick flip of her skirt as she exited through the revolving door.

The drive back to Redondo Beach was lonely. Coley Doctor and Beryl were now on the *New Territories*. They were due in Los Angeles in four days. Weather permitting, they would drop anchor in the small harbor at Redondo Beach on Friday evening. No doubt Phipps would go aboard to be with Beryl. A smile flickered across her face. I wonder how Beryl and Coley Doctor are getting along, she mused. She would have to get a full report from Alexandros. Phipps had never made an issue of promiscuity among his colleagues. But Beryl was different. How would he react to his protégée's weeklong affair with the big basketballer?

There was something incongruous about Coley Doctor, Onyx thought. The man was just too smooth. He had made believers out of all of them by killing Ginny Du Bois, in a fiery auto crash, over a cliff no less. She had known callous hit men who would have trouble terminating a beautiful woman in that manner.

Onyx concluded that Coley Doctor must be something pretty special and decided that she would shoot a few baskets with him just as he had offered.

Nevertheless, she would question Captain Alexandros very carefully about Coley and Beryl. Her relationship with the captain actually predated that of the people involved in the whole smuggling operation.

It was at the Idiot Club in Macau that Onyx Lu first met Captain Alexandros. In the wee hours of a Sunday morning she had come upon him alone in a room deep within the bowels of the old mansion, where a dominatrix had left him in a straitjacket and leg irons. Obviously at that point his appetite had exceeded his tolerance.

He had made a direct proposition. "Get me out of here and I will give you a half kilo of cocaine."

It was as simple as that. It was the start of a long relationship that would lead them to Logan Phipps. Later Alexandros told Onyx that the people at the Idiot Club had been paid to kill him because of all he knew.

The lunch crowd usually started coming to the Black Lamp about 12:30. That was an hour and a half away when Onyx arrived. The chef and his staff were busy in the kitchen. The maître d' was receiving reservations at his podium. Carlos was late, which was very unusual.

Onyx slipped unnoticed into the elevator and pressed the button for the third floor. She unlocked the showroom and flipped a wall switch, which bathed the room with light from a quartet of floodlamps. Without the show lights, the laser show, the spinning glitter and the pounding beat, the room looked like nothing special. Only the individual cages that held the La Sex Ménagerie drew her attention.

She walked backstage and then along a small passageway that led between the walls to an ordinary stepladder. She climbed the ladder, opened a small panel and crawled into the cage. From this point of view she could see every table in the cabaret. She flipped the switch on the small spotlight attached to the cage, which hung about twenty-five feet in the air. As she maneuvered it, the powerful spot pinpointed every nook and corner of La Sex Ménagerie. Onyx sat on the floor of the cage and contemplated the room below. It would be perfect. With the ear-splitting music, no one could possibly hear a gunshot.

"Onyx!"

The voice of Carlos startled her. She spotted him sitting at a table in a far corner of the room, dressed as usual in a handsomely tailored dark silk business suit. She wondered how long he had watched her play with the lights. She could have sworn that she had looked earlier at the table where Carlos now sat.

"Carlos, I'm glad you're here. I want to go over a couple of things with you. I'll come down." Onyx slipped through the panel and down the ladder. In thirty seconds she stood next to him.

"What brings you here, Carlos?"

"When you turn any lights on in this room, it activates the security cameras. I came here to investigate and found you, perched like a bird in a cage."

"Carlos, you could have said beautiful bird. If you would just work at it, you could be quite charming. Really, Carlos, you embarrassed me in front of Lolly Penrose. All it would take would be a little smile. You don't even have to say anything; just a smile, Carlos."

The unexpected happened. Carlos did smile.

"There, you see, Carlos. It is so much better for people to see you that way. Miss Penrose would have been impressed. You are a handsome man, Carlos, when you smile."

"I smile because you are stupid, Onyx. It was a chance letting me come face to face with Lolly Penrose. I drove her home the day before I terminated Hatcher. Hatcher raped that woman all the way home in the front seat while I watched. It is very lucky she was too drunk to remember about me. If she remembered, I have to kill her."

"Oh, lighten up, Carlos. She obviously didn't remember. The woman is a drunken whore." Onyx spoke the words with relish. She had heard herself referred to as the Macau whore too many times.

Onyx effortlessly moved her legs to sit cross-legged in the chair in front of Carlos. The minidress slipped back to fully reveal her womanhood.

"Carlos, I saw you looking at the mimes in the cages the other night. I saw you stare at their sexual tableaus."

Carlos glared at Onyx with contempt. "What

woman, Onyx, would make a display of herself such as you are now doing? It takes a Macau whore to do something like that."

Quick as a blur, Onyx's hand slashed across Carlos face. He quickly stood and backed several steps away from the table. Onyx continued to sit motionless in her all-revealing position.

"It is a shame you are so stupid, Carlos. We have so much energy to give to each other. It would be like two gods fucking."

Carlos strode toward the elevator in the outer lobby.

"Hey, Carlos! You fool! I could teach you how to make your Luisa Maria the happiest señorita in Jalisco."

The scowling hit man turned and shook his fist at the grinning Onyx. Then, without saying a word, he spun around and entered the elevator. The door closed behind him.

Onyx thought he looked like a man who wouldn't hesitate to kill her.

58

Willy Hanson paused to talk to the cabdriver and slipped him a tip that would encourage him to wait for them. They were chancing one more visit to the *Tashtego* to pick up a few things before they continued to the airport for their trip to Los Angeles. Willy and Ginny had agreed that if Whitcomb appeared, they would bring him more into their confidence. He had trusted them and now they would return the favor.

Willy propped the old stepladder up against the transom of the *Tashtego* and followed Ginny aboard. Down below, he withdrew the .38 from his belt, dropped the bullets from the cylinder and wrapped the weapon in plastic. That done, he opened a bilge hatch and tossed the gun forward into the lower compartment, where it clattered somewhere beneath the engine. Alaska Air would certainly frown on the weapon. He would have to acquire a new one from his subculture friend in San Pedro after they landed.

He crammed a few pieces of clothing and personal gear into a duffel bag and climbed back into the cockpit. Ginny was staring at a point in the parking lot a couple of hundred feet away. It was the blue Malibu. Mark Whitcomb was already walking straight toward the *Tashtego*.

A twinge of apprehension gripped Willy. What if Whitcomb was coming to arrest him?

Whitcomb didn't stop at ground level. He climbed up the ladder and boarded the *Tashtego* without skipping a step.

"I hate to disappoint you folks, but this vessel stays right here. I hope you weren't planning to put her back in the water."

Whitcomb eyed Willy carefully, then looked at Ginny. "You must be Miss Du Bois. You don't look dead to me." He gave a little laugh.

"You really know how to dish out a compliment, Mr. Whitcomb." Ginny decided to keep it as lighthearted as possible.

Whitcomb turned back to study Willy. "Where is that pop-gun thirty-eight of yours?"

"That's funny. Coley Doctor calls it a popgun too. Actually, I just tossed it into the bilge." Ginny was smiling now. It no doubt made her feel **good** to hear Willy speak truthfully to the FBI.

"Now, why in the hell would you toss it into the bilge?" Whitcomb sounded genuinely puzzled at these two people, who insisted on playing cops and robbers with Hong Kong drug lords.

"I don't think Alaska Air would appreciate me bringing it aboard."

"So you're going south, are you?"

"That's right. Redondo Beach. We'll be staying at the Porto Sol. How's that for cooperation?"

"What if I say you can't go?" Whitcomb looked quite serious.

"Then I suppose Ginny and I would have to pounce on you and kill you with our bare hands." Willy said it with a hint of a smile, but Whitcomb was not amused.

"You know, Hanson, the biggest favor I could do for you and your lady here would be to get you off the street and put you both under protective custody. You haven't got a chance against Logan Phipps. He plays hardball, day and night, all year 'round. Do you have any idea why we're not taking you into custody?"

"You're using us as bait."

"You're damn right, Hanson. And I'll tell you something else. I hope you don't stop your stupid chase. You and this pretty lady are going to get killed. But we are going to win. The FBI will win. I can tell you that there stands a good chance of a real bloodbath down in L.A. And you are going to be right in the middle of it."

"Thanks, Whitcomb. Thanks for taking the

heat off Ginny and Coley by planting that news-paper story. I owe you one."

Whitcomb looked Willy squarely in the eye and moved close enough to tap his chest with his forefinger.

"Private citizens who play vigilantes are an abomination to the system. I don't know how you can play that game and pull Miss Du Bois into it. Whether you know it or not, Mr. Hanson, we've got you on a leash. You are going to lead us to the whole sorry bunch. But just remember that cockroach on the pantry floor I told you about. You ain't got a chance, Hanson."

Willy and Ginny climbed down the ladder and walked to the waiting cab. Willy turned and nod-ded to Whitcomb, still in the *Tashtego*'s cockpit. The agent gave him an almost imperceptible nod in return.

59

Foul weather engulfed the *New Territories* along the Oregon coast. Captain Alexandros made an unpopular decision to ride out the storm near the mouth of the Columbia. Six- to eight-foot seas had pounded the trawler steadily for the next hundred miles. Under Alexandros's scowl, Coley had retreated from the bridge to his own cabin. The sea-sickness he had earlier fought off now took charge of his body, and all the skillful and provocative diversions Beryl could offer were ineffective.

"Beryl, I want to die."

"Don't say that, Coley. No matter how you feel you should not say that aloud."

"Beryl, why are we in such a godawful hurry? L.A. ain't goin' anyplace."

"Alexandros promised Phipps we would be there in four days. He will keep his word. Actually, the captain is having fun. The *New Territories* is well equipped to handle seas like this. There is nothing to worry about, Coley."

The big trawler rolled about twenty degrees as it slid through the trough of an unusually rugged wave. Alexandros was conceding nothing to the storm. He was plowing ahead as if he were on flat water.

Coley moaned and retched. There was absolutely nothing left inside him to come out. Turning on his bunk, he saw Beryl decked out from head to toe in foul-weather gear.

"I will go below and see if Fallon has anything stronger than he's already given you."

"Hey, isn't the captain going to be pissed off? He don't like women out there."

"Coley, I am completely covered by this grotesque yellow slicker and boots. I am sexless." Beryl opened the door to the stateroom and went off into the howl of the wind.

Coley shook his head helplessly. She was some kind of woman, even if she was a cocaine-peddling killer.

Beryl found Fallon resting in his cabin and was surprised to see that he wasn't making out too well with the rolling *New Territories* either.

He gave her pills, grunting, "Take one every couple of hours."

As Beryl left Fallon's cabin she came face to face with KoKo.

"Captain must see you right now. He no can wait. Right now!" The trawler rolled under them, pitching them both against the handrail. KoKo's arms encircled Beryl tightly, much too tightly to suit her.

"Keep your hands off of me," she hissed. "I can handle the going without your help."

KoKo just grinned at her without speaking. For a moment she wished she had bothered to put clothing on under the foul-weather gear.

When they reached the bridge, KoKo started to enter with her, but was motioned away by a frowning Alexandros.

"Stand by outside to help Miss Beryl get back to her quarters after I'm finished with her. We won't be more than a few minutes here."

The grinning KoKo gave a nod of assent and took up his post just outside the entrance to the bridge.

"Not the kind of a day to be out on deck, Miss Beryl." The captain's scowl deepened as he spoke.

"I'm doing just fine getting about, Captain. I would probably do better if you would instruct KoKo to keep his hands to himself. If he touches me again, Phipps will hear about it."

"Sorry, Miss Beryl. I suppose he thought he was helping you. I'll tell him to mind his manners."

"Just tell him hands off, Captain. Okay? Hands off!"

The captain nodded.

"Miss Beryl, I have some distressing news about our other passenger. Inasmuch as you seem to have developed a . . . shall we say, good friendship with Mr. Doctor, you should be informed immediately that he may not be what he seems to be."

The captain stared gloatingly at Beryl.

"Let's don't play games, Captain. What is it? What is it that brings me to the bridge in a storm like this? Being aboard your ship in these circumstances is hell, Captain. Phipps will hear about it, you can be sure."

Alexandros broke into a smile that showed how unconcerned he was about Phipps. "It seems there is a very good chance that Mr. Coley Doctor may be lying to us."

Beryl's great dark eyes widened as she waited.

"We have a man named Larkin. A very reliable man, is this Larkin."

"Yes, I know of Larkin. In Bay Area." Beryl was perplexed. What could Larkin have to say that was so important?"

"It was Larkin who spotted the *Tashtego* as it headed north. So I sent Larkin to Seattle to keep his eye on her where she sits in dry dock." The rain was now hammering against the windows of the bridge. Alexandros paused to take a look at his chart.

"Two days ago the *Tashtego* was boarded by three people. One of them was Willy Hanson.

There was another man and also a woman in her thirties who fit our description of Ginny Du Bois."

Beryl stepped forward next to Alexandros, who was watching the rain pelting against the bridge.

"Impossible! I saw Coley leave the restaurant when he kidnapped her. KoKo and Leyte did also. The newspaper said there was a body."

"I have sent Larkin back for more information. There are ways of checking out the identity of the body. Larkin has checked the newspapers and there has been no mention of the woman killed in the accident since the very first reports. I think that strange, don't you, Miss Beryl?"

"By all means we must bring Logan up to date."

"I intend to do that, Miss Beryl."

The captain had trouble looking directly at Beryl when he talked to her. She was so dominant. She was Onyx Lu all over again, looking exactly as she had looked in the Idiot Club back in Macau. He groaned almost inaudibly, but loud enough for Beryl to hear him. the juices of the old perversions began to flow as he visualized the dominatrix Onyx Lu from the old days.

"Captain, I will return to my quarters. Fallon has given me seasick pills for Coley, who is not a person of the sea like you and I."

Alexandros turned to gape at Beryl, flicking his eyes up and down the tiny female hidden beneath the foul-weather gear. Something had suddenly changed his demeanor. Her intuition told her that she should rip her raincoat wide open right there on the bridge and stand nude before him, and she came very close to following her instincts. Only the presence of KoKo outside the door stopped her.

She turned to open the hatch. KoKo was still there. Alexandros stepped close behind her. "We are about two days' run from Los Angeles. The weather flattens out a great deal once we pass San Francisco. We will make port in Monterey for a few hours to take on diesel. If you find it more comfortable on the bridge, then you are welcome to visit." He watched her as she made her way along the handrail of the companionway to join KoKo.

"Leave her alone, KoKo. Leave her alone!" It was a menacing growl meant only for the ears of KoKo, but Beryl could hear it very clearly.

As she entered her quarters, she noticed Leyte slumped in a lifeboat a few yards away. She guessed Coley Doctor had become his assignment.

She bolted the door to her cabin, Coley eyeing her appreciatively as she shed the ugly foul-weather gear. He was obviously feeling much better.

Beryl opened the vial of Dramamine and popped a capsule into her mouth, then scrambled under the sheet that covered Coley and squirmed to a position where their faces met. She forced the capsule between his lips with her tongue and continued to explore his mouth until she felt swelling against her legs.

"Ah ... the pills work very quickly. You are feeling much better, Coley."

"I'm supposed to tell you how I feel."

"You feel marvelous, Coley. I want you to follow instructions. Can you do that?"

"Certainly."

"I want you to lie perfectly still. You are not to move a muscle. You are to lie there as motionless as a stone. I shall move ever so slowly for ever so long. I will polish this beautiful stone to a high gloss."

Coley gasped as he entered her and continued to pulsate with a barely perceptible rhythm.

"Don't gasp again, Coley. You are not to say anything. You exist just to enjoy the polishing of the stone."

Beryl tossed her hair back, then let her chin rest lightly on Coley's chest.

"Coley, watch my eyes."

He looked down and their eyes met. Beryl's great dark impassioned eyes locked on his own, as her pulsing rhythm slowly accelerated. Then, without flickering an eyelash, she spoke.

"Captain Alexandros says Ginny Du Bois is alive and well in Seattle. He will probably kill you tomorrow, Coley."

Coley could see it all now. The scheming bitch had set him up. He lay underneath her trying to concentrate on sustaining his rigid passion. Any collapse of his ardor at this point would be interpreted by Beryl as a confession that he had lied to them. Please, God, he thought to himself, I

361

have no right to ask, but don't let the body fail me now.

What Beryl hadn't counted on was the bizarre excitement of fielding a death threat in the midst of passion. To his amazement, he found himself fortified and rejuvenated as they went on and on into orgasmic spasms.

About a half hour later, Beryl again looked up to meet Coley's eyes.

"Coley, I'm sorry. I had to find out. But you did enjoy my little test, didn't you?"

"It's all bullshit, kid. Hell, you saw me with her the last fifteen minutes of her life. Where in the hell did Alexandros get that crazy idea?"

Beryl sat up cross-legged on the bed.

"We have this man, Larkin. Alexandros sent him to Seattle to keep his eye on the *Tashtego* after Wong died. He saw Hanson aboard the *Tashtego* with a man and a woman who must have looked something like Ginny Du Bois."

"Hell, Willy Hanson's got more girlfriends than a junkyard dog has fleas. That woman could have been any one of a dozen."

"Well, he has sent Larkin back to get more information. I will try to get Alexandros to call him back. No need to waste manpower like that."

Beryl turned in the bunk to part the small curtain concealing a porthole. The rain was still pelting down on a tossing sea. Just outside she could see Leyte in his lifeboat.

"Coley, would you do me a favor?"

"Sure."

"I am afraid of Leyte. Will you kill him for me?"

"Sure. As soon as I get the chance, baby."

"That's nice, Coley. Captain Alexandros says we will be putting in for fuel in Monterey in the morning. It will be nice to get on land and stretch our legs. From there he says it is less than two days' run to Los Angeles."

"I could use a little stroll on the beach."

Coley's mind was going a million miles a minute. He would love to get to a telephone and reach his voice mailbox. Perhaps he would be able to do that from Monterey.

"I'd like it done before we get to Los Angeles. Can you handle that for me, Coley?"

"Handle what?"

"Leyte, Coley, Leyte. Sometimes I don't think you listen very well. It probably could be best done while the storm is still raging. In the night, perhaps."

"Does Leyte carry a ball-peen hammer like KoKo does?"

"I've never seen him with one. He does have a rigging knife. A rather large one, with a six-inch spike. I would be careful of that."

"No problem, sugar pants. I'll sure watch out for that sucker."

Beryl smiled. Coley had passed the sensual test she had devised. Killing Leyte would be proof positive that he was an ally she could trust implicitly. Leyte was a menace deserving the worst of fates anyway.

"Beryl, I'm afraid I have to confess something," Coley said quietly. "I am a private investigator. Killing is not my business. Getting rid of Ginny Du Bois was the hardest thing I ever did, and I almost botched that up by getting trapped in the car myself."

Beryl studied him, measuring each word he spoke.

"But damn it, I will try. And I will try to get it done before we get to L.A. I suppose he could fall overboard. Let me put my mind to it."

Beryl wrapped her arms around his broad shoulders.

"You'll get it done, honey. You can do anything you really want to do, Coley."

60

The taxicab ride from Los Angeles International Airport to the Porto Sol took only about fifteen minutes. Using his handy Caleb Jones credit card, Willy registered for a second-floor suite in the classy little hotel that overlooked the entire sweep of the coastline from Palos Verdes to Los Angeles. Under different circumstances it would have made an ideal lovers' hideaway.

A frothy surf was crashing onto the rocks of a long jetty that formed the sole protection for the snug harbor of Redondo Beach. Inland, behind the hotel, rose dozens of low-level homes and condos, all with magnificent views of the colorful harbor. Dozens of fine restaurants and discos were sprinkled throughout the area. One of these was Lolly Penrose's Black Lamp, just two blocks from the harbor.

"I have a package for you, sir. It just arrived this morning." The words were spoken by the desk clerk, one of those sleek, scrubbed blondes so prevalent along the Southern California coast.

"That's unexpected." Willy was puzzled. No one really had time to know they were there. He had made the reservation from Seattle only yesterday.

The clerk produced a small but heavy box, about eight inches by four inches and a couple of inches deep. The return address was illegible. Willy handed it to Ginny while he completed the registration.

Their suite was large and elegantly furnished, particularly in contrast to the *Tashtego*. Their attention was completely taken by the box that now sat on the coffee table.

"Coley recommended this place," Ginny said. "It has to be from him."

"But Coley has been at sea for at least two full days. This was sent same-day parcel delivery." He hefted the heavily taped package carefully. "It ain't candy, baby." Willy began cutting through the tape with a small pocket knife and managed to cut the entire end off the package.

Out plopped a .38 revolver, tightly sealed in plastic wrap. Also inside was a small leather tobacco pouch containing a dozen hollow-point .38 cartridges.

Willy recognized the gun immediately. It was the same snub-nosed .38 he had tossed into the bilge of the *Tashtego* the day before.

"Whitcomb! The FBI is actually watching over us. Whitcomb is our mother hen! That son of a gun got inside the *Tashtego*, scrounged around in the bilge and fished my gun out."

Ginny was all smiles. "We ought to nail him for breaking and entering. I hope he locked the hatch again." As much as she hated the weapon, at least it gave them an ounce of security. "He no doubt had a search warrant when we saw him on the boat. He probably takes a dim view of breaking and entering. I think he is really rooting for us, Willy."

"Hey! Remember that he compared us to cockroaches. When Phipps or Onyx get close to us, we become expendable. We're not the object of his investigation. Our staying alive is just a convenience for him."

"Okay, so he is helping us stay alive for a while. I kind of like that idea, Willy. I still say he's rooting for us."

Ginny had peeled all the plastic wrap off the revolver and was lying on the bed now, twirling it on her trigger finger. She smiled at Willy, knowing that the careless handling of the weapon would annoy him.

"Whitcomb thinks we're amateurs. Doesn't he realize we are actually vigilante geniuses?"

"We're not geniuses, Ginny. We just do a lot of fancy screwing in a lot of fancy places." He carefully took the gun from her. "Now that we've unwrapped our surprise package, I want to call Coley's voice mail." He leaned over and planted a lingering kiss on her lips as he reached for the telephone.

Nervous apprehension swept over him when the mechanical voice reported that he had three new messages. He hadn't really expected any because Coley was at sea on the *New Territories*. He quickly motioned for Ginny to get close to the receiver so that they could both listen.

"Hi, old pal. I am gonna have to talk fast because I might be interrupted at any minute. I'm at a bar in Monterey. We're taking on some diesel. We're due to arrive in Redondo Beach sometime Friday P.M. Everyone on this boat belongs in an insane asylum!"

There was a pause as noise in the background drowned out his voice.

"I'm in a hallway where waiters go in and out of a kitchen. Every time the door opens it gets noisy. Sorry about that. Ginny's cover might be blown. Alexandros had another spy up north who saw Willy, another man and a woman on the *Tashtego*. I told Alexandros it was probably one of your many girlfriends. I don't know whether he believes me or not. However, Beryl does and she's the boss. We spend a lot of time shooting buckets. Hey, I see her outside this joint right now. Got to hang up."

There was a click, a pause and then the second message began.

"Hi, pals. Everything's okay. I ducked into the men's room and she left so I'm back at the same

368

phone. Remember the big house on Ventana Drive that you told me about? Carlos wants to talk to me about it. Seems Onyx is kicking up a storm since they got rid of Wong.

"Didn't you tell me your agent, Reinard Gossman, used to date Lolly Penrose? See if he can find out from her what the hell is happening down there. There seems to be big trouble in paradise. Maybe Onyx talks to her.

"Hey, guys, there is this sawed-off tank named Leyte who carries around this big reefing knife. I may have to deal with him before I see you in Redondo. If the worst happens, dump it all in Whitcomb's lap and then try to vamoose to Tahiti. Ta-ta . . ."

Willy waited for the third message, fully expecting it to contain more bad news from Coley.

"Hi. Reinard here. I hope you're somewhere in the L.A. area and that you have a manuscript for me. Ha ha ha . . . I guess I should know better. Going to be at the Century Plaza Thursday through the weekend. I'm seeing Lolly Penrose just for old times' sake. Seems she has a lot to talk about. She is a restaurateur now. Supposed to be a four-star joint. Be nice if we could all get together. Bye now."

Reinard sounded just the way he always sounded. He was the ultimate spectator of life. He had become one of the most successful literary agents in the world simply by listening to a vast number of movers and shakers who took him into their confidence.

"Wonder if it's too late to catch him tonight?"

Willy called information for the Century Plaza and then dialed the number.

"Reinard Gossman, please." The hotel operator rang the room.

"Hello, Gossman here."

"Yes, it is! The world's greatest agent. I know, because he sells manuscripts that do not exist!"

"Willy. This is luck. I called your number only an hour ago. Where in the world are you?"

"Right here in the land of milk and honey. Say, I want to thank you for recommending Coley Doctor as a private investigator. He is some piece of work, although he may be in a little hot water right now."

"He's a good one. Has super law enforcement connections, you know. He is a little unorthodox."

"Reinard, I would rather save all that for later. Can Ginny and I horn in on your dinner tonight?"

"Hey, Lolly would love that. It would be like old times. Are you above ground now? Have you surfaced yet for all the world to see?"

"Absolutely not, Reinard. We are still very much on the run. Maybe it's a bad idea. We would have to meet somewhere off the beaten track."

"Same old Willy. I know the perfect spot near Redondo. Very remote. Lolly is bursting with a desire to talk about her new business partner. It terrifies me, you know. I can't imagine anything legitimate abut Onyx Lu."

"Lolly's choice of friends was always a little peculiar. Except for you and me, of course."

"But she is loyal, Willy. She still thinks you are the salt of the earth."

"That's just the trouble. She thinks everyone in the world is the salt of the earth. How is she doing with the booze and the coke?"

"She sounded great on the phone. Says she has been on the wagon for a few days. Maybe this time it will stick. Willy, I think I'd better level with you. Lolly wants to bounce some information off me about a homicide. Did you read anything about the Aussie rock star Evan Hatcher?"

"A little. Had a car accident. Ran off a cliff down near San Diego."

"Lolly says it was murder, and she knows who did it. Some guy by the name of Carlos."

"Carlos! Coley talks about Carlos! Listen, where do we meet? You better warn Lolly that Ginny and I are coming. She may change her mind about her dinner date."

"Not a chance. Maybe we can help her this time. I'd like to see her stay off the sauce. Meet us at the El Valdiz right near Sepulveda and Manhattan Boulevard. I think that puts it in Manhattan Beach."

"Seven-thirty?"

"Fine. By the way, are you still carrying that heater?"

"Reinard, it's the only insurance policy I've got."

Willy hung up, then paced the floor as he fed bullets into the cylinder of the small revolver. They had been in Southern California for only a few hours and things were already starting to heat up.

He looked at the snub-nosed .38 and for a moment felt a little better. Whitcomb was out there someplace with his eyes on him, hopefully right there in Redondo Beach.

61

Logan Phipps had been enraged by Onyx's behavior when she paid her visit to Sino-America's offices. The brandishing of the weapon revealed intolerably bad judgment. Now she was insisting that Saturday night's festivities at the Black Lamp would include not only Lolly Penrose, but also a number of highly visible West Coast supermodels.

It was all part of her marketing plan. No cocaine would be offered for sale that night. Her plan was the same as that which had been so successful in the past. Build up a large celebrity clientele and offer them cutting-edge fun and games with the press all over the place. Over a period of several weeks the crowd would be culled to include only those beautiful people who would welcome an exclusive haven for drugs. La Sex Ménagerie would then change over to a private club, and the press would be barred, unless some were allowed to join. Onyx would have complete control over all membership decisions.

The plan was all well and good, but in this case it was taking far too long. Onyx had been diverted by her compulsive vendetta against Willy Hanson and her emotional attachment to the expendable Wong.

The gun had been the clincher, though. He had been forced to kneel before her or she might have pulled the trigger. That was the last straw. It would not happen again.

Onyx must go. She was now on the list of the expendable. She would have to be terminated.

Phipps had thought very carefully about a plan. It was his personal hope that she could be put on a plane and sent back to her native Macau under some as yet undetermined pretext. In Macau, the job could be done quietly, without causing even a ripple in the water.

A single tone sounded from a small speaker behind him. That would be Henry in the lobby. Carlos was several minutes early.

"Yes, Henry, please send him right up."

Carlos appeared before him, natty as always in

a meticulously pressed silk suit. There was only the slightest hint of a bulge where the nine-millimeter was concealed beneath his jacket.

"Carlos, you have been staying very close to the Black Lamp."

Carlos nodded slightly.

"That is good, Carlos. You have no doubt learned a lot about the running of the restaurant and the cabaret. At a time like this you have become invaluable to us. You will be able to take over the full management of the complex beginning on Sunday."

Carlos frowned, then smiled slightly. "Mr. Phipps, has this been discussed with Onyx?"

"No, Carlos. Nor will that be necessary, you see, because Onyx Lu will be terminated following the gala festivities on Saturday night."

"Terminated!"

"Yes, Carlos, I mean that quite in your sense of the word. Her life must be brought to some appropriate conclusion."

Carlos, who had been standing, sat down in one of the ornate rosewood chairs opposite Phipps.

"As usual, Carlos, there is no point in going over the reasons for this. Let's just say that Onyx has run amok."

"I will need a few hours to think about this. The how, the when, and the where will have to be worked out."

Phipps was amazed at Carlos's composure.

"Oh, there is no great rush, Carlos. Take a few days. I thought we might easily cook up some pretense to send her back to Macau or Hong Kong. You would accompany her, of course. The task could be completed there without a lot of fuss. What do you think, Carlos?"

"That is an interesting possibility, but not really necessary. I can take care of this in my own way. I assure you that she will be visible one minute, then no one will ever see her again. In time, people will ask, 'Where is the one called Onyx?' We will just shake our heads and tell them that one day she did not show up for work."

"Carlos, you are a wonder. I leave the decision totally in your hands. And by the way, Carlos, congratulations. I think you will be a fine manager of our restaurant and club. Beryl and Coley will assist you in whatever way they can."

Carlos stood, believing that their business had been concluded. Just as he turned for the door, Phipps raised his voice again.

"Oh, Carlos! I take it that our inventory is still in the greenhouse on Ventana Drive."

"Yes, sir."

"How much do we have there now, Carlos?"

"There are one-hundred-thirty-one kilos there under the tarp in the greenhouse."

"Who knows of this?"

"Only Onyx and myself."

"Obviously, when Onyx is no longer with us, only you and I will know. I would like to keep it that way. Okay?"

"Of course."

"Keep in touch, Carlos. I would like to get a re-

port from you every day. If there is nothing to report, say just that."

Carlos nodded and exited to the elevator. Once
inside, he smacked his fist into his palm several
times. A broad grin crossed the usually stern hit
man's face. "This one is going to be fun!" He
couldn't resist saying it aloud.

62

The *New Territories* was plowing through a light chop just north of the Channel Islands near Moro Bay. She was moving as smoothly across the water as a Caddy on the open road, in contrast to the rolling and pitching of the two previous days. It was about 3 A.M. and an ebony night on the water. A moonless sky left the visibility nil as a light scud of clouds covered the stars.

Alexandros had requested that Coley stand night watch with him on the bridge. When Coley had arrived at midnight, the captain had excused KoKo and Leyte from duty and told them

378

to catch up on their sleep. During the storm, the two able hands had gotten little rest.

Coley was surprised when the captain asked him to take the helm. Of course, Alexandros sat on a stool at his elbow, checking the compass to make sure Coley was on his heading. Once again Coley Doctor was actually enjoying himself. Standing at the helm of a brawny vessel like this was exhilarating.

At one point Coley saw a flicker of light to his port side. But it vanished immediately. It was probably Beryl or Fallon peeking through a port curtain for a moment.

With Coley and Alexandros safely sealed away topside, Beryl opened her stateroom door to the port companionway and slipped quickly outside. Pausing for just a second to make certain she could not be seen from the bridge, she went quickly to the lifeboat that held the dozing Leyte. She crawled into the lifeboat and under the tarp that covered Leyte, now wide awake.

"Leyte, are you glad to see me?"

"Yes. Oh yes!"

"I'll bet you have been peeking in my porthole between the crack of the curtains, haven't you?"

She could see Leyte grin broadly in the dim light. "Yes, I peek! I see you all over."

"Well, Leyte, you do not have to peek anymore. Now you can touch and feel. Do you like what you feel, Leyte? It is much better than just peeking through a curtain. It is much better for me too."

Beryl slipped her arms tightly around Leyte's waist. The bewildered seaman lay back eagerly, allowing the aggressive woman to explore wherever she wanted. He closed his eyes in sensual delirium as Beryl reached down to withdraw the already open reefing knife from her boot.

Very carefully she explored Leyte's back to find the exact spot she wanted. Then she plunged the knife in with all the strength she had. The long, thin spike, honed to ice-pick sharpness, did its job quickly, eliciting only a feeble cry and several gasps.

In a matter of seconds, she was back in her cabin carefully washing away the evidence. The reefing knife, Leyte's own, was left buried in the broad back of the muscular hand.

Alexandros and Coley Doctor were still on the bridge when the dawn began to break. The Channel Islands lay off to port. Alexandros had taken the seaward side of the islands to avoid small craft, which could be a nuisance in the occasional fog patches.

It was after 7 A.M. when Beryl emerged from her cabin, dressed in foul-weather gear against the crisp morning air. She walked up to the bow pulpit and stood brushing her hair for some time under the scowling scrutiny of Alexandros.

She walked down along the rail toward her cabin and paused, leaning against the lifeboat, to continue brushing her hair.

With Alexandros and Coley both watching, she hesitated by the lifeboat and lifted the corner of the tarp. She stood absolutely rigid for a moment and then let out a piercing scream. She came running toward the bridge.

"Captain! There is something wrong with Leyte. He looks dead in that lifeboat." She shivered and put her arms tightly around Coley.

"Take the wheel, Coley. I'll find out what is bothering this woman." He walked quickly over to the lifeboat. "KoKo! KoKo! Fallon! On deck! The captain's voice boomed repeatedly as he stared transfixed into the wide-open eyes of Leyte.

"What's going on over there?" Coley asked the still clinging Beryl.

"Leyte has been stabbed, of course. Thanks, Coley, I was afraid you had turned chicken."

"Oh no you don't. I wish I could take credit, Beryl, but I have been right here on the bridge with the captain all night."

"It's okay, Coley. You can level with me. I told you to do it. Remember? I've stood watch with the captain many times. He dozes a lot at the wheel, doesn't he? I am so proud of you, Coley!"

Coley was watching the captain. "What is the old buzzard going to do now?" He was leaning over the lifeboat with KoKo, apparently discussing the matter.

"He can't do anything, Coley. If you were on the bridge with him all the time, as he thinks, he would have to blame it on KoKo or Fallon. Thanks again, Coley. For this I will always be beholden to you."

"Beryl, I didn't do it! Believe me, I know I

promised you I would do it if and when I found the opportunity. But I didn't do it."

As he was talking, he suddenly realized the truth. There was really no other possibility. Leyte was KoKo's pal, and Fallon was hardly capable. Beryl had sneaked into the lifeboat and done it herself! Now she was testing him to see if he would take responsibility. She was testing him again and he had passed with flying colors.

Far off in the distance Coley could see the California coast. It was probably Santa Barbara. They now had only a short distance to go, but he still wondered whether or not he would make it alive.

"Beryl, I know you did it. You killed Leyte. There is just no other answer. I'm sorry you got to him first. I really wanted to do it for you. You could have gotten yourself killed. Killing like that is man's work."

Beryl put her arms around him and held him tightly. Coley shuddered. Everyone aboard this ship was totally evil.

Captain Alexandros came back to the bridge, took over the helm and without saying a word pointed the *New Territories* due west. Coley's pulse gave a jump. They were now headed away from Los Angeles.

"We'll hold this course for about twenty minutes." The captain's voice was barely audible. "We will have a burial at sea. Leyte would like that. It will also save us a lot of questions when we get to Los Angeles. The damn fool fell on his own rigging spike. But imagine trying to tell that to some investigator."

About forty miles at sea Alexandros cut the *New Territories'* powerful engine to an idle. Leyte had been bound to a slab of wood skewered to a piece of heavy sheet metal, and at this moment was balanced over the starboard side, held aboard by KoKo's weight as he stood on the end of the plank.

Captain Alexandros emerged from his quarters with a Bible. As they all stood around the body of Leyte, he opened the Bible and read several passages silently. His lips were moving, but his voice could not be heard.

Then, after several minutes, he read the Lord's Prayer aloud.

This done, the captain offered a brief observation. "Dear Lord, we are turning Leyte over to your care. He is an able seaman. You can trust him on any ship in your fleet. I want to thank you, Dear Lord, for allowing him to perish by a cherished tool of his profession, his own reefing knife. Leyte would like that. Amen. Let him drop, KoKo!"

Coley gulped. He wanted to vomit.

Following the funeral, the *New Territories* came about and pointed full speed toward Los Angeles. They arrived in Redondo Beach and anchored just outside the jetty well before their 10 A.M. deadline.

Alexandros had called ahead to Phipps at Beryl's request. Phipps himself stood on the pier awaiting the small runabout, which was lowered to take Beryl and Coley ashore. Fallon dropped them off, then headed back to the *New Territories*.

If Phipps was upset by rumors about Beryl and Coley, he didn't show it. There was a faint smile on his face and he seemed to show some genuine warmth when Coley praised Alexandros and his vessel.

Logan Phipps did say there had been some developments that they would all have to discuss Sunday afternoon at a meeting in his office. He brought them up to date about the major publicity splash Onyx was having on Saturday night at the Black Lamp. Coley was instructed to meet Carlos there in a couple of hours. Then, without speaking a word, Beryl climbed into Phipps' Jaguar and sped away with him.

For the first time in days, Coley Doctor was alone. He heaved a heavy sigh of relief as he watched the Jaguar pass the exit of the underground garage near Redondo Beach pier.

Coley felt incredibly alive. He wanted to shout to the whole world that he had just gotten off a hell ship and was alive. He looked at his watch. He thought about his sneakers and wondered if he had time to run up and down the court a few times and slam-dunk a few. Alexandros had asked him to call anytime, and Fallon would pick him up in the runabout when he wanted to return to the *New Territories*. Coley Doctor was all smiles. Hell, he might never go back.

63

Willy and Ginny were sleeping late. Their meeting the night before with Lolly and Reinard had been a gabfest that had lasted until the El Valdiz had closed.

Ginny was the first to awaken. She stared out across the harbor and began to think about the amazing story Lolly had told them the night before. Lolly had been extremely candid, revealing all the details she could recall about the rape. And then she confided her suspicions about the murder of Evan Hatcher. She had even preserved the answering machine tape, she said, that had recorded Hatcher's telephone call.

Early in the evening, Ginny couldn't help feeling hostile toward Lolly Penrose. After all, she was Willy's ex-girlfriend. But as the evening wore on, she had grown to like Lolly. At times during their conversation Ginny was almost hypnotized by her, as if she were being drawn into a film.

Willy was fascinated by Lolly's description of Carlos. Coley had reported that Carlos was not getting along well with Onyx. Though he sounded like the scum of the earth, Willy realized that Carlos somehow was the key to trapping Onyx.

Ginny tried to sort it all out in her mind as she rose to sit on the edge of the bed.

This very morning Lolly was to take Luisa Maria shopping. Luisa Maria, the daughter of some big generalissimo in Guadalajara, was also the intended fiancée of Carlos. Wow! What a last chapter this would make for Willy's book.

Reinard had been pretty nasty about the book, Ginny thought. Their lives were in danger and all he could talk about was getting his goddamn manuscript.

Ginny slipped off the bed, careful not to awaken Willy, who needed all the sleep he could get. She walked to the window. It was a brilliant morning. The fog had lifted and the Palos Verdes Peninsula was etched in fine detail on the south horizon.

During the night a large vessel had dropped anchor just beyond the jetty a couple of hundred yards from their hotel. Ginny squinted to see better, then gasped in disbelief. The name was emblazoned on the transom: the *New Territories*, home port, the Crown Colony of Hong Kong. It seemed impossible that this could be the same vessel that had dogged them down the San Juan de Fuca Strait almost two thousand miles away.

Willy was stirring in bed. Her audible gasp awakened him.

"Willy, darling! Look outside! You won't believe it."

"Does this mean I have to get out of bed?"

"Look Willy! It's the *New Territories*!"

Willy was suddenly fully awake and out of bed. He looked out near the jetty and read the name himself. His mind began to race.

"This means Coley might be here any minute." But how long had it been there? Why hadn't Coley contacted them?

Then the telephone rang, almost as if they had willed it. Willy let it ring a second time and then picked it up.

"Hi."

"Hi yourself. Are you Caleb?"

"Coley! Thank God! We've just been looking at the *New Territories* right out our window."

"We got in about an hour ago. I got to you as quick as I could after the funeral."

"Funeral?"

"Yep. Beryl nailed some guy with a reefing knife and sent him to sailor heaven. We buried the son of a bitch at sea. It's a rough way to start a day, Caleb, but it's been better than most days."

"Why don't you come on over? Where are you now?"

"I don't know how smart that would be. I might be carrying a tail. If you look north along the coast a half mile or so you will see the Renaissance Hotel. I'm using a phone in the lobby. I have a meeting with Carlos in just a few minutes. After that we'll try to get together. Onyx wants to shoot some buckets with me later on."

"Onyx! You must mean Beryl."

"No, I mean Onyx. I ain't no one-woman dude like you are. She wants to tell me something. Hey, you got a heater?"

"Yes, your friend Whitcomb dropped one off in my mailbox."

"Good for him. By the way, if you see some strange guys hangin' around it's probably Whitcomb with his personal SWAT team. They are expecting a really big show, ya know."

"I've got a feeling they'll get one too. We had dinner with Lolly Penrose and Reinard last night. Believe it or not, Lolly is out shopping on Rodeo Drive right now with Carlos's fiancée. Says Onyx made her do it. It's all supposed to be a big surprise for Carlos."

There was total silence from Coley for about fifteen seconds.

"Coley, you there?"

"Yeah. Man, you just told me something I didn't know. Man! Carlos is really gonna be pissed off. Luisa Maria is the world's last virgin and he don't want her seeing the likes of anybody connected with any gringos that peddle drugs. I'm gonna find out if he knows anything about her being around. He's a mean dude to get mad at you. You sure Onyx set this up?"

"Yep."

"Hell, man. This might be one of those straws they always talk about."

"What's that?"

"You know, the ones that break the camel's back."

"What about the kilos, Coley? Have you found them yet?"

"Maybe . . . maybe. I've got to be sure though, man. We'll talk again after I talk to Onyx and Carlos. They are my best buddies in this company, you know. Hey, Caleb. Have you given my raise any consideration? I'm going to be out of a job over here in a day or two."

"Are you sure of that, Coley?"

"Talk to you later. If you leave there, we'll talk to our voice mail. Ta-ta."

Willy hung up the phone to find Ginny back under the covers, the sheet over her head. Her voice came from beneath the sheet.

"Jeepers, Caleb. It's getting scary, isn't it? It makes me want to do something that would clear it all right out of our minds for a while. Can you think of anything that would do the trick, Caleb?"

64

Once out of the underground garage at Redondo Beach, Logan Phipps stopped the Jaguar on Pacific Coast Highway. He got out and insisted that Beryl drive. It was a simple matter of his wanting to watch her face as he asked her questions about the Seattle visit and the trip down the coast aboard the *New Territories*. He was a great believer in the concept that many times people's faces were actually more revealing than the words they spoke.

"What of this business with Leyte?" he asked. "Captain Alexandros insists that he fell on his own reefing knife, but that hardly sounds right, does it? Leyte was a good hand. The captain will miss him."

"I think Coley killed him, Lo. Alexandros claims Coley was on the bridge with him for the entire watch, but the captain does a lot of dozing when he has someone else on the bridge. I know that from my own experience."

"Why Coley?"

"Because I asked him to arrange it. The captain and I were troubled by the news reports from Seattle that the name of the woman killed in the car crash had never been released. In fact, I questioned Coley carefully about the woman. I am convinced he killed her just as he said. However, Alexandros always had some doubts about Coley."

"Did he say why?"

"Alexandros sent him to a doctor he knew in Seattle to have a wound cleaned. He had him followed. For some reason Coley shook off his tail and walked back to the *New Territories*."

"Why would he do that?"

"I've thought about that endlessly. I have come to the conclusion that Coley would do that as a game, a mere game. But I asked Coley to take care of Leyte anyway, just as a test, to see if he really could do something like that."

"Why poor Leyte?"

"Leyte was a monster. His hands were all over me whenever he had the chance. He would hide it from others but when no one could see, he was all over me. Many times I caught him at my porthole at night. To tell the truth, Lo, I really didn't think that Coley would do it."

"It sounds like you've gotten to know our Coley Doctor very well."

Phipps stretched his arm across the seat back to massage Beryl's neck as they drove. Her usually straight face broke into a broad smile.

"I have, Lo, I have. But you know that you taught me how to always separate the mental and important from the physical and trivial."

"That is fine if you can completely separate those feelings."

"But you and I scramble them all together."

"Now don't try to convince me that is love."

"We have no time for that, Lo. That is what you taught me also."

The ride to Newport Beach went swiftly. Miraculously, the San Diego Freeway moved without a hitch, and the sleek Jaguar purred along quietly at eighty miles per hour.

"Do you want to drop me off, or would you rather stay at my place this evening?" Beryl asked, hoping that Phipps wouldn't stay with her. It had been a physically demanding four days. She and Coley had experienced some especially exhausting trysts, and she needed serious sleep now.

"Beryl, I am glad you asked, because I want to do just that. There are many things I haven't told you. And there is something that only you can do for me."

"Oh, wonderful, Lo. We will share a bottle of

wine and each other." She hoped Phipps was unable to read her true feelings.

Fifteen minutes later they were in Beryl's condo on the waterway in Newport.

"You must excuse me, dear. I want to shower and get comfortable. The *New Territories* is excellent, but showering on a boat is never as satisfying as it should be. Make yourself at home. You know where everything is."

She left Phipps on a couch digging into an accumulation of newspapers and business reports. As she stripped for the shower she glanced into the mirror. On the inside of her arm, starting at about her elbow, there was a narrow brown streak that ran almost to her armpit. It was the encrusted blood of Leyte. He had been dead only about ten hours now. She wondered if the sharks had got him yet. Beryl turned the water on full force and stood under it for quite some time.

When she returned to Phipps, he had changed to a swimsuit and a robe. He was sitting outside on a deck chair sipping a glass of wine. He kept a full closet of his own at her condo.

"Lo, it is so great to see you relax. You do this so seldom."

"Beryl, I must tell you of a decision I have made concerning Onyx Lu."

Beryl sat down across the small redwood table from him and listened.

"We are removing her."

"Removing?"

"Yes, I have instructed Carlos to handle the details. I suggested that he have her transported back to Macau or Hong Kong, but he seems to have a more efficient plan in mind. Onyx will be in charge of the Black Lamp until after the publicity feast she has planned for La Sex Ménagerie Saturday night. After the party, you and Carlos will take over. I want Coley Doctor to stay around with us too. I had no idea he would turn out to be such an efficient hit man."

"I suppose I know all the reasons why Onyx must go without you telling me. She is an obsessed madwoman, Lo."

"She has even gotten worse since Wong was killed. It seems that she had a real attachment. She let the physical get scrambled up with the mental. She actually drew a gun on me other other day."

"Really! Then you are doing the right thing. I wonder sometimes if she is not back on the stuff again. Her addiction to Wong was dependent on his complete subservience. She used to give and take. Now she only takes."

They both sipped the wine and stared off into the distance at the Pacific. The day had become remarkably clear, and the light chop on the water sparkled all the way to the horizon.

"Lo, when we were talking in the car, you said that there was something only I could do for you."

"Yes. I have been thinking. I have never seen the Black Lamp and La Sex Ménagerie. I would like to see it in full operation tomorrow night, especially because of the Onyx decision. When we talk about it in the future, I want to be able to visualize the whole operation." Phipps hesitated. "Ah . . . you know how I feel about my identity. It has always been my policy to protect the identity of board members as much as possible. There are fewer than a dozen people in this whole country who recognize me on sight and I would like to keep it that way."

Beryl broke into a confident smile. Here, she knew, was where her real power over Logan Phipps lay.

"Oh, we will have such fun. I still have the stunning outfit you wore in Maui last summer. Let me show you."

They went inside to Beryl's large bedroom. Phipps sat on the edge of the bed while Beryl went into her closet and began looking through an assortment of trendy evening wear. Beryl was probably one of only two or three people in the world who knew of Logan Phipps's penchant for cross-dressing. He regarded it as a weakness and tried to veil that weakness by contending that it made for a successful disguise. The secret, kept by Beryl, had cemented a deep bond between them.

"Here is the dress and the pumps you wore in Maui. And here is the lingerie. Remember how smooth it felt. I remember how it turned you on, Lo."

Phipps reached for the flimsy silk.

"Saturday night we will dress together. Then we will spend the whole night here afterwards."

Phipps walked back out onto the deck. It was difficult for him to cope with his fetish, even with

Beryl, who had discovered it in Hong Kong many years before. Beryl had followed him out to the deck.

"I have the perfect wig for you, Lo. We will work with it in the morning. It will be so much fun, the makeup, the wig and all the clothes. You will be so beautiful. You will see the Black Lamp and La Sex Ménagerie as my guest at a private table."

Phipps was now smiling and rubbing the stubble on his chin which would have to be shaved closely tomorrow.

"And who will you tell them I am?"

"Let's say that you are a governor's wife. You are a Madam X who cannot be identified. There are fifty governors and no one there would know all of their wives."

"You will tell this to Onyx, Carlos and Coley?"

"Of course we cannot fool Onyx. She attended the party in Maui, remember? But Carlos and Coley will never suspect. They will be very busy with the evening's festivities. Don't worry about it, Lo. Let me handle everything. Think of the fun we will have when we get back here tomorrow night. Think, darling, of how you will feel in all that silk!"

"Beryl, please, let's get off this subject for a moment. There is something I must tell you. One of my greatest secrets has been kept from you, and it is time that you should know."

"What is that, Lo? What is it?"

"Remember the old estate in Palos Verdes that we used to visit once in a while?"

"Oh yes. It was on Ventana Drive."

"That's right, Beryl. 12755 Ventana Drive. Write that down."

"I will remember that forever, Lo."

"It's where Onyx lives now. Carlos lives in the guest house."

"I know all of that."

"Do you know the greenhouse?"

"The greenhouse?"

"Yes. There are one hundred thirty one kilos of cocaine hidden under a green tarp in the greenhouse. When Onyx is terminated, only Carlos and I would know where it is. Now you know. It is the company's ultimate secret, and now you know."

65

Onyx Lu nosed the vintage white Cadillac out of the gate of 12755 Ventana Drive. She drove leisurely the half dozen miles to Redondo Beach and parked the battered old vehicle in the underground parking garage. She was careful to back the car into a parking slot so that the trunk was flush against a wall. She wanted to get rid of the old thing. It made her think about the miserably stupid Wong every time she saw it. Now at least it would serve some useful purpose.

She exited the vehicle and, casting a glance around the garage, inserted the trunk key into its slot. She walked slowly toward the stairwell leading out of the parking facility, satisfied that the trunk key was invisible at the rear of the car.

As she turned into the stairwell, she saw KoKo walking toward the car from another direction. He was carrying a large suitcase.

Onyx ascended the stairs to a second level. Then she entered a phone booth and removed a cellular phone from the large purse she carried. Captain Alexandros, aboard the *New Territories*, answered on the second ring.

"Alexandros here."

"Captain, this is Onyx. Everything is fine. I just saw KoKo heading toward the car."

"Tell me, Onyx, is this going to be like the old days?"

"Of course, Captain, except this time it will just be you and me."

"Now tell me, Onyx. Why in the world did you leave the thirty-one kilos in the greenhouse? Why did you argue about that?"

"Captain, by tomorrow night you will understand thoroughly. By the next day you will read about it in the papers, except of course, we won't be around here to read the papers. Remember, tell no one about this transfer. Not even our Phipps. All of our lives depend on it."

"Yes Onyx. What goes on between you and me concerns no one except you and me. Those are the orders I have from Phipps."

Over the years they had sworn each other to secrecy many times. Onyx was always the go-between for moving shipments from Baja or Panama. There was no reason now to question her.

She turned off her telephone, put it back in her purse and walked the couple of blocks to the Black Lamp. She looked at her watch and realized she would be a few minutes late.

As she strolled along, Onyx wondered about Coley Doctor and his constant references to shooting buckets. Now she would find out once and for all what the big bastard was all about.

The Black Lamp was empty. The lunch crowd had not yet started to arrive. It was very quiet. Coley Doctor and Carlos were sitting at a table staring at her as she walked toward them.

Neither spoke. Onyx could feel the tension. Both men had their fingers clasped together, their hands on the table. She walked toward them and sat down. Still not a word was spoken.

Carlos dropped a hand inside his silk jacket to touch his nine-millimeter Glock. He spoke first.

"Onyx, you will rot in hell. Whatever I do with the rest of my life, I will promise that I will make certain along the way you rot in hell. I guarantee that." Carlos slammed his clenched fist on the table. "You mangy bitch! Because of you, my Luisa Maria is out shopping on Rodeo Drive with another whore like you. Lolly Penrose, who keeps her name in print by screwing people in public. You have my Luisa Maria out shopping with a hopped-up Hollywood whore!"

Onyx froze, aware that she couldn't possibly fish the small automatic from her purse before he had time to use the Glock.

"I meant it to be surprise. How did you find out, Carlos?"

"She called here! She called the Black Lamp looking for you! I realize, Onyx, that you do not know what it means to be naive. She had no idea that I would answer the phone. You stinking whore. The idea of you entertaining my Luisa Maria makes me want to puke on your face. But believe me, Onyx, I will do much worse than that."

Onyx was trying to think of anything that would defuse the situation. Coley was staring straight at the mirrored wall behind her, mute.

"I am sorry, Carlos. She does have her mother with her, you know."

"Thank God! I have invited them to have lunch here tomorrow. Arrangements have been made to get them on a three o'clock plane for Guadalajara. They will not attend your obscene party. She will no longer mingle with whores."

"For a man in your profession, dear Carlos, you certainly make a fuss over morality."

Coley leaned over and now put his open hand between them, fearful that Carlos would explode. Carlos slowly stood up and walked to another table, his hand still fingering the hidden Glock.

"Onyx, you sure know how to get a dude upset." Coley mumbled the words, trying to cool the situation down before breaking the bad news.

"Oh, he'll get over it, Coley. I think the nature of his business makes him grouchy."

"Well, I guess it is up to me to get to the business at hand." Coley pulled his chair in closer as he spoke. "When I finish talking, I want you to stand up and look directly behind you in the booth just next to the front door. You have a visitor and his name is Willy Hanson."

Onyx appeared suddenly nervous and started to fumble with her purse.

"You'd better leave the heater alone. Hanson probably has one himself. Besides, Carlos might think the ticket is for him."

"Are you sure it's him?"

"About ninety-nine percent. There have been some strange folks up and down the sidewalk too. He just wandered in as Carlos and I were waiting for you. He asked to speak to Onyx Lu. I told him you weren't here and he said he'd wait. He said to tell you that your old pal Willy Hanson had come to call."

Onyx put both palms on the table and tried to collect her thoughts. Her timetable had already been set in motion. KoKo was probably on his way back to the *New Territories* now with the one-hundred kilos. Any kind of violent showdown here would end in real disaster.

She stood and turned toward the door, dangling her purse by a long strap. She recognized him immediately. Willy Hanson was sitting in the booth next to the door, partly obscured by the brightness from the outside. She walked over and sat down directly across from him in the booth.

"Hi Willy, it been long time."

"Jesus! You're exactly the same! Beautiful, sexy and forever young. How do you do it?"

Onyx grinned. "I lead a clean life, Willy."

She slid her hand toward the large purse on the seat beside her and pulled it close.

Willy dropped his hand to the .38 that was jammed in his belt and leaned over the table to whisper what was meant for her ears alone. He was praying that Coley had Carlos covered.

"Keep your hands on the table and away from that purse or I will blow your brains all over this booth. You are going to hear what I have to say and then you can have those goons over there shoot me if you dare."

"Okay, Willy, so I listen. Incidentally, you look great yourself, and I bet it is not from clean living. You and I have so much fun together. Remember?"

"Onyx, I'm here to make peace. Life without Ginny is hell. Blasting your brains out would be very satisfying to me, but it would not bring Ginny back. I also realize it was not you who kidnapped her and took her away. I saw her in Schooners Notch. She wore a wig. She looked like you, but was much younger. I realize that even more, now that we sit face to face again."

"Someday, Willy, I will help you find that woman. Okay? I did not want them to go after Ginny." It was true, she thought, but only because she had wanted to go after them herself.

"Onyx, you just hit the nail on the head. I am willing to bury the hatchet if you will identify that person for me. That person will pay the price. Hell, Onyx, you have already been exonerated by a jury. I think you owe me for that. I skipped out on the warrant to testify against you."

"Yes, Willy. I know that."

Onyx began to consider his request seriously. If Willy was on the level, he was playing right into her hands. The one-hundred kilos were already aboard the *New Territories*. Everything was falling into place. In three days' time she would be in Cabo San Lucas, far from the yoke of Phipps and Beryl. She would be rich and there would be plenty of time to shoot buckets with Coley, the captain, and whoever else might be amusing.

"Willy, you've got a deal. We are having a big publicity party tomorrow night at the Black Lamp. In honor of old times, I will make you special guest. The person who kidnap Ginny will be at that party. I will introduce you to her. Then ball in your court, Willy. Deal?"

"Hey, Onyx, nothing special please. I would just like to tag along with Lolly Penrose. We're seeing each other again, you know."

"Oh, really? That great news! It will be so much fun to see you and Lolly together again. Hey, Willy, I think we should seal this big deal with hot kiss, no?"

Willy leaned forward and Onyx met him halfway. Their lips touched and lingered together over the middle of the table.

The two hit men, the real one and the ersatz one, were so captivated by the scene that their hands folded comfortably on the table. Both nine-millimeters were temporarily forgotten.

Willy Hanson left the Black Lamp arm in arm with Onyx. They walked for a few moments on the sidewalk out front, then kissed again and departed in different directions.

Coley walked over to the table where Carlos sat and pulled up a chair. The maître d' arrived and the telephone began ringing for lunch reservations.

"You know, Carlos, I didn't feel much like killing anyone today anyway."

Carlos looked at him, face clouded with his darkest scowl. "Who were you going to kill, Coley?"

Coley shrugged his shoulders. "Maybe Willy Hanson."

Carlos looked him right in the eye as if he was trying to solve a great puzzle. "Coley, it wasn't the time or the place."

"I guess you're right." Deep inside Coley could feel that Carlos must know he wasn't a real hit man.

"Tomorrow night at the big party, Coley, we might do a little business."

Then Carlos shrugged, rose from the table and walked back toward his security office.

Coley felt like a freshman center on a high school team. He would give Willy a little time to get back to the Porto Sol and then call to find out what had happened.

66

The weather along the coast of Southern California is usually good. However, on the day of Onyx Lu's grand publicity bash at the Black Lamp, the South Coast was being buffeted by a howling Pacific storm. Deluges of wind-driven rain sent row upon row of massive white-capped breakers pounding at the sand and rocks. Captain Alexandros had his hands full early in the day until he moved the *New Territories* to a point just inside the breakwater.

It was almost as the devil himself had picked this rare day to celebrate the carefully orchestrated media event. The selected guests would begin arriving at 7:30 P.M. to dine at the Black Lamp. Most of the handpicked crowd would then be shown to the third floor and La Sex Ménagerie for the special show, dancing and all the cutting-edge bombast of lasers and electronic fireworks.

It was 1:15 when Señora Dolores Rodriguez and Luisa Maria arrived with Paco, the general's personal aide, who had accompanied the two women to Los Angeles. Lolly Penrose and Reinard Gossman had escorted the three from Beverly Hills, where they had visited several shops. They had all enjoyed themselves, despite some early tension concerning Carlos's insistence that they cut their trip short and leave for Mexico in midafternoon. Carlos explained now that he needed to leave town that evening and would therefore be unable to go through with previous plans.

Onyx had made arrangements for them to be served promptly at half past one, but alas, there was no Onyx. After a few minutes Lolly suggested that they begin their lunch.

Having Reinard there turned out to be a godsend. He spoke Spanish fluently and got along famously with Paco and Dolores, who were greatly entertained by his anecdotes about his famous clients.

Carlos was a nervous wreck. Luisa Maria was distraught about the change in plans and disappointed at not being able to meet Onyx Lu.

Carlos looked again at his watch. Missing an appointment like this was unlike Onyx. And where was that mysterious bastard, Coley? Perhaps they were together. But if they were, why? Carlos had been feeling very uneasy ever since yesterday's surprise visit by Willy Hanson.

Early that morning, instead of shooting baskets, Onyx had prevailed on Coley to go a small-arms range for target practice. Coley's PI license gained him access to a shooting range where he could take her as a guest.

Onyx had described a long-barreled .22 target pistol to him that she had acquired and was eager to test. Once they got to the range, she quickly proved how good she was. She put seven out of ten within the bull's-eye at twenty-five yards.

"That's a nice weapon, Onyx, when you're as good as you are. It is a little bit hard to conceal, though. Unless you are a sharpshooter it doesn't leave much of a margin for error."

"That okay, Coley. I just having fun. Tomorrow we have big, big fun. Today I have much business left to do for tonight. Thanks for shooting with me, Coley. You keep working at it and you be good as me!"

"Thanks, but long-barreled peashooters aren't my game."

"What your game, Coley? Tomorrow we play any game you want."

"That's a deal."

Onyx had something on her mind that Coley couldn't figure out. She dropped him off at Torrance Boulevard and then wheeled the Jaguar north in the opposite direction from Redondo Beach.

About thirty miles later she got off the freeway on Colorado Boulevard in Glendale and drove a few blocks to a small Thai restaurant. She looked at her watch. It was almost 1:30. That bastard Carlos would be having lunch with his prissy little missy at the Black Lamp.

She entered the small restaurant. There were only a half dozen tables, two of them occupied. She walked over to where a dark-haired young woman sat alone. The woman grinned broadly as Onyx approached.

"Glory! You sweet little bitch. Did you bring me what I need?"

"Of course." The woman held up a small gym bag. "It's all in here. I hope it all fits."

"We are same size. You no forget I have seen your body. We are same."

Onyx handed Glory two hundred-dollar bills rolled tightly into small tubes, along with a small embossed velvet bag.

"You doing me a big favor. It will be fun seeing La Sex Ménagerie as everyone go crazy. Thank you, Glory. Keep our secret and Onyx come back and make big fun with you."

"Onyx!"

"No, no, I must go. Must make plans. See you next week. Enjoy night off."

She returned to her Jaguar and drove to the Golden State Freeway, wound around Griffith Park and ultimately streaked south on the Harbor Freeway. At its end, she leisurely climbed the

Palos Verdes Peninsula and Ventana Drive. There seemed to be a lot of gardening-service trucks around. She thought about that for a second and decided that the rain was probably creating washouts that needed tending to.

She would skip the Black Lamp today. Let Carlos sweat it out with Coley. She would concentrate on providing a finale to their party that would be remembered forever by those who stayed among the living.

67

Ginny wore a pageboy wig that not only disguised her identity very well but gave her an exotic flair that outshone the glamorous Lolly Penrose, who was Willy's date for the evening. Reinard would escort the remodeled Ginny.

The foursome met at Lolly's condo before heading for the Black Lamp. Reinard watched Willy pull out the snub-nosed .38, check it, and then stuff it back into his belt above his left kidney.

"Look, all of you. Maybe you ought to stay home. Who in hell knows what will happen? I wouldn't carry a weapon if I didn't think I might need it."

Ginny shook her head decidedly. "No, Willy. I've followed you four thousand miles already and I'd rather die than not go with you tonight."

"Bravo! Bravo!" Lolly Penrose clapped vigorously as Reinard thrust his two thumbs up.

"Besides," Ginny offered, "Coley says everything looks good."

Willy shook his head. "Ginny, I never heard Coley say anything like that."

"Well, he implied it."

"I know one thing." Reinard ran his eyes up and down the two gorgeous women. "The Black Lamp has never seen two such gorgeous patrons. Now let's get a move on. It's after seven."

The giddy banter died away as they piled into the waiting limo and tore off into the stormy night. As they approached the Black Lamp, they could see the *New Territories*, tossing and bobbing visibly in the stiff onshore wind, dark except for one dimly lit porthole near the water. The ominous blackness of the rogue trawler brought a quiet sobriety to the four.

The Black Lamp was already jammed when they entered and were led to Lolly's table, set for four people. Dinner was superb, all the rave reviews obviously deserved.

It was a crowd with a lot of celebrities. Lolly began to point them out as best she could. Several people came over to greet her. Lolly tried to be gracious, but came off as rather abrupt much of the time. In truth, she just wanted to get on with the evening. Much as she hated to admit it, she was once again drawn compulsively to La Sex Ménagerie.

For different reasons, most people felt the same way. The tabloids, fed by the gossip campaign Onyx had unleashed, had piqued the interest of the jaded party crowd. When news sped around the room that the elevator was taking people up to the cabaret, a line formed immediately. Once the patrons reached the third floor, they were greeted by cocktail waitresses who were elegantly dressed in black shirts, white ties, and satin pumps. They were otherwise nude. Drinks were served in large double glasses, and champagne pourers circulated among the guests to keep the glasses full.

By the time Lolly and her group found their way up to La Sex Ménagerie, it was already jammed. A large part of the crowd was on its feet and rocking to a reggae rhythm.

Clothing was diaphanous and skimpy. Bosoms swung freely to the pulsing beat, derriéres ground to repetitive electronic detonations that rendered conversation among the guests impossible.

The lights became dim with sporadic strobe-like flashes. Then came a wild trumpet solo that wailed slowly up to a piercingly high pitch, ending when the room was dark save for a single pencil-thin laser beam that traced each suspended cage of La Sex Ménagerie. In an instant the cages were barred in vivid orange. The mimes in each of the four cages, apparently nude, began their repetitive tableaus, running the full gamut of erotic expression. The disco beat became softer but intensified slowly.

Lolly Penrose reached across the table to grasp Reinard's hand tightly. She knew exactly what was happening when the laser beam traced a single brilliant circle on the ceiling. The circular stage began descending as the familiar beat of Ravel's "Bolero" filled the room.

One of the performers on the stage was skillfully made up to look like Lolly Penrose, and a bony duplicate of Evan Hatcher was beginning his degrading role. The audience began to stand and clap to the cadence of the defiling performance. Though the performers were sheathed in sheer body suits, they made the imaginary performance more realistic than the original event. The crowd roared encouragement for the tasteless display.

"Lolly! Lolly! Lolly!" became the deafening two-syllable chant as the mortified star buried her face in Willy Hanson's chest and tried to hide from the world.

"Where is Onyx? I want to kill her."

Willy had been asking himself the question ever since they had entered the room. The chair where she should have been sitting was empty. Coley Doctor was sitting next to Beryl, and next to them was an elegant, tall blonde he could not identify.

Lolly Penrose continued sobbing in Willy's embrace as he scanned the jam-packed room.

Mercifully the circular stage started ascending into its home in the ceiling. The two performers were now standing arm in arm, bowing in acknowledgement of the applause, which was amply laced with catcalls and obscene suggestions for an encore.

Once the stage disappeared into the ceiling, the disco beat began again and the caged mimes resumed their work to edify the crowd.

Coley Doctor allowed his eyes to roam the room. When he spotted Willy, he gave excuses to his tablemates and then struggled his way through the crowded room. When he reached Willy's table, he looked directly at Lolly, still wrapped in Willy's arms.

"Miss Penrose, I'm sorry. I didn't know what they were going to do up there."

Lolly did not respond. The disco beat was steadily quickening and growing louder.

"Coley! Where the hell is Onyx!" Willy was actually shouting to make himself heard.

"I haven't seen her all night, but I am more worried about that other son of a bitch."

"Who!"

"Carlos. I haven't seen him either."

"Hey, there he is, he's sitting next to Beryl, right where you were!"

Coley looked over his shoulder and saw Carlos in deep conversation with Beryl.

"Who is the woman?"

"Beryl says she is some governor's wife. Whoever she is, she doesn't talk. Seems to be scared to death of this scene."

The music and the laser show were now combining to present what could best be described as an indoor fireworks display. The pulsating percussion formed staccato patterns of ear-splitting detonations. Lights pulsed from dim to dazzling in the four cages holding the sexual performers.

It was the cage highest on the wall that captured the interest of Coley Doctor. There was a nude woman on all fours, saddled like a horse, complete with bridle and a sparkling bit clinched in her teeth. High in the saddle rode a diminutive equestrienne. She was clad in a full-sleeved short kimono. One arm was held high in the air, gripping a riding crop.

Coley strained to see through the flashes of light, pointing and urging Willy above the din to look also. A glint of metal reflected off the riding crop as it was leveled toward the crowd below. The electronic detonations became deafening as a flash spurted from the end of the riding crop.

"It's her, Willy. It's Onyx and that goddamn long-barrel."

A succession of piercing screams came from a table not far away. Coley and the others turned to see Beryl screaming for Coley. Her beautiful woman companion lay face down on the table.

Coley rushed to her side through the panicking crowd. He bent over and gently tried to lift the woman. A wig fell to the floor.

Coley's huge basketball hands held the head of a man whose wide-eyed stare was punctuated by a small, neat red hole in the middle of his forehead.

There was no question about it. Logan Phipps,

the leader of the massive international drug-smuggling cartel, was stone dead.

"He's dead, Beryl. He's been shot."

Beryl looked directly at Coley. "Wait here, Coley. Tell people that he has just fainted. I will get Carlos to cover the door so she can't get away. This has to be the work of Onyx."

68

Beryl pressed open the panel that led to the security room. When she entered, Carlos was standing there with the nine-millimeter in his hand.

"Latch the door behind you. I will throw the master fuse switch and the entire building will become dark except for a few auxiliary lights. Stand right there at the top of the stairwell and I will lead the way to the street."

When the building was plunged into darkness, a chorus of screams and shouts rang out from beyond the thin wall. Beryl and Carlos reached the alleyway within moments. Carlos, gun drawn, checked outside and saw no one; then he and Beryl raced to her black Jaguar, parked less than a hundred steps away. Beryl got behind the wheel, and in seconds they were speeding along the Coast Highway toward the Palos Verdes Peninsula. Carlos was shaking his head.

"I don't get it. This is too easy, Beryl. Where in the hell is Onyx?"

"She is probably still in the building trying to get out. Let's not sell ourselves short, Carlos. This was the contingency plan in case anything happened to Lo. As he used to say, always have a contingency plan."

"Beryl, there is the possibility that Onyx might have beaten us out of the building. In that case she might be ahead of us."

"You're right, of course." She pushed her foot down even harder on the accelerator. They had reached the broad curve that would spiral on up the peninsula.

"Carlos, when did you last check the stock? Is it still in the greenhouse?"

"Phipps told me I was the only other person who knew besides him."

"He just told me about it. He must have known things were going to get rougher. Is it still in the greenhouse?"

"Of course it is. I just checked it this morning after Onyx left."

"So relax. We'll have it all in our hands in just

a few minutes. We'll take it to Newport and stash it in my condo. Then we'll lie low for a time. Perhaps you can spend some time with your Luisa Maria."

Carlos again began shaking his head. "This is just too easy, Beryl."

"We have more time than you think, Carlos. Most of those people are still in that building. There will be a long investigation. They will have a problem finding out who the dead man is. Logan Phipps has concealed his identity too well."

"What about Coley?"

"He killed that woman for us in Seattle. You know that, don't you, Carlos?"

"I never believed him, Beryl. Maybe . . . maybe he did."

Beryl turned onto Ventana Drive. Carlos had her slow down and park about fifty yards from the gate. He wanted to make sure they were not being followed.

Finally, with his nine-millimeter in his hand, he motioned for her to open the gate with the remote button.

Nothing inside looked suspicious. The estate was dark except for a row of low-intensity garden lamps lining the driveway. Beryl guided the Jaguar to the rear of the house and then backed it up so that the trunk was next to the greenhouse. They both got out. Carlos unlocked the greenhouse door and entered. He flipped a light switch and pointed to a green tarp that appeared to be covering a pile of clay pots.

"It's right there, Beryl."

Beryl flipped the tarp back. Several kilos of cocaine were visible. She got down on her knees to examine the cache.

"Carlos, it is here, but—"

She never finished the sentence. Powerful spotlights flooded the greenhouse and the area adjacent.

A voice boomed through a bullhorn. "Don't move!"

Carlos spun on his heels and began firing at the sound, managing to get off several shots before a hail of bullets came at him from several directions. The hit man died instantly.

Beryl had hit the ground and scrambled under one of the potting benches. Miraculously she had escaped the gunfire.

With an icy calm, she crawled out from under the bench to face agent Mark Whitcomb.

"FBI, Miss Beryl. I find you a little short of the expected inventory here." He kicked at the cocaine. "Care to tell us about it?"

"You kill my boyfriend. Why?"

One of the agents came forward to apply handcuffs.

"Okay, if that's the way you want it. Listen carefully now. You have the right to remain silent . . ."

Whitcomb left the shed, shouting instructions to several agents. "Mop up on things here. Make sure we've got everything we can find. Finish the search of the premises. I'm going to take some of you back to Redondo."

Whitcomb climbed into a van with several other members of the task force and proceeded to a helicopter port less than a half mile away. They would be in Redondo Beach in a matter of minutes.

69

Several pocket flashlights had materialized from the crowd, enabling Lolly Penrose to locate the panel leading to the stairwell. It took only a couple of hefty kicks from Coley to pop it open.

It was the screaming of the people trapped in the elevator that had saved the day, attracting the attention of the maître d' in the restaurant below. He had immediately called the fire department.

Leaving Lolly Penrose and Ginny in the restaurant with Reinard, Coley Doctor and Willy sprinted the two blocks to the waterfront. When Willy reached the boat landing at the end of the pier he suddenly realized that he was sprinting alone. He turned around and Coley was nowhere to be seen.

"Don't move! Don't move a muscle!" Willy turned back to find himself staring down at four men in an open boat, each holding a shotgun aimed right at him. The scene spelled FBI.

"Is Mark Whitcomb around?" Willy boldly boomed out the question to the quartet of men facing him.

"Who wants to know?"

"Willy Hanson."

He heard his name repeated several times by one of the men in the open launch.

"Leave him alone. He's okay. Whitcomb says he's okay." One of the men was talking into a two-way radio, evidently in touch with Whitcomb.

The man on the radio looked at Willy and suddenly asked a question. "Where is Coley Doctor?"

Willy again looked behind him on the dock. Coley was nowhere to be seen.

"I don't know. He was right behind me." He looked around again, unable to believe that Coley had left him all alone.

"Hey! There he is!" Willy pointed to a tall man in a small outboard skiff racing toward the *New Territories*. Coley looked as tall as the skiff was long.

Suddenly there was a rumble from the powerful engine of the *New Territories*, and the rattle of the anchor winch.

"Okay, guys, Whitcomb says go. Come on aboard, Hanson. We'll take care of you later."

Willy climbed aboard the launch, to be immediately relieved of his .38.

"Just relax. There ain't going to be any shooting here."

"Oh Jesus, look at him." Willy pointed out to the transom of the *New Territories*. The small harbor was well illuminated with lights along the pier and the adjacent marina.

Coley Doctor had brought the tiny skiff alongside the *New Territories*. Onyx Lu extended a helping hand as Coley vaulted over the rail. But Coley shoved the tiny woman to the deck with a sweep of his long arm and ran forward toward the pilothouse.

The big trawler was under way, picking up speed rapidly as the agents kept pace with the launch now alongside. One of the agents tried to communicate with the trawler with a bullhorn.

Captain Alexandros kept revving up the big diesel and fishtailing against the launch in an effort to swamp her.

Seeing an opportunity, Willy stood up in the launch and flung himself at the handrail of the *New Territories*. He struggled aboard and raced forward, stumbling over the prone figure of Onyx Lu.

Willy reached the pilothouse to find Coley in mortal combat with KoKo. The muscular seaman had Coley pinned down and was trying to free his wrist, holding the heavy ball-peen hammer. Willy delivered a sharp karate chop to the base of KoKo's neck, and then another and another before the massive hulk of a man fell limp on top of the exhausted Coley.

Willy kicked in the door of the pilothouse and jumped on the back of Alexandros, who clung doggedly to the wheel. When he succeeded in wrestling Alexandros down, the *New Territories* went out of control and began to lurch and scrape against the rock jetty. By that time agents were swarming around, and the whir of the helicopter thumped above.

The big trawler then tried to do something it was not built to do. It tried to climb the massive stone jetty. The *New Territories* roared to a stop and then became silent, marooned on the dark side of the jetty outside the harbor.

Whitcomb and another unit of his team came aboard a few minutes later. Spotlights were set up. After determining that the settling trawler had stabilized, they decided to set up a base on the jetty and wait for daylight. The vessel had to be searched thoroughly, and there was some concern for the safety for those who would go below.

"No thanks to you, Hanson, we didn't have casualties." Whitcomb was delivering a lecture. "We could have lost men in an accident like that. By the way, Coley said he saw Onyx Lu aboard."

"I saw her too, Mark. She was lying unconscious aft of the fish locker."

"Not now, she isn't. She either fell overboard or is hiding somewhere below. We'll keep the place well lit and conduct a complete search at daybreak. We'll also send a party to walk from both ends of the jetty right now to make sure she didn't walk away."

Willy stirred uneasily. They had caught some big fish, but he didn't want Onyx to get away.

Mark Whitcomb came over to speak to Willy privately.

"Hanson, I owe you one for leading us to these rats. Logan Phipps is dead. We nailed Beryl with her fanny on thirty kilos of cocaine. Carlos is dead. The *New Territories* and her captain are out of business forever. It has been a great day, Hanson. But after tomorrow, I never want you playing cops and robbers again."

"I hope we find Onyx."

"Hanson, get off it. She's dead. Look around. We'll probably find her on the rocks. No swimmer could make it alive in a rough sea like this pounding the jetty. Hell, Hanson, she was the smallest fish of all. She was just a marketer. Nothing more than that."

All the next day, an elaborate search was conducted along the entire jetty. The hulk of the *New Territories* was combed inch by inch. Scuba divers searched the relatively shallow waters all around the jetty.

Late in the day, one-hundred kilos of cocaine were found in a waterproof compartment inside the aft fish locker.

Willy, Ginny, Lolly, Reinard and Coley all had dinner that evening at a restaurant there on the pier in Redondo Beach. The *New Territories* lay dead on the rocks right outside the restaurant window.

Willy, sipping a brandy, turned to Coley and asked, "How many kilos did you say they found in Palos Verdes?"

"Thirty."

"And there were a hundred aboard the *New Territories*."

"Yep."

"Thirty and one hundred make one hundred thirty. Carlos and Beryl always said there were one hundred thirty-one."

"So all we are missing is Onyx Lu and one kilo."

Ginny had the last word. "Willy, I don't want to hear any more. It's over."

"What now, Willy?" Reinard was no doubt thinking about the unfinished book.

"Your manuscript is in the *Tashtego*, high and dry in Seattle. I'll mail it next week before Ginny and I start our trans-Pacific. I've grown to prefer the water. It's the highway that goes anywhere."

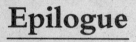

Epilogue

Six months later on the island of Cheung Chau, a part of the Crown Colony of Hong Kong, a Star Ferry landed and put ashore a new English teacher en route to a small private school for the affluent residents of this remote island in the South China Sea.

Cheung Chau lies southwest of Hong Kong Island, perhaps twenty kilometers from the ferry landing at Aberdeen.

The new teacher, mature but arrestingly attractive, came upon one of her new students playing on the sandy beach.

"Hello, I hear you are to be our new teacher," the five-year-old girl said. "What is your name?"

The woman smiled and said, "I want you to play a game. My name is the same as one might call a precious stone."

The little girl grinned. "Is it Diamond?"

"No, but you have the right idea. Guess again."

"I know, because you are so pretty. It's Emerald!"

The beautiful lady became very quiet as she walked with her new student across the white sand.

"Emerald, you say. Well, that is a very pretty name. How did you guess so quickly?"

"Because you are so pretty! Is that really your name?"

"Of course it is. You may always call me Emerald. Emerald Lu."

HIGH-TENSION THRILLERS FROM TOR

BESTSELLERS FROM TOR

THE BEST IN
SCIENCE FICTION

Buy them at your local bookstore or use this handy coupon:
Clip and mail this page with your order.

Publishers Book and Audio Mailing Service
P.O. Box 120159, Staten Island, NY 10312-0004

Please send me the book(s) I have checked above. I am enclosing $ _____
(Please add $1.25 for the first book, and $.25 for each additional book to cover postage and handling.
Send check or money order only—no CODs.)

Name _____

Address _____

City _____ State/Zip _____

Please allow six weeks for delivery. Prices subject to change without notice.

MORE OF THE BEST IN SCIENCE FICTION